Royal Blue

a novel

Christina Oxenberg

Simon & Schuster

SIMON & SCHUSTER
Rockefeller Center
1230 Avenue of the Americas
New York, NY 10020

DESIGNED BY BARBARA M. BACHMAN
Manufactured in the United States of America

10   9   8   7   6   5   4   3   2   1

Library of Congress Cataloging-in-Publication Data
Oxenberg, Christina, date.
    Royal blue: a novel / Christina Oxenberg
        p. cm.
    I. Title
    PS3565.X3R69   1997
    813'.54—dc21   96-52207
                                                 CIP

ISBN 0-684-80093-4

Acknowledgments

If I were to attempt to draw up a list of names of all those who have offered assistance along the way, that list would easily outnumber the pages of this book. Furthermore, any level of accuracy would likely be at odds with my slim and shaky memory.

Therefore, I would like to take this opportunity to express my profound gratitude to all: family, friends, and foes.

This book is dedicated to:

Lauren Shuler Donner
for the kick start

❦

Manuela Dembeniotis Simpson
a.k.a. Homer
and
Kate Hall
a.k.a. Gatito Corridor
for their enduring friendship

❦

Oh . . .
and
Bob Asahina
a.k.a. Editor Bob

Royal
Blue

Six MONTHS CHUGGED SLOWLY BY BEFORE I saw Tino again. And to tell the truth, I hardly thought about him. His purpose, as far as I had seen it, had been exploited, and his memory held no more consequence than an empty husk. Besides, I was quite taken up with studying finance and with the Houdiniesque complications of the straitjacket budget I had rigged, allowing for three meals a day—at $1.25 for a cup of coffee and a toasted corn muffin soaked through with butter— subway fare to and from work, and one movie a week. A former stepmother very kindly undertook the challenge of finding me some form of employment, and since my credentials in the workforce were nonexistent, seeing as I had never attended university and could not type, file, or even spell, one can only say she was inspired when she thought to introduce me to Omar Lahood, movie producer. After I failed to accurately answer any one of his many questions, he hired me on a trial basis at $100 a week. I toiled unhappily, attempting to reduce whole scripts to a mouthful of words and fit the pages into jazzy plastic folders, and watched them pile up on the boss's desk, unread, used occasionally as a coaster for his mugs of steaming ginseng. Most often I was sent on errands, to buy bulk soft-pink lightbulbs or jars of particular pickles, or to return the forgotten earrings of a starlet the boss might have auditioned on the sofa in a private room upstairs, above the offices. My nights were even more desperate, spent scouring the real estate section of the *New York Times* in search of a home. My very temporary lodgings, on the sofa bed of the housekeeper of the mother of another ex-stepmother of mine, were nearing a natural end, and daily it became more imperative that I move on. Not that Zelda, the housekeeper, wanted me to go; she claimed she liked the company. But the smell of five wide apathetic cats and their individual litter trays, compounded by the painted-closed windows, was proving a formidable obstacle to the benefits of $40-a-week rent, utilities included.

One night I went to dinner at a restaurant on the Upper East Side, and there he was, dining with his wife and three children. I knew it must be them by the way Tino ministered to them, fussing over them, looking relaxed and bored. His wife is quite beautiful in a dramatic Nordic way, and the children, for what they lack in organic good looks, are well compensated for with fine manners and stylish clothes.

"Maria!" Tino exclaimed as he shoved his chair back, threw his napkin on the table, and walked toward me with a smile so intense it unsettled me. I had hoped to go unnoticed, to observe from a distance and then depart. "Where have you been?" he demanded, taking both my hands in his, completely ignoring the three people I was with. I did not answer. Instead, I looked across at his wife, who seemed to be pretending that he had never left the table, clucking over her brood like a concerned hen. "Answer me, goddamn it!" Tino said, his smile broad, totally engaging. "I've been asking after you, and nobody ever knows where the hell you are or what you're doing. You're not leaving tonight without giving me your phone number." Only then did he inspect my companions, frowning. "Is one of these hoodlums your boyfriend? I'll kill him if you tell me yes!"

"No!" I said, laughing, looking at the two men and the one

girl I had come to dine with. I found it impossible not to be se-
duced by Tino's enthusiasm. "I want you to meet Madeleine," I
told him, turning to introduce a pretty French girl I had recently met, who had offered me a room of my own in her spacious Park Avenue apartment. I could stay as long as I liked. She
would charge only $10 a week more than Zelda, her home was
airy and bright, the windows opened, and more important,
Madeleine was closer to me in age, which I hoped would allow
me to make acquaintances beyond the small circle of meringue-
coiffed housekeepers Zelda played rummy with in the evenings.

Tino ignored her completely and asked me, "Where have
you been?"

"I've been away. I walked all over Saudi Arabia and I just got
back, a few days ago, in fact."

"How ridiculous! Saudi Arabia? Who did you go with?"

"Countless suitors!" I said, laughing. "I've been here, reading
scripts for a movie producer. I'm beginning to suspect he pro-
duces nothing more than a different pretty girl to cast on the
office couch every afternoon. All I know for certain is that the
man likes pink lightbulbs, and I've been entrusted with the du-
bious honor of carting crates of them to and fro. In between
boiling the scripts down to one-liners. My biggest fear is that
I'll be tracked down by an author one day and stabbed to death
with a thousand Parker pens!"

"What are you babbling about?" he asked as he tightened the
grip on my hands. His striking blue eyes made me smile. "If I
hear you have a lover, I'll never speak to you again." Then, as if
he had only just remembered, he glanced around at his wife.
His mouth shut in a hard, pinched way. "I'm here with the bat-
tle-ax. She insists on making me take her to dinner once a
week. Such a bore. Except that I love my kids. If it wasn't for
them, I wouldn't bother at all. Now give me your number."

"I'm not living anywhere," I told him, suddenly uncomfortable with the speed of the attack. Not to mention the fact that Madeleine, who stood a foot away, had only just that evening suggested I come stay with her. "I'm not settled."

"You must be staying somewhere, you little fool, and you're not disappearing on me again." He produced a pen from his breast pocket and handed me a book of matches. "Now stop being an idiot and give me the number."

His hand lingered on my fingers when I returned the matchbook. His touch was warm, as warm as his smile. Then he turned and went back to his family.

He called me at work the following morning, interrupting my digestion of a seafarer's tale of woe and piracy into a scant five lines. For months after, he never failed to call me at ten o'clock. "Good morning, little dummy," he would say. "What did you do last night? Where? Who with? You'd better tell the truth. How do you know you're not being trailed as it is?"

"I was at home," I would say. "With Madeleine. And then fourteen strapping men came over and we had an orgy. It was all quite dull, really."

"Why do you torture me?" he would yell. "I've made you feel far too comfortable, showering you with attention. If I were a games player I'd ignore you, then you'd be begging to see me."

"Go on, then," I would say. "Make me beg."

"I'm not going to waste my time on you if you're going to be an idiot," he would say, sounding dark and menacing and totally unconvincing. "Maria, I can't stand the thought of you with another man. If you won't be with me, promise me, at least, you won't be with anyone else."

"I promise," I would say, wondering what I meant by this. Something about his obsession made me afraid to encourage him and yet afraid to give him any reason to free himself. I worried that if he ever got to know me, he would find out I was not whatever it was he had conjured up in his active imagination.

Occasionally I would run into him at a restaurant or a party. There were always women around him, and the sight of them would pierce my stomach, a primal, territorial response. But then he would catch sight of me, and that wonderful, warm smile would spread across his face. He would leave whomever he was talking to, come toward me with arms extended, cup his hands around my face, and kissing me, he would say, "Why do you have to be so beautiful? Every man in the room is going to want to take you home." He would hold me at arm's reach, by the shoulders. "Woman was designed to ruin man," he would say, and I would feel a surge of some kind of twisted pride. The consistency of his affection was totally addictive. I was fascinated with him despite the fact it made no sense. It was all so exotic to me that a grown man would bother at all. And the very man both my mother and my father despised.

"I knew you'd be here," I would tell him, lying, taunting him only because he had no recourse. "But I saw you talking to a woman. Tino, our friendship is over."

"Her!" he would exclaim, looking around. "She's a bimbo! What do you expect me to do, when you'll have nothing to do with me? I'm a man, for God's sake! Who are you here with?" he would interrogate, instantly on the offensive. "Which unlucky lover are you going to destroy tonight? Tell me, so that I can warn him about you!"

MY INDENTURE WITH Omar Lahood was slowly but steadily working to stamp out any hopes I might have garnered for a more stimulating life, and yet I continued, in great secrecy, to sneak away on my lunch hour to attend a dizzying montage of job interviews, where I was inevitably thanked and politely refused. Always something wrong, always some requirement I could not possibly meet or even bluff; or, most traumatizing of all, the suggestion that five years of my precious life be signed over to the typing pool of some enormous corporation, after which, at the ossified old age of twenty-three, I could expect to earn a decent wage and tackle a relatively interesting job. Five years! Was this the gulag of democracy? I would leave these interviews weak kneed, desperate, and bereft, and beg my two departed guardians, Alison and Charlie, to think of something fast to save me from this awful path I seemed destined to trek pointlessly along. My future loomed clearly before me—bound to the employ of Omar Lahood for a pittance, a veteran though unhirable interviewee, and in-house shrink, maid, and best friend to Madeleine. Depression began to weigh heavily on me. Taking yet another ride on the panic train in my head, I desperately tried to think of a way out of this mess. But I never could come up with anything beyond traveling here and there, planting shallow roots at the homes of hospitable friends, living off the charity of others.

To cheer myself up, one Saturday afternoon in late spring I ambled casually up Fifth Avenue. A game I liked to play was to stand in front of Van Cleef & Arpels and stare at the huge jewels on their appetizing black velvet stands. I thought that if I affected a look of deserving need, some man, an older, kindly gentleman, would approach and say, "Little girl, you look like you really want that. Let me buy it for you. No strings attached." That was the important part, "No strings attached."

"Maria, is that you?" The voice jolted me from my reverie. It was Tino, approaching with books stacked in the crook of his arm. "What on earth do you think you're doing? Choosing something for one of your lovers to go broke buying you?"

"Of course," I said, happy to see him. The sight of him made me smile, warmed me. "Shall we go in and see if the tiara suits me?"

"A tiara, indeed!" His eyes were bloodshot, and he was swaying slightly on his feet. There was no life in his ashen face.

"Don't tell me you've turned out to be as pretentious as that ridiculous mother of yours!"

"What's the matter?" I asked him. I felt uneasy. "Are you ill?"

He stared at me, not saying a word. His lips trembled, and his usually bright blue eyes seemed to have trouble focusing. The people passing and car horns blaring blended into a muted backdrop. I saw and heard nothing except for Tino, who by the second became less and less familiar.

"What's the matter?" I asked again, unable to conceal the edge in my voice.

He took a step forward and lowered his eyes to mine. "You should have taken your chance when you had it," Tino said, billowing steamy alcohol fumes into my face. "I don't feel anything for you anymore."

He turned and walked away, and I watched as he tripped on his unsteady feet, weaving an uneven path through the crowd.

The harshness of his words ricocheted, shattering the confidence built from his affection for me. Pellets of salt water fell down my face, and all at once I was unable to see, unable to think. I felt sick. I slumped against the glass pane that sheltered the gleaming jewels.

"Wait!" I yelled at Tino's back. Frantic, I ran after him, pushing people aside. He was hailing a cab. "Tino! Please wait a minute. I need to talk to you!" But he was gone, the cab gunning to make the changing light.

That night I paced up and down Madeleine's living room, where I still resided despite my hostess's ever more insistent hints that my welcome had waned. When I was not wearing a path across her Persian carpet, I sat on the edge of one of the many uncomfortable little hard-backed chairs. Gold-gilt faux bamboo with velvet seats, chairs Madeleine had shipped over from her former home in Paris, where no doubt they better fit the mood of a life she had led with a disastrously drab-sounding chairman of the Paris Metro.

Two packs of cigarettes saw me through to dawn as I waited for the ornate gold clock on the mantelpiece to strike ten and, hopefully, for Tino's daily phone call. Insipid morning light gradually lit the day, glowing around the fringes of the long green-and-white curtains. At six o'clock, birds began their morning song, and the merry chirping made me wish I had a peashooter. To drown the sound I began pacing again, from the front door in its little hallway, which Madeleine had painted a glossy red in a fit one weekend—some sort of primitive response to expiate a bad mood she had become ensnared in on account of a shabby New York relationship, one of those that begin with, "He's it! He's the one! Sensitive, charming, funny, good looking. . . . And he's mad about me!" and end with, "Why didn't I listen to my instincts? I knew there was something wrong with him when I first laid eyes on the son of a bitch."

Sucking on my cigarette, I paced back into the living room to the green-and-white sofa that matched the curtains, and circled the coffee table, a low rectangle of glass with sharp corners to nick the skin off of your shins. The table was piled high with unread books on painters and their creations. I flicked ash into one of five Hermès ashtrays, more of Madeleine's French imports, and then began the journey back to the front door, in the red hallway that made you feel as if you were walking into someone's mouth.

At nine o'clock Madeleine came out of her bedroom looking the very picture of health in her pink silk robe. Fluffy blond hair surrounded her delicate Botticelli angel's face.

"This place smells revolting!" she declared as the fog of cigarette smoke hit her. She dashed across the room and dramatically drew back the curtains. My tired eyes flinched at the bright light.

"We've got to have air in here!" she said, struggling with the windows to let great rushes of cold spring air into the room. With her hands on her hips she addressed me in a stern, authoritative manner. "Maria, I think it's time we had a talk."

"Not now, Madeleine, please?" I begged, slumping into the sofa. "I've had a bad day, I mean a bad night. Actually it's been a god-awful day and night, and if Tino doesn't call me this morning, I'm definitely going to die."

"Maria," she said, not listening to a word of mine. "When I told you to come and stay, it was supposed to be for a reasonable length of time. Do you know you've been here almost two years? Now, you know I adore you, and obviously you needn't leave until you've got somewhere to go, but really, two years!"

Madeleine crossed the room to a vintage record player she was reluctant to render obsolete, preferring the retro-chic of imperfect sound to orchestral-quality compact discs. "Too modern!" she would say, passing a definitively damning sentence on the matter. She chose a David Bowie album from a formidable pile. Her delicate white fingers removed the record from its sleeve and placed it on the turntable. "China Girl," her favorite for laconic moments such as these, began to play.

"Madeleine, I'm sorry. You're absolutely right, we do have to talk." I started pacing again, trying to keep the oxygen flowing to my head. The sad sounds of Bowie were suffocating. I barely had the strength to think at all, let alone offer an ingenious plea to extract another month's lodging out of my obviously disillusioned hostess. "Couldn't we talk tomorrow, or next week perhaps?" She crossed her arms and tapped her little pink foot beneath the hem of her robe. "All right, later maybe," I acquiesced. "After I've had some sleep. I just couldn't right now. My life is dissolving all around me, and I might even be in some sort of coma. Sleepwalking, you know? A zombie. Perhaps I'm dead. Don't I look dead?"

"No," she said. "You don't look remotely dead. But you're

rambling like a maniac. Get some rest. I'm going out, and when I come home we'll order in and have a little chat. And whatever you do, don't speak to Tino in this condition. You're likely to say something you'll regret."

I snatched the receiver up from its berth so quickly the phone barely had the chance to ring. "Tino?" There was no answer. "Hello? Tino, is that you?"

"Yes," came the slow response. "You're awfully friendly this morning. What tricks are you up to now?"

"No tricks," I said. I sat, cradling the receiver against my head, curled up on the sofa, deliriously happy to hear the familiar voice with its familiar tone. "How are you today?"

"Fine!" He laughed. "All the better for hearing you in such a good mood. You know I'm leaving for the summer? I've rented a house in Cap d'Antibes from now until September, and I was hoping I could persuade you to come and visit me."

"Definitely."

"What?"

"I want to come," I told him unhesitatingly. "When?"

"You'd better not be pulling my leg. Are you serious?"

"Yes." I was emphatic. "Yes, yes, yes. Let's go now."

"What about your job?" he asked. "Will they let you go?"

"I'm quitting first thing tomorrow morning!" I said, laughing, the thought only just springing to mind. "I've had it with those bloody scripts! You know, my boss never even reads a damn word. He uses the reports as coasters! It's all an enormous waste of time and it's depressing. I need sun, I need to go to the Côte d'Azur. I need to go right away. Let's leave immediately and stay away for a long time. Can we? Please say yes!"

"What on earth has come over you?" he asked suspiciously.

"It's because . . . " I closed my eyes. Somehow it made it easier to speak. "When I saw you yesterday . . . I ran after you in the street. Didn't you hear me? I cried all the way home."

"What are you babbling about?" he asked.

"What?" I thought he must be teasing. "Outside Van Cleef. You had horrible things to say to me! Don't tell me you can't remember."

"Remember what?" Tino said, sounding confused and mildly amused. "I never left the house yesterday."

PART ONE

New York, April 1994

AN ERRATIC TRUST FUND ENABLES MY mother to glide from one month's expenditures to the next. The sum is just large enough to prevent the need for employment and just small enough to allow her to flirt with the notion of being destitute. A favorite theme is to announce with wide-eyed shock, "I'm flat broke! I'm going to have to get a job!" But then the monster seems always to have been laid to rest, because her life continues as before. I suppose one might call her modestly extravagant. She is not often prone to bouts of frivolous shopping. She might, however, temporarily adopt some aspiring art student and educate him at her expense.

On occasion, over the years, she has trained her sights on various obscure moneymaking schemes. Most times she is approached by vultures who see her as a name to be exploited, and for a time she might be inclined to indulge the fancy. One summer she met Hobart Cray, the famous cowboy jewelry designer. She agreed to act as the European distributor for his limited-edition Mount Saint Helens lava necklaces. By the time the merchandise was shipped eastward my mother had lost interest in the enterprise. Crates remained stacked in the dining room of our home in London for months, for as long as it took my mother to disburse the contents to friends and guests who happened by and admired the baubles.

One time I found her sitting cross-legged on her bed, surrounded by dozens of scruffy bits of paper. She was arranging
the placement for a dinner party, and when I interrupted, she
said, "I don't know how people with jobs do it. It's taken me
three full days to get this in order."

My mother's apartment consists of the two top floors of a
brownstone on the Upper East Side. Stuffed with heirlooms, it
is a showcase of her heritage and her destiny. Priceless bejeweled boxes and fussy Fabergés sit beside a feather presented to
my mother on a recent visit to a reservation, a pile of sapphires
she scratched off a mine wall in Sri Lanka, a signed photograph
of the guru who runs an ashram she likes to visit in Moose Jaw,
Saskatchewan, Canada. Fat, quilted armchairs face each other
with a low coffee table between, a table covered with art
books and a faded pink porcelain tea set on its own faded pink
tray. No inch of wall is spared the baroque, gold-framed paintings of ancestors in fancy dress, crowns atop haughty, stiff
faces.

We sat side by side, my mother and I, on a sofa three-feet
deep in tapestry cushions and folded cashmere blankets: pink
and raspberry and chocolate brown. Her pampered, untroubled face is beautiful. Clear, soft white skin, unlined when in re-
pose, smooth as cream. You can see the light dusting of powder,
confectioner's sugar. Her famous green eyes are as dark as a
reed-choked pond; her mascara a little heavy. People say we
look alike, but it is only our coloring that is similar. Pale skin,
dark hair, dark eyes. Except that mine are brown, and my
mother's a legendary green. Otherwise we are quite different.
We have never shared an idea, a thought. We do not understand
each other. This lack of understanding has built a barrier between us, an insurmountable obstacle of preconceptions. I
think I frighten her. I know she frightens me.

As a child when she would scold, I would stare at her, my
mind a complete blank. "Say something!" she would shout. All I

heard in my head was, "I have nothing to say." I could not even say that.

I have never liked the fire-engine red lipstick she wears. To me it looks like the bloodied mouth of a predator. The lipstick left a mark on my cheek when we kissed hello. She jabbed her thumb over the impression, smudging it into my face.

"Darling, what a lovely surprise to see you! That's so extra-ordinary, I was just thinking about you! Isn't that remarkable, darling? I was just thinking about you, and here you are! You're looking marvelous," she said, the way she always did when I saw her, not a trace of sincerity in her voice. Or was I imagining things? "I'm so glad you came to visit. Ralph and Cecelia are coming for tea; I know they'd love to see you. Will you stay?" She picked up a small pile of paperbacks from the floor. "I know you hate it when I ask you to read anything, but I would so appreciate it if you'd take a look at these and tell me what you think." I could see the covers were devoted to galactic life-forms against dark backgrounds, tow-headed monsters with lighthouse beacons streaming out of their faces, odd-shaped limbs holding baskets of what looked like wheat shafts, though maybe it was gold, maybe it was money. Space money, I thought; very handy. "Give them a chance, darling," she begged. "The man who writes these books is quite brilliant. I met him at a conference I went to about aliens and UFOs. He says that there's plenty of proof aliens came to Earth six thousand years ago. We are all descendants of the aliens . . . Don't look at me like that, darling; it makes complete sense. After all, before the Sumerians, man was nothing more than a shaggy beast striking rocks together in a cave. Then all of a sudden, too suddenly for evolution, there's reading and writing and culture. Aliens!"

"I don't know," I said. I was smiling. "I don't think there's much point in me taking these home. I know I'll never read them. I'm sure they're fascinating, but it's just not quite my thing."

"Oh, please," she said, shoving the books into my lap. "I bought lots. I have a set of my own."

"Thank you, Mama," I said, and I placed the books by my feet, where I had dropped my dilapidated brown leather suitcase. I looked away, at a portrait of a gentleman with a stern face and a great many medals on his golden-brocade breast. Beside it hung a little etching from Castle Cairngorm, with new glass protecting the huddled, eternally sobbing couple. It was both surprising and comforting to see that it had survived the upheavals when so much else had gone astray. There was something charming in its very existence, an admirable tenacity. "I want to talk to you about Prockney Hall." I looked her in the eye, checking for a flicker of reaction.

She leaned forward and began to rearrange the delicate pink teacups on their porcelain tray. The pink is faded, and where it is especially light, it is almost white. A rim of gold circumnavigates the tops of the cups, the upper cupola of the teapot, the lip of the creamer, the edge of the tray. They tinkled mutedly as my mother moved the three cups about on their saucers, adjusting their position. She wears no jewelry. No rings on her soft, not quite beautiful hands. Our hands are alike, and I study mine. They are rounded where they should be tapered. The palms of my hands are almost entirely square. Strong hands, I am told. People often seem surprised by my hands, belying as they do the conventional signs of good breeding.

"I want to tell you about the school, Mama." I began to lose courage. I was hoping she would turn to me and hug me and put an end to this ordeal. But she said nothing. She sat back into the sofa, the cushions puffed up around her like wings. Protection. She examined her hands, splaying them out on her lap, milky white starfish against her black trousers.

Her head was slightly bowed, and I could see the strip of white roots that ran down the center of her skull like a river on a map, bordered by the too-dark dyed hair. "There was a boy there. Roland. He used to hit me, Mama. I never told anyone, because he said he'd kill me." I looked down now at my lap, where my sweating hands were rubbing into each other as if they wanted to wear away the skin, get down to the bone. "I . . . " I faltered. "He used to . . . " I gave up. My head hung like a dead weight, tears fell into my hands, wetting the hot, red-worn skin. I wanted to go on, but I simply could not. Words clogged with salt water.

My mother leaned forward and hugged me. With one hand she smoothed my hair. "Darling," she said in that slightly scratchy voice she has, "Remember the time I sprained the same ankle twice in six months? Everything in life is a learning experience. I'm sure you learned a lot from being at that school. Much more than you even realize."

"Three years is a long time," I maundered breathily, my stomach knotting as it occurred to me that I had never once voiced these thoughts before. Their very unfamiliarity frightened me. I pulled away from her embrace and watched her through unclear eyes, like a smudged windscreen in the fog. I felt very far away from her, though we sat a foot apart. "Mama," I said, almost in a whisper. "He, he did things . . . "

"It's all so long ago! It's a little late to bring this sort of thing up!"

"I was afraid," I murmured, staring down, not wanting to encourage the tears.

"Well!" she said, stretching a tissue from a box, presenting it to me. "What do you want me to do about it now?" She looked hurt, resentful that I should have brought up something unpleasant.

"Nothing, really," I told her, lying, blowing my nose, the noise effectively sounding the end of the round. "I guess I just wanted to tell you about it. I feel like I have so many secrets to hold in my head. Sometimes I feel like a freak."

"You're not a freak, darling." She got up; she wanted to get away. "Can I make you some tea? That'll make you feel better. A warm cup of Darjeeling." She stood at the kitchen counter with her back to me, filling the kettle, choosing cups and saucers from a cupboard at eye level in front of her, tinkering with silver spoons from a drawer. "I hope you'll stay. Did I mention that Ralph is coming for tea? I know he'd love to see you."

Friends of my mother's began to arrive. The room was immediately filled with a crescendo of "darling's" and "It's so divine to see you's" and little yelps of delight coating the "You are too sweet, you shouldn't have's" that accompany the unwrapping of a gift. She devoted herself to her followers, pointing to the coatrack as she greeted them, patting the back of an armchair as she beckoned them to come sit. I said hello, doing my best to appear enthusiastic. I watched the merry band of misfit moths that flit around my mother's glittering flame. The prototype is fat, maternal, middle-aged women who can dispense worldly, commonsense advice and who never object to being the target of my mother's prankster humor. The men are most often homosexuals, designers, singing coaches, transcendental meditators. Ethnic is a plus. Everyone must worship the princess. Any efforts to curtail or hamper her desires are met with swift and final expulsion. An interchangeable group whose members I have seen come and go.

The noise level surged and I thought my head would explode. If I had to tell one more person, "I'm fine, thank you, and yourself?" I thought, I would scream. Instead I collected my leather suitcase, made my excuses, and backed out of the gathering, shaking hands and kissing cheeks.

"I hope you're feeling better, darling, now that you've spoken about it?" my mother asked, following me to the door with the pile of books I had overlooked.

"Yes," I said. I took the books from her. I smiled because, ultimately, she is impressively impervious.

"Must you go, darling? Ralph promised to tell us all about his mother's funeral! It was hilarious! The priest was blind drunk and tripped into the grave! Do stay and listen to Ralph tell it, you'll be weeping by the end! Have you ever heard anything so wonderful? The fool fell flat on his face on the coffin!"

"Thanks, Mama," I said, uncomfortable with her exuberance, which always left me feeling as if I had been run over by a train. "I'm on my way to the Hamptons for a dinner party tomorrow night. And to visit Dad. I just stopped in on a whim."

"You must always feel like you can come talk to Mama. I hope it won't be years again before you come to see me. You know that I never could talk to my mother? Darling, please let me know what you think about the books." She kissed me on the cheek and closed the door.

M Y   M O T H E R   W A S born a princess, inheriting a rusting title from long-defunct European royalty. She is therefore genetically inclined toward encouraging serfdom in the folks who loiter in her life. As her mother was fond of saying, "Snobs? They're our best friends!" At no time since I have known my mother was she not surrounded by at least one court jester, one confessor, one secretary to plan and organize a schedule of lunches and hair appointments and intrepid expeditions up the Nile or down the Amazon with modern-day Marco Polos, and all for free because, of course, the princess has very little cash to dispense. We hope the honor will suffice. Sometimes she vigorously eschews overusing her peculiar status, refusing to be escorted to the theater by anyone other than her Alabama-born Cajun astrologer. Or she might insist that her dinner guests sit on the floor of her home and balance on their knees the heavy crown-crested silverware and the twenty-four-karat-gold plates, passed down from better times, while they try to find a resting place for the acidic Spanish wines served in chunky crystal goblets carved with the initials of a former reigning monarch. Equally, she might drop the full force of her unusual and evocative name on an inattentive maître d' and so secure a better table, or call a talk show and book herself an hour or so of prattle time to air her princessly views on foreign wars or female subjugation or the paltry level of hygiene in the Third World—and holding her nose to express herself more graphically, she might add, "The countryside is very beautiful, but my, the natives stink! I think it ought to be mandatory to open Body Shops all over the world!" a natural presumption coming from a descendent of a long line of bossy types who inflicted laws and regulations on voiceless minions. In the confines of her home my mother prefers for the maid to address her as "Your Highness." This tends to make me smile involuntarily, until, of course, I notice glimpses of my mother's contradictory ways appearing in my own personality, and then I feel obliged to remove myself, sometimes for years at a stretch, praying the infection is due to proximity, rather than lying dormant in veins of royal blue blood.

A F E W B L O C K S from my mother's home, at the entrance to the subway stairs, a man stood tapping a pair of thin wooden chopsticks against the brick wall. White eyes facing the sky, his head swayed gently while he thrummed his steady beat, *t-clack, t-clackity-clack.* "Oh, Lordie, are you listenin'? Can you see me, Big Man in the sky? I'm flyin' around in the underground like a bat, like a rat, like a man po-zessed! Lordie, tell me, am I Satan or am I singin'?" Footsteps of passersby would halt the tune momentarily. "Can you spare a penny, sir or madam? I'd be ever so o-bliged."

I neared with coins bunched in the warm cavity of my hand, swimming in a droplet of sweat, preparing to drop them in the upturned cap that lay at his feet.

"Ladies and gentlemen, citizens of the world, I beg you t'

look into yo' hearts, as our savior did on the downtrodden and
the o-pressed." *T-clack, t-clackity-clack.* "Sweet Lordie in heaven,
won't you come take me up to see you soon?"

A foot away from him I let the coins drop into the cap.

"I know you's a young lady, I can hear it in yo' step and in the
smell of your purrfume! But don't you know that pennies come
from heaven, little lady? Don't you know that the Lord saves us
and that the weak shall inherit the great planet Earth? And what
would you say if I told you that it's a little lady like yo'self that
I'm most in need of? Can you spare a kiss, miss? Can you spare
a tender moment fo' an old blind fool?"

I raced down the stone steps two at a time and jammed a to-
ken into the turnstile, heard the ticking of the rotation, and
stepped onto the platform. I leaned back against one of the
many movie posters that lined the tunnel wall, and hugged my
mother's gift of books close to my chest with one arm, my suitcase dangling from the other, flimsy shields against the pit of
steel girders and sunken tracks, where the rats meandered and
oily puddles shone.

At Pennsylvania Station, I exited. I stopped to buy my
ticket from a woman with a lisp so confounding I had to ask
her to repeat everything she said at least three times, until, by
the end of the transaction, there were sparks of fury flying between us.

Immediately I was sorry I had lost my temper. Walk away, I
counseled; be strong and walk away. But I could not. The fear I
felt building in my stomach over my impending visit with my
father was partly due to the financial aid I still relied heavily
upon and partly due to the hope, somewhere very deep, that
one day we might be friends. One day. It made me queasy, and
haltingly I trickled down the cement steps to platform 19,
where two grumbling trains lounged like giant snakes ready to
race. Searching for a mostly deserted carriage, I settled in the
last seat, facing west, where I removed my coat, tucked my suit-

case beneath my feet, placed the books on my lap, and proceeded, as unobtrusively as I could manage, to observe a family
of five children and their weary-looking mother. I caught the
eye of a girl, maybe ten years old, and we smiled at each other.
This made her shy, and she burrowed her head into her
mother's bosom. Then, slyly, she turned her face toward me
and smiled again. If I were a scout for a modeling agency, I
would have solicited her. Her eyes were wide almonds that rose
at the ends; her skin, a faint mocha, was flawless; and her young
limbs were long and sleek. She reclined against her mother like
a Modigliani muse. Just muscle and bone and an angel's face.
Where is she from? I wondered. And where is she going?
Home, perhaps, but home to what?

I cannot remember a place being home since my mother left
England. Up and went in a day. Sold the house and moved to
America and forgot to mention it. That was half my lifetime
ago. I still dream about that house and my bedroom and the little objects I fussed over, my prized possessions, miniature treasures that I treated with the utmost consideration. The love of
miniature things was a strange passion I shared with my maternal grandmother, the most beautiful lady I have ever known.
Tall, soft like powder, and a glint in her green-blue eyes. Looking into her face was like looking at a dawn-brightened
Mediterranean Sea. That was my grandmother's face. And yet
her manner was stern, even frightening sometimes. It was
many years before I found out that she was, in fact, more afraid
of people than anyone ever was of her.

As a very special treat she would sometimes bring me upstairs to her bedroom in the house in Madrid where she had
lived with my grandfather for almost forty years, a room in
subtle shades of gray and blue. Behind a screen was a bed half
concealed, fitted with starched Irish linen sheets edged in lace
peaking out from beneath rows of rose-petal pink satin pillows
that rested one upon the other like fresh-cut headstones in a

quarry. Everything in the room was old, though nothing was worn, still beautiful and apparently untouched by the century, like my grandmother.

My grandmother would unlock one of the many wooden drawers of a bureau across the room and lay out her collection. There was a silver tea set that had come from Russia, decorated with carvings of flowers. Delicate porcelain cups sat on matching saucers in translucent whites painted with bees and berries and butter yellow butterflies. There were tiny gold boxes with precious stones sunk into the tops and the sides. Our favorite was one so small it could not comfortably have held a single postage stamp, and yet, inside it, lay a doll with real clothes and a sprout of the softest brown down-feather ends for hair. The doll was dressed in red trousers, a white shirt of cotton, and a black-and-white waistcoat done up with buttons that cannot have been any larger than a dot on the back of a ladybug.

We would spend hours taking everything out, laying it all carefully on the leather-topped bureau usually reserved for letter writing. There was no need to speak, just an intense satisfaction that passed between us as we handled the diminutive objects. A secret obsession, ours alone to indulge.

Every once in a while one of these treasures would be passed on to me in a ritual of the deepest solemnity. "I think perhaps it's time you took this home with you," my grandmother would say, pointing at one of the treasures. "I can't look after everything myself forever, and there's no one else in the family who appreciates these like you do."

The Russian silver tea set—teapot, creamer, sugar bowl with its own tongs—that was my prize. It sat alongside Nymphenburg porcelain cups, tiny wine red leather-bound books, crystal-topped hat pins, all of them along the back of the desk in my bedroom in London. They were all entirely useless, but I adored them. They provided the basis for my fantasy life; they were a springboard to enter my even more private world of dreams.

The train eased into a station, wheezing to a low rumbling idle as a disembodied voice announced where we were and how long we might expect to stay. The woman across from me corralled her five children toward the doors. She talked them through some familiar drill, preparing them for the disembarkation, wearing herself down even further. The eldest girl, the pretty one with the almond eyes, looked so much more frail now than she did when she lounged against her mother. She looked gawky and bony, and even her spectacular eyes looked sad. When I sprang across, extending the books my mother had given me, pressing them into her hands, she looked terrified, opening her mouth while no words came out, gulping at me like a fish. But she accepted them, folding them in an embrace, a wordless exchange between us, a tacit bond. The doors closed, dividing us forever, and I settled back as we heaved off in that peculiar electric way. If the law of averages was anything to measure life by, we would most likely never see each other again.

The train rambled deep into the countryside of eastern Long Island, whipping by malls of a thousand movie theaters and the distinctive colored roofs of fast food conglomerates and the flag-bannered lots of car dealerships, all of it vanishing slowly into the twilight like a sinking ship.

I do not like to think about the house, but when I do, I see it streaked with sunshine sneaking through the leafy branches of an oak tree that grew in the courtyard in front by the street. A tall house of brick with a circular blue-and-white plaque claiming some famous former tenant's tenure. Indoors, wooden shutters folded back into recesses in the wall. Thick curtains hung down beside them, curtains to stand and hide behind and watch the busy world of cars and people passing on the street. Sunlight-warmed squares of floor beneath the windows, where the cat would bask.

A dumbwaiter traveled all the way from the basement,

where the kitchen was, to the very top floor, and I would ride it up and down like a tiny elevator, folded into a crouch so as to fit between the shelves, pulling myself up by the thick ropes. A patio behind the house, surrounded by a high wall, was filled with hip-high burnt sienna pots growing baby orange trees and my mother's prized gardenia plants. Every thick-scented white bloom was treated like a great occasion, and my sister and I would be called outside to admire the open petals, encouraged to lean forward and inhale the sweetness. That is a home to dream of.

I T O Y E D W I T H a bowl of soggy cornflakes as I sipped my coffee and gazed at the thumbed-through newspaper left on the breakfast table. The sound of a car coming up the driveway caught my attention, and I looked up in time to catch sight of a silver fin, the tail end of my father's Cadillac, silver Sedan de Ville with red interior. The one time he tried to teach me how to drive, I rammed the silver grill into an oak tree.

A car door slammed. Footsteps ground steadily across the gravel driveway. *Crunch, crunch, crunch.* Then silence for half a minute as he crossed the flagstones in front of the front door. The screen door creaked breathily open.

"Anybody home?" my father yelled out as the screen door clacked shut behind him. "Hello?"

I sat quite still, coffee cup suspended, and listened to him walk directly toward the breakfast room, toward me.

"When did you arrive?" He stood at the open door, filling the frame. His dark tan showed off brilliantly against his sweat-drenched tennis whites.

"Late last night," I said, my tone pitching up defensively.

"Whatcha doing today, kid?"

"Nothing," I said, with a little too much emphasis.

"Don't be a wiseass, Maria. Nobody likes a tough broad!" he

said, holding his racket like a golf club. He swatted at a plant by his feet. An overflow of rubbery, glossy green leaves poured up and over the wicker basket. Looping my spoon beneath the cornflakes, I watched the milk splash up the sides of the bowl, cover the handle of the spoon. I could feel my father's eyes boring into me. I did not like to look him directly in the face when we spoke, because there was always the worry that I might raise an eyebrow or frown in some way that could offend him, spark off his temper. I preferred to concoct obscure, untraceable methods of attack. So I kept my gaze downward, jabbed the milk with the end of my spoon, and watched the flakes spin.

"Why don't you ride your bike over to the club and get a game together?"

"I think I might go to the beach," I said, staring at the cornflakes floating peaceably about the bowl. I made a concerted effort to sound inoffensive, while I knew my choice of words would enrage my father. "I want to read."

"You hate tennis," he spat out in the same tone one might use to accuse a person of being a racist. "Look at me when I'm talking to you!" he hissed. "You have no respect for me. You don't treat me like a father!"

"Well, the jury's still out on that one," I muttered daringly, working up a camouflage of noise in my cereal bowl.

"What's that?" He charged, beheading a leaf or two.

"Dad, I need to talk to you," I said, fairly whispering into the cereal. My stomach tightened, and yet I knew that this effort would be as swiftly aborted as all the others, and so the impact of anticipation was greatly reduced.

"What about?" he asked, plucking the strings of his racket.

"Prockney Hall," I said, a lead weight flattening any further words into the back of my throat.

My father stared at me as if he hoped the anger in his eyes might burn me to ash so that this tiresome topic could be swept up by the slightest breeze and dispersed permanently. The rubbery plant by his feet lost another few leaves to the face of the tennis racket. "That's between you and your mother."

"It never would have happened to Miranda," I said, hoping that this new slant might spark a shred of remorse. "You never would have left her in a place like that."

"Leave your sister out of this!" he snapped, leaning slightly forward, so that I pressed back in my chair, defeated. "I never saw the school! It was your mother's responsibility! I like your mother, but she's crazy. You know that, don't you? She's the most abnormal person you'll ever meet!"

"You married her!" I said, eager to get as far away as possible from the unsavory subject of Prockney Hall, and yet annoyed at having had it buried so artfully, so irretrievably.

"She married me! I divorced her!"

"Otto Harris Sr. invited me to a dinner party tonight," I said, and as I spoke I wondered how the unlikely revelation would affect the joust, hoped it would both placate and infuriate, all at once.

"The truth at last! I didn't think you'd travel this far just to see your old dad!" he said, sounding surprised. The tennis racket still thwacked the leaves of the potted plant. "Did he ask your sister?"

"No. Least, I don't think so," I said, hiding my delight at his consternation, and sent the cereal on another tour of the bowl.

"Why not?"

"Why should he?" I said, too fast. "She's busy with her billionaire. I think she said he's flying her to Paris for some escargots and then on to Kenya for a cup of coffee. Or was it Java? I forget! I get it all mixed up!"

"Your sister knows how to merchandise herself. She gets that from me," he said authoritatively, an eyebrow raised for emphasis, as though he were revealing the meaning of life. "If we're lucky, you'll meet a rich doctor tonight. A shrink. Think about it, you could have free medical help for the rest of your life!"

• • •

"HOW NICE OF Otto to invite you to a dinner party. Of course, eighteen years old is about the right age to start going out," Patricia said as we drove in her navy blue Mercedes, an anniversary present from my father, down streets bordered by ten-foot hedges and immense, draping oak trees. The car had to have been twenty years old, more perhaps, and still, each time you opened the door, pulling on the silver latch, the sweet, heavy scent of leather engulfed you. "Formally, I mean. This is a grown-up dinner party."

The car turned into a driveway between a set of brick gateposts. We coasted up toward the house, slowing to meet the gloved hand of a butler who would open my door for me. My mind was elsewhere, though. I did not really know this house by night so much as I used to know it by day. Alison and I used to ride our bicycles side by side down these same streets, either to her house or to mine. Our bikes would slow as the front wheels lurched into the blue pebbles of the driveway, and we would stand up, pedaling as hard as possible, guiding the bikes with stiff arms, arched backs, until we reached the crescent of flagstones, the hem of the house. Then we would let the bikes drop, deserted chariots, and dash through the house barefoot, across the hand-painted sisal and out the sliding glass doors at the other end of the living room. Feet plunging through the hot sand to the ankle-deep surf, we would swivel around, arms flailing, and fall backward into the freezing, salty waves, shrieking, laughing.

"I wish I wasn't so nervous," I told Patricia in a half whisper.

"You'll be fine. I'll come pick you up at eleven o'clock, so keep an eye on your watch. You are wearing your watch, aren't you?"

"Yes." I glanced at my wrist, where I had fastened a scuffed gold-faced watch with Roman numerals and a once-glossy brown leather strap. It was too bulky for my dress, but it was a reminder of a previous life, one of my very few possessions that had survived my mother's impulsive move to America.

I entered the low-lit room, my heart thumping. The gathering of people at the other end looked like one cohesive mass of confidence. Everyone chatting animatedly. Tiny dresses, white slacks, navy blue blazers. Gold flashed from waists, from wrists, around necks. I stood, immobilized, by the door. I wore a yellow linen dress of Patricia's that, in her dressing room, had seemed appropriate, even elegant. Yet here I felt very much out of place.

I might never have crossed the room if Otto Harris Sr. had not seen me and come to shepherd me across a stretch of terrain more familiar to a time long past. All the furniture had been changed from when I used to come, and as we walked, I searched for signs of that other lifetime. The hand-painted sisal was gone, and instead I walked over downy-soft carpet that indented with every step I took. I supposed this was the handiwork of the new wife, Rachel, whom I had never met.

"Maria, my little Maria," he said, smiling. "I'm so glad you came. I was beginning to worry." The big, bearish face calmed me; his warm hand holding mine, leading me toward the guests, was reassuring. We saw each other rarely, and when we did we never spoke about Alison. I always wondered why this was, but there was something about him that silenced me.

"Hello, Mr. Harris. You didn't think I wouldn't show up, did you?" I was horrified that he could consider such a thing, but he was not listening to me. He was introducing me to a woman whose name I did not catch and whose limp little hand she held out for me to grasp like a handkerchief.

"This is my little Maria Moses, who I've known since she couldn't have stood much higher than my knee. She was Alison's best friend," Otto Harris Sr. said, explaining me to a man beside the limp-wristed lady. The man had wicked, liquid blue eyes and a touch of arrogance in the hard line of his square jaw.

The two of them stood in front of a wall of blackness, reflecting glass doors, doors I only remember being wide open for Alison and me to dash past on our way to the beach. "And tonight we present her to the world."

"I thought," the man with the blue eyes said as he crunched on a cube of ice, "you were celebrating Rachel's decision to stay in Paris another week, you old rogue."

"A second week in Paris is going to cost me more than any fun I could have here. I'm telling you, that woman is going to be the end of me!"

"Any relation of Sammy Moses?" the man asked, fixing me with his intense blue glare.

"Her father," Otto Harris Sr. answered for me. "You know him, don't you?"

"Who doesn't?" the man said, eyeing me with the unabashed curiosity of a child, a sly smile creasing his face. "I know your mother even better! As a matter of fact, didn't I meet you in Scotland years ago? At Charlie Cairngorm's?"

"Perhaps," I mumbled, unable to place him, embarrassed to have to speak at all. I quickly looked away. "I don't know."

I watched the three adults in front of me, the sounds of their conversation blending into a gentle hum. I hoped that they would forget about me. For whatever reason, I was mesmerized by their teeth, three sets of jaws opening and closing, spitting out words. Whenever I felt their eyes on me I would smile, a mounting panic building within me, and burrow my fingers into the folds of Patricia's yellow dress, bunching it together, praying that I would not be expected to speak. When I felt sufficiently forgotten, I looked around beyond the crowd, a chattering morass of peroxide manes and shiny pomaded pates bobbing and undulating and exhaling shafts of smoke. Everyone seemed to have so much to talk about, and the noise swelled as laughter cut in like refrains in a song.

An old man, obviously once thick limbed and grand, was in

fact singing. "Tra la la, la la!" he sang with his head tilted, a
shaggy thicket of white hair hanging down his back. He faced
the ceiling with his mouth open, directing the throaty warbling
upward. He was dressed in one whole piece of orange cloth
swaddled around his corpulence, his tanned, lined face emerging at one end, sandaled feet at the other, like a turtle standing
upright in its shell. "Tra la la, tra la la!" Insidiously his rich baritone stirred up dormant recollections, jolting my senses about.
Scenes materialized before me, scenes from a time when these
sliding glass doors had been open. I thought I could feel the
cool breeze on my wet bathing suit, thought I could detect the
heat of the sun on my arms and legs, and the sunburn that
would peel in white sheets. I looked around more carefully and
tried to see beneath the layers with which time conceals the
past.

My eyes strayed to the stairs that led up to a landing I knew
by heart. Alison's bedroom, where she and I had spent so many
midnight hours wide awake, telling stories, making pledges. I
could barely suppress the urge to walk away and go up there,
look around, sit on one of the two beds, prop a pillow up behind me, and lean back against the wall. See if I could find a way
to travel back in time. Nostalgia fell around me like a soft summer rain, exposing memories long since buried.

"If you'll excuse me, I'm neglecting my other guests. Mademoiselle Celeste, would you accompany me on my rounds?"
Otto Harris Sr. said insistently, his thick, deep voice reeling me
back to the present. He linked his arm with the limp-wristed
woman, Mademoiselle Celeste. "Miss Maria Moses, may I introduce Tino Brooks? Constantine Brooks, Miss Maria Moses."
He spoke with his arms slicing the air like a conductor's, and
then he turned and whisked Mademoiselle Celeste away with
him. Tino Brooks! I had been standing next to Tino Brooks all
this time and not suspected a thing! My father's archenemy. The
one member of my father's social set whom he actively and

openly loathed. This would be a supreme irritant, and I could hardly wait to tell him of this chance meeting at breakfast to-morrow.

"You don't look a bit like that wretched father of yours," Tino said, grinning, devouring another cube of ice.

"That depends who you think my father is!" I said, spinning off lines I knew by rote, part of my battery of clever comebacks that sounded far more spontaneous than they ever were, leaving me free to observe this sworn foe of my father's.

"Why d'you say that?" Tino said evenly, swallowing fragments of ice. Tino is a wonderful-looking man, cut square from some granite quarry. His face is hard and his stare is stern and unforgiving, yet there is a warmth in the way he smiles, a charm that softens and smooths the rough edges of his interrogatory style.

"According to Mama, you always know who your mother is, but you can never be sure about your father!" I said, still unraveling my oft-repeated quips.

"According to Mama!" Tino fired laughter at me with a force like hail. Grabbing my hand, he turned it over and back again, as if he were handling a dead fish in a marketplace, checking if it was fit for sale. "Do you have blood on your hands too?"

"What?"

"Did Mama ever tell you what she did with poor old Charlie Cairngorm?" Tino asked, tipping his drink back, sucking in the slabs of ice, still clutching my lifeless fingers.

"What do you mean?" I said as coldly as I could manage. He opened his hand, and very slowly I reeled mine back in, crossed my arms, looked him right in the eye. Tino was imposing and dense, but not frightening. "Charlie Cairngorm was a friend of my mother's. And mine."

"Tell me something, do you get along with that ridiculous mother of yours?" Tino asked, chewing his ice, smiling at me in direct contrast with his oddly combative tone.

"Do you?" I fired back, one eyebrow raised and an inkling of a smile on my face as I began to get the hang of his debriefing methods.

"It's a long story," he said, swilling the last of his drink around his glass. "For now, all I'll say is I can't stand either one of your ghastly parents. Your mother's a self-centered, gold-digging tart, and your father is a shameless social climber. As for your sister, she's one of the most beautiful cold bitches I've ever met! I like them with a little blood pumping through their veins! Hope you don't mind me speaking my mind?"

"By all means!" I was impressed by the rampage. I had never heard anyone take on all three of my immediate family with such velocity. And though I knew I ought to have been insulted and stood valiantly by my ravaged relatives, I found instead that I was amused by this opinionated man with the steely blue eyes and the jaunty swagger. "But you're wrong about my mother; she's not a gold digger. She's not the least materialistic."

"Not materialistic?"Tino said, his taunting eyes conveying his feelings, the lids raised into his wrinkling brow. "You're either a very good actress or you're hopelessly uninformed! At a guess, seeing as you come from such a uniformly untalented family, I'd say it's the latter!"

"Blessed with psychic powers! How lucky for you!" I said, laughing, less and less bothered by his bombastic manner. He did not intimidate me; if anything, his provocations inspired retaliation. I liked him.

"Is she still beautiful, your mother?"Tino asked, a hesitant, self-conscious smile on his face. "I'm sure she's still an idiot, but how does she look?"

"Always beautiful," I replied, and quietly I added, "I went to see her yesterday. I, uh, I wanted to talk to her about something but . . . I don't know, we just don't seem to be able to . . . communicate." I was fiddling with the folds of Patricia's yellow dress, plucking at the embroidered flowers. "It's as if we speak different languages."

"So you're an ally?" he proposed, ruffling my hair as if I were a dog.

I smiled radiantly as I thought how extraordinary it was that in such a short time we should have made peace, or at least forged a truce. Tino's fearless theatrical manner was beguiling and entertaining, and I knew I had found a kindred spirit, who saw the truth and was not afraid to speak it. A jingling of bells stole into my thoughts. A man in dark trousers and a white jacket stood by the entrance to the dining room, a small silver bell in one white-gloved hand, dwarfed and absurd, chiming emphatically. "Dinner is served, ladies and gentlemen," the man said, straining his vowels, sending his mustache up with every word, thin strings that hung like a cowboy's tie.

"Men should always be flanked by beauty. Then there would be no great wars!" Tino said, steering me with his hand on my back as we strolled toward the dining room. "If Josephine had shown up at the front lines, those northern brutes would have welcomed the French with fanfare."

I rolled Tino's words around in my head, wondering what sort of significance to attribute to them, but I could not confidently make out his meaning, and I was not inclined to reveal the looming depths of my ignorance.

We dined in a room I barely recognized, with three tables covered in white linen and chrysanthemums and gold-rimmed plates. Tino sat at the head of the table nearest the windows. I was seated to his left, Mademoiselle Celeste to his right. It took all my imagination to see through the darkened, candlelit room with the painted, dusted faces of grown-ups breathing in on their cigarettes, tipping back dark red wine, huge diamonds catching the light. I wanted so much to feel the midday sun come streaming through the windows while Alison and I sat at the lunch table hurriedly downing sandwiches, glasses of milk, dusky brown limbs frosted with sand, sand that crunched in the sandwiches.

" . . . you realize that Anna Karenina was a morphine addict?"Tino blasted gruffly, jerking me back to consciousness. "It wasn't love that sent her under the train tracks. She was a junkie!"

Tino stared at me and I examined his face, searching for clues. Did he expect me to answer? Words collided, building up like a highway crash. I was not certain of what to say.

"What have you been doing with your youth? Don't you read?"Tino's blue eyes brimmed with a strange opalescence, absorbing light from the candles. His words were harsh, but the smile that flickered on his face reduced the impact.

"I've been searching for your books but I can't seem to find them anywhere," I lied, panic building as I realized I had no idea whatTino did, and I prayed he was not about to quiz me. "Don't you write? What have been doing with your adulthood?"

"You are ridiculous!" he said, clearly enchanted. His eyes fixed on me. "Ballsy but ridiculous!" he told the room, despite the fact that only I listened. "My guess is that Maria Moses is headed for a whole lot of trouble! I knew a young girl just like you a long time ago, . . ."

I studied this man who sat beside me, entirely conscious of wanting to grab his attention, and trap it forever. As he spoke, never directly to me, never to me alone, but to the four of us closest to him, he checked to see that my eyes never left him. I felt certain that my jumble of feelings, like waking from a coma, were fully reciprocated by him. The notion was intense, hypnotic.

"Do you see that woman over there?"Tino asked, pointing with his chin at the table behind us. "The dame with the tight face. She used to work at Madame Claude's."

"Really, Tino!" Mademoiselle Celeste said, dangling her silver fork as if it were too great a weight for her filigree fingers. "How uncouth!"

"Pffff!" Tino spat, flicking his hand through the air impatiently. "Women should personally thank Madame Claude for satisfying the cravings of frustrated men!" Tino rolled up the sleeves of his blue button-down shirt, preparing for battle. "But if that old hooker doesn't watch herself, she'll become the next victim bled dry by our wonderful eccentric Nate!"

"Who's Nate?" I asked as Mademoiselle Celeste clutched her throat. Was she hoping to catch the words before they surfaced, prevent herself from saying something she might regret?

"You don't know who Nate is?" Tino asked, pursing his mouth in a smirk, as if he were not sure whether to be embarrassed of me or for me. "You've never heard of Tolstoy! You don't know what your mother is up to? You must be the most socially unaware person I've ever met!"

Tino was smiling as he chastised me, and though I could feel my face prickling, at the same time I felt an odd sense of pride. There was something in the way Tino smiled as he scolded that left me feeling I was a fool but that he found it charming, that it did not matter at all.

"So who's Nate?"

"Well, for one thing, he is the ex-husband of Mademoiselle Celeste. For another, he used to be a neighbor of your father's," Tino said, raising an eyebrow as he spoke. With his chin he pointed at the fat man dressed in orange cloth, and with his voice substantially lowered, he added, "And lastly, Mr. Abernathy Ford is sitting four bodies away from you, attempting to seduce the trollop. No doubt as a means of financing his artistic endeavors for the next few years!"

"I know, I know! Filthy old fat-assed Flasher Ford!" I whispered forcefully.

"Keep your voice down!" Tino ordered, tapping me on the head. "You're worse than me!"

"I remember him! He married an Indian lady, and there was something about money and death and I don't know what else. Am I right, is that it?"

"In a sense," Mademoiselle Celeste said sadly, her hands propping up her exhausted head, her bejeweled fingers dangling under her chin like an unkempt beard. "Tino, really, you shouldn't encourage the child like this. Especially things you don't entirely understand. Nate has been the victim of some terrible bad luck. He is to be pitied, treated with the utmost consideration and care." Her voice rose dramatically as the arch of her painted eyebrows peaked into pyramids.

"Celeste!" Tino said, gesturing grandly. "He wiped you out! Took every penny and left as soon as the coffers were bone dry! Left you for this ridiculous bimbo! I don't know how you stand to be in the same room! The funny thing is, I like him. He's eccentric and completely mad, but how could you dislike a man who loves opera as much as he does?"

Dinner ended and I followed the exiting women into the sitting room. Without Tino I felt awkward and lost. Mademoiselle Celeste, out of Tino's sights, seemed uninterested in occupying the same hemisphere as I and drifted away with sighs and mutterings both times I attempted an approach. Conversation with a cygnet was of no interest to this game of swans, and I sat at the edge of a sofa and listened vaguely to the chatter as thoughts drew me away to a distant time, thoughts easily triggered by a thousand references around the room.

It was a relief to see Patricia, on the dot of eleven, that wonderful smile always in place on her beautiful face. "Time to go home, Maria," she said, a little too loudly for the sake of my pride. I returned to the dining room to thank Mr. Harris for having invited me to his dinner party. As I left the room, walking past Tino, he grabbed me by the arm.

"Don't you have any manners, young lady?" he shouted at me, making my heart falter. "Come say good night to an old man." Holding my shoulders with his hands, he drew me to him, kissed me on both cheeks; then he let me go and I saw he was smiling. There had been a moment when I thought I had offended him. His warmth thrilled me, and I knew that I had carved a niche for myself somewhere on the rock face of his soul.

"It was very nice to meet you," I said, beaming at him, meaning it. "Good night."

T HE S UN W A S up before me, and I arrived at the breakfast table to find my father almost finished with the morning's newspapers, piling up the gray-and-white pages in an unruly stack.

"How was the party last night, kid?" he asked from behind the *New York Times.* "Got any stories for me?"

Slithering onto one of the leather-backed chairs that creak as you sit, I reached for a box of cereal. "Yes," I said, the rehearsed lines on a loop in my head. I knew I ought not to go on, but it was somehow too late. The best I could do was lower my voice to a murmur and work a delay into my script. "Mr. Ford, the man who used to live next door, was there."

"That fuckin' schmuck! I thought he'd be dead by now!" my father said, speaking into the pages of his newspaper so that they billowed, rustling in a ghostlike way. "Who else?"

"Tino Brooks."

The newspaper descended, crumpling into his lap. My father stared at me. I thought his gray-blue eyes looked paler than usual. "Is that so?" he said, his thin lips shivering with the effort of controlling his predictably quick temper. "Why d'you tell me this?" As he spoke he picked up the knife beside his plate and began to tap the table.

"Dunno." I followed the line of the cornflakes tumbling into my bowl. My heart was pounding, blood coursing through the veins in my head so fast it was hard to think. "I don't understand what the fuss is all about," I said, trying to stay my shaking hand so that I did not pour milk all over the table. I swirled my spoon around beneath the cereal, creating whirlpools, watched the flakes spin, hoping to hide the fear I felt. "I liked him."

"Is that so?" he said, still tapping the knife. Then he flicked it forward and it fell like a toy soldier shot dead. Shoving his chair back from the table, he stood up and jammed his hands into the pockets of his tennis shorts. When he reached the door he turned and said flatly, "Tino Brooks is abnormal, and if you like him it's only because you're abnormal too, just like your mother. You know, of all her husbands, I'm the only man she ever loved! She still loves me. D'you know that, wise guy?"

"Is Mama suing someone?"

"Why do you ask?" my father said. "Did Tino tell you about that too? Anything he has to say is a lie. He's an evil human being. Your mother may be crazy, but Tino is evil. What your mother's doing right now is her business, and as far as I'm concerned, let her get the bastard's money. Why the hell not? I'm not going to support her!"

"Why do you hate Tino?" I asked, trying to sound impartial, hoping to appease with the good graces of neutrality.

"I don't hate anyone! Except for my mother, the tough broad!" he said harshly. "Tino Brooks inherited a lot more money than brains. He likes to think of himself as an intellectual, but he's a troublemaker, and don't you forget it!" He turned to leave and then stopped again. "I'm convinced it was Tino Brooks who blackballed me from the Bath and Tennis Club when I applied years ago. It's a secret ballot, but I know it was that asshole who ruled against me. The son of a bitch! Fuckin' cowardly way to express his anti-Semitic views. Let him come say that kind of thing to my face, I'll give him a shot right in the eye!"

"He's not anti-Semitic. By the way, he says you're the best tennis player outside of the pro circuit," I lied, curious to see if flattery would overrule his distaste for Tino.

"Vitas Gerulaitis once said if he practiced as hard as I do, he'd be ranked number one in the world!" my father said, a short laugh shooting out through his large white teeth. "Poor old Vitas, that was a hell of a nap! Whatcha doing today, kid? Play a little tennis? Why don't you get a game together? It's the best thing for your social life."

"I'm taking the noon jitney into the city. I have work tomorrow."

"D'you need some money?" my father asked, digging into the flap of his tennis shorts, retrieving a stack of green notes. He slowly unfolded five twenties and tossed them on the table, an unnatural smile creeping across his mouth. He looked mesmerized. "There you go. Don't say I never gave you anything!"

"Thanks, Dad!" I yelled as the dining room door swung closed. In a shallow, casual way there was affection between us, buried deep beneath the bubbling-hot surface.

I tried to imagine my father, at his advanced age, fighting anyone. I pictured his tanned, tennis-clothed figure standing, poised with his fists held high, telling Tino to get his "fuckin' cowardly anti-Semitic fists up" while Tino laughed, crunching on his cubes of ice, taunting him. There was a childish thrill in the luxury of conjuring up such an image in the privacy of my mind, and yet I could not refrain from choreographing a handshake between the gentlemen. White flags of peace run up. I stuck my spoon beneath the soggy cornflakes and raised them, dripping like a haul in a fisherman's net.

PART TWO

THERE WERE TIMES WHEN THE SUMMER FELT as if it would never end. Long days with Alison at the beach, hurtling to shore on the tops of the waves, eyes closed, mouth tight. Shake your head against the turgid froth. Cross your fingers and pray you have not miscalculated, that you are not about to get sucked down and gargled in the undertow.

Bruised and spent from fighting the waves, the sharp taste of seawater in my mouth, I flopped down onto the sticky sand. I stretched out, driving the coarse granules into my back, and listened to the swelling bass drum of the curl, the splash on the cymbals as the water fell; rolling up a foot or two before dribbling back, dragging open airholes for the hermit crabs, stealing shells and parched wood. Over and over, a lulling drowning of the senses.

"Hey, girls!" my father called. "I'm leaving in twenty minutes. If you come say good-bye, I'll give you some money."

"Okay, Dad!" I hollered through cupped hands. I rolled over, but he was gone. A bird trolled its shadow across the expanse of beach, shimmied it over the pale green dunes, swaying like seaweed, and landed on the handrail of the weathered pine bridge to the house. Above the hem of dune grass I could see the roof of my father's pink-brick summer house with the terra-cotta tiles suffused in sun. The little brown bird shook out his feathers, tucked his red beak beneath a wing, and plucked at the downy fluff. The distant hum of an airplane cutting a white path through the sky caught his attention; he looked up and let out a velvet-soft coocooing in reply.

"How much?" Alison asked, wading out of the water, twisting her long dark hair like hemp.

"Twenty minutes."

"Money, Sherlock!" Alison shrieked, laughing. "How much money?"

"Dunno," I said and watched the startled bird flap away, a white feather clamped like prey in his beak.

"Come on, lazybones, let's have an adventure!" Alison said, squeezing the seawater from her hair onto my stomach so that I leapt up. "It's time to pay filthy old fat-assed Flasher Ford a visit. Unless, of course, you've lost your nerve." Alison's voice trailed behind her as she loped off, swinging her arms wide like a tiny windmill. I followed her across the bridge and down the steps into my father's property. We skirted the swimming pool at a trot, jumping the deck chairs and the red potted geraniums, and skipped across the lawn. Two acres of beech and ash surrounded my father's mock-Spanish hacienda, silver leaves tickling the breeze so that the air sounded, at times, like a fast running river. Passing beneath an oak tree's dense panoply, a cathedral of shivering leaves and fine filtered light, Alison was camouflaged in shades of green and gold. She ducked into the hedge and vanished.

A murderous screech pierced my head and I leapt backward, knocking into the molting bark of an oak tree, sledding on the mulch of leaves. "Cripes!" I yelled as scaly shards attached themselves between my shoulder blades. I spun around to slap at my back, dislodge the creepy-crawlies.

"Shhh!" Alison hissed, reappearing. She steadied me with a hand to my waist. "Don't lose your nerve on me."

"I'm not losing my nerve," I said indignantly as I patted down the gooseflesh on my arms, brushed away the filaments. "Something screamed in my ear! Like a ghost!"

"You mean Billy?" Alison said, her suntanned arms crossed over her white bathing suit, the heavy twist of dark hair still in place, reposing on one shoulder. "Billy Bluster? Our own personal crow, who screams every time we pass by? You're losing your nerve. You better stay behind me and watch for signals." With a wink she turned and reentered the green wall of hedge.

"I'll do no such thing!" I huffed, following.

"Shh!"

"Okay," I whispered. "But we're equal."

Mr. Ford's terrain was barren and dry, covered with a rubbery grass with fat, squashy leaves that felt springy underfoot. Hills of sand, blown in by the seasonal hurricanes, had collected haphazardly, and we used these bunkers to hide behind on our approach to the house. We crept, bent over, scurrying a few paces at a time. The house was sprawling and low; dark brown wood hung with an unfriendly collection of rusted metal. Mr. Abernathy Ford, "that schmuck next door," as my father referred to him, was a sculptor. His property was a veritable dump, littered with swirling masses of metal with teeth and spikes. The impression was of the aftermath of a desert battle. Most of the windows were boarded over, and Mr. Ford had occupied himself by painting these boards with his version of guests inside his house, milling around in a sociable manner, normal except that the guests were animals. On one panel a silver wolf, tuxedoed and dapper, snapped greedily at a buzz of moths about his head. Alison disagreed, but it looked like Dad to me.

Strenuously quiet as we neared, we eased our way around the jaws of sculptures and stepped gingerly over stacked crates. A particular worry was not to tip the empty beer bottles and send them scuttling and so alert Mr. Ford.

Outside Mr. Ford's studio we dropped to a crawl, scraping

our knees on the sand-dusted flagstones, and assumed our customary positions beneath a tall casement window. Hot currents
filled with the smells of tar and molten iron pressed themselves
against us, invisible and suffocating.

"Sherlock, d'you read? Over," Alison murmured, covering
her mouth with her hand, eyeing me excitedly.

"Roger, Watson, what's up? Over."

"Approaching enemy target, all stations red alert. Over and
out."

The sounds of opera, like an encroaching thunderstorm,
boomed threateningly. A lady singer's sad lamentations jagged
like lightning, accompanied by a tremendous drumming and
Mr. Ford's throaty baritone. The operatic reverberations slunk
down my spine, snaked inside the marrow of my bones. A moment was spent composing our thumping hearts before Alison
held one hand above her head, the signal; and, achingly slowly,
we stretched up and peered in.

Naked except for brown gloves and a helmet, Mr. Ford
lunged at a slab of metal, carving it with his blowtorch. The studio was dark, like a cave, with pale patches of daylight entering
through the windows and, of course, the bright red of the fire-
spitting weapon in Mr. Ford's hands. Mr. Ford was easily the
largest human we had ever seen, and it was an unparalleled joy
to watch him waddle around, swaying from foot to foot, mas-
terfully accompanying the incomprehensible lyrics. That he was
naked was, of course, the primary appeal.

The lady singer's voice rose higher and higher, warbling with
intensity, and Mr. Ford, lost in the raptures of sculpting, attempted to follow, blasting the foreign words out with such
force that his jowly cheeks shook. He jabbed at the metal,
working his blowtorch up and down in huge, swift moves while
bellowing out his tune, so that his entire body rollicked and
roiled like high seas in a tempest.

"Alert! Alert! The enemy target is going to carve his dowacky off!" Alison whispered loudly, stuffing her hands into her mouth to stall the laughter that invariably engulfed us when we spied on Mr. Ford.

"Right you are, Sherlock. Code seven standing by!" I replied giddily, both of us exploding with giggles.

Mr. Ford froze momentarily, his arms above his head gripping the blowtorch that spat fiery spittle ineffectively into the darkness of the rafters. He hung his head to one side as if he could better receive any stray sounds from this position, distinguish the telltale signs of intruders over the wail of opera. Very slowly he turned toward the casement window, pivoting on the balls of his feet. With surprising speed Mr. Ford lumbered over the bare wood floor, shaking layers of flesh, charging with his blowtorch flaring ahead of him, so that he looked like some demonic rhinoceros.

"Code seven! Code seven! Abort mission! Abort mission!" Alison yelled, scrabbling to her feet. "Repeat, abort and run for your life!"

"Lost your nerve?" I yelled, sprinting alongside her. "Last one home's a toad."

Jostling each other out of the way, we leapt over obstacles, over Mr. Ford's strange crabgrass, and crashed through the hedgerow, tearing ourselves against the spiny shrub. There was a coolness on my father's side of the world, as if the sun's rays were gentler, the breeze softer. I never saw the root that grew above the ground, across the grass, like some petrified snake. My hands extended automatically, protectively. I slammed down hard. Yet somehow I witnessed the fall in slow, drugged time. Some unseen muse of mischief tricked my vision and transformed each blade into swaying, neon coral, and I discerned the cilium fringing every fallen leaf that sat on the tips of the grass, boats on the water. My vision smudged with the shock of pain, and air felt sharp like steel as I forced it into my abruptly emptied lungs. I shook my head to clear the blur before I was up once more, running full speed to the house. Alison stood by the door, holding back the screen, a vague look of concern on her face. "You okay?" she asked. "Either way, I won. I mean, if you're okay or not, I still won."

Instead of slowing, I sped past. "Victory!" I yelled. "Last one in's a toad!"

I was propelled forward as Alison tackled me to the carpeted floor. "No way I'm a toad!" Alison shrieked. "I stopped to see if you were dead, you cheating Brit."

I lunged, knocking Alison off me, pinning her to the floor with all my weight, her wrists pinioned in my hands. "Don't ever call me a Brit," I said huffing, breathless, "or I'll have to kill you!"

"Brit, limey, pom!" Alison said, spluttering through her giggles. "With that retarded accent, you'll never be an American. Anyway it's rotten egg, not toad, nerd face!"

"Calm down, girls. I thought someone had an accident!" My father's voice quelled our excitement. "Why don't you two get up off the floor and sit nicely, like ladies? Don't forget I've got something for you!" He tapped the bulge of his back pocket, lips parted, flashing huge, bright white teeth. His smile was lupine. Caps, I'm told.

"You're so childish," my sister said, her voice languorous and deadly. I looked up from the wrestling hold I had on Alison to see Miranda embedded in the sofa, *Vogue* propped on her lap. In gray silk pajamas and two long strands of pearls, she looked far more sophisticated than the average fourteen-year-old. Lamplight beamed gently from behind her, shimmering on the silk pajamas, so that the gray turned to deeper shades where the fabric folded, like a grim ocean in the fading light of day.

"I hope," Miranda said, looping the pearls around a finger, gazing angelically at my father, "you aren't going to give them money for behaving like savages."

"Spoken like a true Moses!" my father said. As he crossed the room, his Gucci loafers whispered to the carpet; the buckles jangled. He went into the bar, a little room like a horse stall with a half door flung open, and though he was partially concealed, swiveling and reaching, I knew the sound of ice clanking into a glass, the top of a bottle being unscrewed, liquid splashing down, a tiny waterfall. Heading back toward the sofa, he stuck a finger into his glass and mixed the clear liquid.

"You look very elegant, Dad," Miranda said, a coy smile drifting across her face as my father settled himself beside her on the sofa. "You're better looking than Roger Moore when he was in his prime."

"James Bond! That sounds like ten dollars!" my father said, steeped in the compliment. He put his drink down on the glass-and-wicker coffee table, slid a wet hand through his thinning gray hair, and leaned forward to pull his wallet from a back pocket. Brown leather fold-over. "Who's your favorite daddy?" he asked as he waived the bill in front of her.

"You are!" Miranda sang happily and snatched it away. She looked at him adoringly, bright eyes alert, alive. They have the same pale eyes that slant upwards at the ends, so that they appear to be smiling when they are not. "You'll be my favorite daddy forever!"

"That sounds like another ten dollars!" he said, pleasure and embarrassment embracing in a smirk. Whenever my father spoke about money, he adopted a giddy, melodic tone of voice, druggy and seductive, and his eyes shone as though he were hypnotized: the money face. He held a second bill high in the air and let it drop down, wafting its way toward Miranda. "Come on, girls," my father said to Alison and me. "Don't you want to make some money?"

"What do you want us to do?" I asked, sitting up, cross-legged, ready to play.

"Why don't you do everyone a favor," Miranda said, smiling like a hangman tugging open the trap, "and grow up!"

"Why should I?" I spat. "I'm already ten!"

"Enough, you two!" my father said, raising an eyebrow for Alison's benefit. "Come on, let's pretend we like each other! How about we all earn a few bucks? That'll put everyone in a good mood. You agree? What do you have to say about money, Maria?"

"Activate code ninety-nine," Alison whispered, lying beside me on the floor. I looked at her, puzzled. Her dark eyes shone meaningfully above her cupped hand, concealing her mouth, muffling her words. "Operation Insincere As Hell. Deceive parents at all costs. Alert, alert!"

Sipping his drink, my father stroked Miranda's hair and watched me with a quizzical look. Their faces are oval, their narrow noses raised by the merest mention of a bump; implacable bookends. "Listen carefully, Maria, and you could get rich tonight," my father said, crinkling a $20 bill in his hand. "Who do you love better, your rich American daddy"—he swept an arm out to encompass the room, the grounds, and possibly the beach and the ocean and the sky itself—"or your poor English stepfather, who takes you to Scotland to freeze your ass off?"

"I can't bear Scotland!" Miranda said, primly picking motes from her gray sleeve. "It's for savages!"

"It's Mama always making us go up to Scotland," I said, pleased at the rare chance to contradict Miranda. "Not Hamish."

"Idiot!" Miranda said, witheringly. "Haven't you ever figured out why?"

Figured out what? Conversing with my sister always made me feel I had lost my footing on a muddy bank. Code ninety-nine: Deceive at all costs. Whom did I love the most? I had never thought to compare the two before. I was not certain that I really did love one better than the other. "I don't know," I said softly, and held my breath.

My father pursed his mouth into a miniature pyramid of

wrinkles; his handsome face trembled slightly as his blue eyes switched from me to Miranda to Alison. He reached for his drink and sucked it dry in a single swallow. "Some people don't know how to play the game," he said finally, spitting an ice cube back into the glass, and I knew that if I had the chance, I would have said the same again.

"Ooo!" Miranda moaned. "I love Daddy!"

"Good," he said, no longer smiling. He wedged his wallet in his back pocket, rose, and strode toward the bar. "But you can cut the bullshit, because you're not getting any more out of me tonight."

Miranda lounged against the pillows like a handful of petals. Honey-streaked brown hair spilled around her beautiful oval face. I knew she was beautiful, on account of having been told as much, but when I looked at her, all I saw was Miranda, my prissy, fussy sister, whom I could never take so seriously as she took herself. I thought she was ridiculous. She found me boorish and immature. We had never been friends.

Last year sometime, in London, my mother had suggested I accompany her on a walk. To have a chat, as she put it. "You really are too funny," my mother had declared from the bottom of the stairs when I appeared on the landing, dressed and ready to go out. "Kilts and cardigans on the hottest summer day, and cotton dresses in the middle of winter!"

Clothes and ornament inspired no interest in me, and it was enough to assemble shirt and skirt and shoes without concerning myself about the weight of the fabrics or the colors or the styles. Matching the items to the weather was beyond me. Miranda cared deeply about the style and look of her apparel and spent hours in my mother's cupboards, experimenting with evening dresses and tottering shoes. It was something of a mania with Miranda to have my mother promise that these things she liked would one day be hers, and little pieces of paper were pinned to the inside of hems and glued to weighty rings and bracelets, with Miranda's name on them. Instinctively I fought to distinguish myself by assuming a contrary position. The most we had in common was the extent of our desire to be different from each other.

"Darling, your sister is very beautiful," my mother told me as we walked, my hand in hers, my attention straying, caught by the immodesty of the eye-level miniskirts of the time, "and you're going to have to learn not to get jealous. You must not covet your sister's looks, darling; it will make you rot inside. You have a look of your own. Darling, you're what's known as 'attractive.' "

I was horrified by the revelation. "Why would I want anything she has?" I said, perhaps too emphatically. "I don't even like her!"

My outburst thunderclapped a torrent from my mother. "You have no heart, Maria! You have to develop a loving heart!" she urged, jerking my hand upward with every word. "This world is ghastly enough as it is!"

And now, in the dimming light of day, in my father's summer house, Miranda and I stared at each other venomously. Miranda had a way of overloading meaning into a fraction of an expression that made me want to take off a shoe and hurl it at her. But given the company, all I could do was narrow my eyes and stare back.

"Picture time," my father said, returning from behind the bar with a replenished tumbler and his Polaroid camera with the brown leather case and his initials pressed in on one side. "Suppose you become famous one day; you want to keep records of how it all began, don't you?"

Chuckling to himself, my father stationed us side by side, arms draped across one another's shoulders, one foot crossed in front of the other. He steered Alison between Miranda and me, possibly to prevent us from inadvertently clawing at each other. Miranda pushed Alison's arm away from her shoulder, took a step away, separating herself.

"Wait!" Miranda said, rearranging her hair, running her fingers through the long honeyed lengths and pulling it forward so that it surrounded her face like a lioness.

"Everybody say 'caviar'!" my father said, the camera obscuring his face except for the bright white teeth framing the emerging words. "Don't move! I'm taking one for each of you. Say, 'Please, Daddy, more caviar'!"

My stepmother came *clack-clack*ing in mules along the stone corridor. "Hi, everybody," she said, her pretty face illumined by a smile. Deep turquoise eyes, a plump chignon of Spanish gold, and the palest pink mouth, always smiling. Patricia put her hands on her slim hips, forcing the tan cashmere cardigan that hung on her shoulders to spread out like wings. Something about her made me think that if Mr. Ford were to paint this scene, it would be of a butterfly recklessly entering a cave of ravenous bullfrogs.

"You got the car keys?" my father asked, replacing the camera on the bar; he braille-read the contents of his pockets, clumping the material.

"We can take mine," Patricia said, pulling a gold chain from her purse, a tiny gold tennis racket dangling amongst the keys.

"It's a piece of shit!" my father said. "What have you got in your hair? You look like you got a job in Honolulu airport."

"Sam!" Patricia said, a frown dampening her smile. "It's a hibiscus. I grew it myself. Girls," she asked us, one hand raised toward the flower, "don't you think it's pretty?"

"Yes, Patricia," I said, barely glancing away from examining my developing photograph. Miranda's slightly tilted head and Mona Lisa smile and her elegant grey silk pajamas came into focus standing beside Alison and me draped on one another in bathing suits and straggly hair, staring straight ahead, grinning toothily.

"Why don't you stick it in your button hole?" Miranda suggested, flicking her version of the photograph onto the coffee table. She slumped back into the sanctuary of the deep sofa cushions and smiled wanly, her cold eyes betraying the disdain I knew she felt. Miranda found Patricia 'common'. Being 'common' was an incurable affliction Miranda attributed to anyone who had no claim to a fortune of their own. She thought Hamish was common, too. Along with his entire family, all the teachers at our school in London and most everybody else.

One day Hamish had come home from work bearing gifts. Warm clothes he had bought Miranda and me in preparation for a Christmas visit to Castle Cairngorm. I pulled the red and white wool hat down low over my ears, strangled myself with the scarf, clapped my hands together to hear the muffled beat of woolen gloves.

Clutching the box that held Miranda's blue and white version I took the stairs two at a time, to deliver her present.

"They're hideous!" Miranda had said after a swift examination, holding the offensive articles by her fingertips before dropping them to the floor. A hillock of blue and white woolens. "And they're from Mark's and Spencer's! They're nasty and cheap!" She walked away, rubbing her fingers on her skirt as if she had dirtied them, or perhaps tainted herself by touching the nasty, cheap things. I was always impressed with the decisiveness of her opinions, though I seldom understood how she arrived at them. To question, I had learned, was unwise.

"Mr. Ford just called," Patricia said, adjusting the flower on her lapel. "You girls weren't over there bothering him, were you?"

"No!" Alison and I said in unison, eyes darting guiltily at each other.

"I'm glad to hear that," Patricia said, smiling. "You'll catch cold lying around in those wet suits. Run upstairs, won't you, and get some dry things on."

"Maria, how many times do I have to tell you to keep away from that fuckin' schmuck Ford?" my father said, slamming his glass down hard onto the bar, a waterfall of flecks splashing his hand. "What's the goddamned attraction, anyway? What's going on over there?"

"He sings opera," I said, a little too slowly.

"Opera?" my father said. "Don't be a wise guy, Maria. Nobody likes a wise guy!"

As cleanly as a set change, my father and his fifth wife exited the sitting room, good-byes and warnings echoing in the front hall, soon silenced by the door as it slammed shut behind them. Miranda sighed audibly, flipping through the pages of her magazine, her earrings held tight in one hand so that only the tips of her fingers were free to turn the pages. "Hideous!" she complained directly to the images before her. "Absolutely hideous!"

"Miranda," Alison said sweetly, "will I ever be beautiful like you?"

Miranda looked up from the engrossing pages of her magazine and stared at Alison, who lay beside me, both of us lounging on the floor. Alison held her face in her hands, like a vase on a stand; her legs, bent at the knee, crossed at the ankle, rocked back and forth, gently shaking fragments of earth and sand from the soles of her feet. Billy Bluster, our sentinel crow, barked manically in the background as we waited for Miranda's pronouncement.

"No," Miranda said, a look of pity on her face as she frowned at Alison, as if the weight of her decision was almost more than she could bear. Suddenly she looked possessed, and her upper lip began to curl, her eyes began to widen, and her face contorted into a twisted grimace. "Yuck! Oh, how disgusting!" Miranda shrieked and tossed her magazine aside. As *Vogue* slithered snakelike to the floor, my sister leapt up so that she was standing on the sofa, pressing against the wall behind her as if it might protect her from her hallucinations. "You filthy pig!" She wailed. "I've never seen anything so revolting!"

I was so delighted with Miranda's comic performance that it was with some reluctance that I tore my eyes away from her to glance quickly outside to see Mr. Abernathy Ford, still completely naked except for his huge gloves and his coal miner's hat with the visor pulled up, standing at the very tip of the diving board, pissing an impressive golden arc into the swimming pool. "Tra la la la!" he sang in his inimitable way. "Tra la la la! La la! La la! Ha, ha, ha! Ha, ha!" The stream dribbled to a halt, and with enormous dignity Mr. Ford swiveled his corpulence and wobbled across the lawn, forcing his way through the uncompromising hedge, accompanied by Billy Bluster's urgent squawks.

"That's absolutely mahvelous," Alison declared in her campiest version of an English accent. "Miranda, tell me you don't think that's simply mahvelous."

"How dare you speak to me like that?" Miranda announced, stepping down from the sofa as she ran a nervy hand through her lovely hair. "That fat pig has poisoned Daddy's pool! I'm going to tell Daddy about this, and I'm going to recommend he punish the both of you very severely. You're both crazy! Totally insane! You should be confined to your rooms for the rest of the holidays! Stop laughing at me, it's not funny! I'll tell Daddy that you think this is funny. He'll be so furious he'll spank the both of you . . . " The doorbell chimed, breaking into Miranda's steamrolling rant. "Well, don't just lie there like fools, go answer the door! It's probably your fat crazy friend. Maybe he wants to pee somewhere in the house. Maybe he'd like to pee on you. Would you like that? Huh? What?"

"Ees a gentleman asking for you, Miss Miranda," said Rosa. Rosa was the shape and hue of a glossy, dark green olive, and at eighteen this gave her an exotic, sultry look. It was very important to my father that the help, as he called them, be chic, that they look good in the house. "Dinner ees ready, girls. Macaroni and cheese and vanilla aysh cream."

"Oh, damn it!" said Miranda, and rather surprisingly she began to undress, revealing a tiny pair of velvet hot pants and an embroidered bustier beneath the silk pajamas, which she whipped off and, with a firm backhand, shoved unceremoniously into Rosa's stomach as if it were a shelf. Then she stalked out into the front hall.

"Wow!" said a young man standing on the porch, staring slack jawed at Miranda. It was Tommy Durban, in khakis and a navy blazer, the eldest son of my father's favorite tennis partner, Swifty Durban, who liked to wear a toupee instead of a tennis hat, despite the fact that he had a full head of hair. It was an irksome eccentricity my father bore because of Mr. Durban Sr.'s athletic prowess. For six straight years Moses and Durban had had their names cut into the round base of the clubhouse's men's senior doubles cup.

"I hope you have a car, Tommy," Miranda said, craning to see beyond her date as she threw a long silver shawl over her shoulders and sophisticated herself by another ten years. "I don't walk."

"Borrowed my Dad's 190 SL. I've the got the top down and the Stones in the tape player, and with you in it we're gonna look ready for heaven!" Tommy said, licking his hand catlike and flattening stray strands. "I'm parked just a little ways down the street, just like you asked, Miss Miranda Moses, discretion with a capital *D!*"

"Tommy," Miranda said, in a voice like silk. "Dad's gone out already, so be a gentleman, would you, and go fetch the car?"

"Ooo la la!" Alison chanted. "Miranda has a boyfriend!"

Miranda and Tommy swiveled to look at Alison and me, lolling in the doorway to the sitting room.

"Ignore them," Miranda said, dismissing us with a flick. "It's just my idiot sister and her friend."

"Back in a flash." Tommy bounded away, stirring up the gravel underfoot.

Pirouetting to gather a purse on a table by the front door, Miranda shot us a contemptuous look, "Grow up!" she commanded, and closed the door hard behind her. Alison raised her hand, flat palm forward. "Gimme five, Sherlock!" The slap echoed in the dusk-warmed hall.

The air became heavy and still, and through the windows beside the front door, we saw the sun swell blood orange. A bloated audience to the orchestra of toads on xylophone, cicadas and crickets on percussion. Tommy's car rumbled down the driveway, heaved to a grumbling halt; the hand break ratcheted. The Rolling Stones swung out into the twilight. Footsteps on the pebbles, voices blended, doors slammed and then Tommy crushed the accelerator and the car careened. I heard my sister scream.

"Why do I have to be related to that wimp?" I whined, leaning against my friend. "I mean, why can't you and I be sisters?"

"How about I ask my Dad to adopt you?" Alison said, as we loped down the corridor to the dining room. "He's only ever in a bad mood if he's lost a tennis game or Mom's trying to get him to go to one of those parties with the Pekingese People. 'Skinny, perfectly groomed and they yap, yap, yap.'" Alison laughed and I could hear her father's voice in my head, complaining about the Pekingese People and how the yapping was going to be the end of him one day. He was always saying that one thing or another was going to be the end of him. I had heard it so many times that I had an image of Mr. Harris Sr. standing alone, arms akimbo, the very last scene in a silent movie with *The End* written in script across his middle.

"Besides, Dad says everything's just a matter of paper money and paperwork," Alison said as we slumped into high-backed chairs encircling the table, a reflecting lake of mahogany. Rosa had set three steaming plates of stiffening macaroni on rush place mats. Alison and I stabbed at the orange tubes, herding them onto oversize forks with sandy fingers.

Rosa appeared behind the swing door, framed by a garish light, tart against the mild tones of matte ocher walls. "Miranda gone?" Rosa asked. Her tired brown eyes reminded me of a bas-

set hound. I had heard my father say she was not likely to age
well, that he would not hire her for next summer.

"Miranda run away with big ugly boy!" Alison said, clutching
her throat dramatically. "Ugh!"

"Silly!" Rosa said, stacking the plates in her meaty hands. "I
get you aysh cream." The kitchen door swung back into place,
obscuring the antiseptic bright light, returning us to dimness.

"Ooh la la! I've got an idea!" Alison said, shoving her chair
back noiselessly over the thick carpet. "Back in a flash!" she said,
imitating Tommy Durban's deep voice and licking her hand to
paste phantom strands. Alison turned sharply, a spray of long
brown hair like the wing of an enormous bird dipping down
into a canyon, vanishing into the darkness of the flagstone hallway. I listened to the sounds of her bare feet running *flack, flack,
flack* against the stone. I thought I heard the crow squawk, Billy
Bluster belting out his warning cries, but the sounds mingled
with the kitchen door closing behind Rosa, until both faded
away.

Alison returned, gripping pens and two huge pads of paper
to her chest. "Tonight we're going to write our wills. My dad
says everyone should do it, that people always leave that kind of
thing until it's too late, and then all the mourners have even
more to cry about." Alison flung her haul onto the table, letting
the pens scatter on the polished surface so that it looked as if
they were pursued, and finally caught, by their own reflections.
"I vote we both leave all our schoolwork and all punishments to
Miranda!"

"My dear Watson," I said. "You must have broiled your brain in
the sun today, 'cause there won't be any of that if we're dead."

"I don't think so, Sherlock, because my dad says you can put
anything you like in a will. That's why it's called a will. You 'will'
someone to do this and that, and they 'will' have to do it. Over
and out."

"I don't have anything that's worth money. Except for my

stash of treasures in London, my teacups and hat pins and things. Would you like them?"

"Roger."

"Can I say I don't want to live in London?"

"Roger."

"And can I say I don't want to be related to Miranda?"

"Roger."

"Ooh la la, I think I like this!"

We worked until four full pages were covered with scrawling ink and the ice cream Rosa had served us was melted to soup. Diligently following instructions Alison swore came direct from her father, we read every page and signed our names to each. "Until death," Alison told me as we traded our rolled and ribbon-bound documents.

"Until death," I replied.

"Adventure time," Alison said, trotting into the unlit hallway, her roll of paper tucked under one arm.

With Alison in the lead, we removed bedsheets and blankets and pillows from my room, set them up on the lawn, and camped beside the crickets grinding out their simple tune in the balmy stillness of an August night. Fireflies, like tiny lighthouses, flashed off and on. An owl yawned. The mild thrum of mosquito engines whirred in our ears as they prepared for strategic landings near blood-sweet veins.

"Dad says old Flasher Ford murdered his Indian wife," Alison said, her words embodied in silver night air, shaking forward like a crazy white wake. "He said Mr. Ford married her for money, and to get it he had to kill her." A long, low, mournful rasp came from the treetops. I sat up quickly. "That's just Billy, you silly limey," Alison said, laughing.

Alison loved horror stories as much for the morbid details as for the reaction she was guaranteed to get out of me. I had never liked the dark. I could see faces in the shadows, I could hear voices in the creak of a branch, could hear my name in the susurrations of the wind. The hem of my shirt could drift across my skin and I would be certain it was the hand of the devil come to escort me down to some antechamber of hell.

I expelled a long, exaggerated yawn. "But they met at a car wash," I said, lying back down, hoping I sounded quite free of agitation.

"Dad says Mr. Ford almost had it pretty good, except that as soon as he got all the money, he lost his marbles. Went loony. Dad says that's the hand of God."

Suddenly I thought I could hear a muffled sobbing, and Billy, the gatekeeper crow, began to bark and flap in the branches above us. I shook violently and wished we could move back inside, to the safety of my bedroom. I tried to make sense of the shadows by squinting at them, but one glance at Alison's mocking frown and I kept my doubts to myself. My imagination jammed into gear, speeding away, and I watched as Mr. Ford strangled his beautiful Indian wife, his swollen naked body lowered over her, a thin woman in a red-and-gold sari, with long oily black hair and a dot on her forehead, his huge gloved hands around her neck. I flinched and tried to dislodge the image from my mind's eye.

"You know that for a fact?"

"For a fact. Dad said so," Alison said, laughing. She rolled onto her side, one hand patting down the grass between us. Why wasn't she afraid? I wondered. Why were the monsters visible only to me? "Let's count shooters. First to ten wins."

Lying on our backs we watched the squid-ink sky and the flashing, inexplicable lights, and waited for the shooting stars. I tracked their fleeting glitter-arc descent and tried not to think too much about filthy old fat-assed Flasher Ford, until Billy, screeching wildly, came flapping and bustling through the branches as if he were escaping the very jaws of death. Ripping through the foliage, he arrived wings extended and beating, screaming as he flew above us, back and forth, grazing the tops of us in his daring aerial display. Following him came a great crashing as a thick shape tumbled through the hedge. "Shit!" it exclaimed, lunging to the ground, grumbling to itself. "Ouch! Shit, shit, shit!"

Alison leapt up, laughing and stamping her feet, virtually jumping in place. "You fat spy, you're going to jail!" she yelled at the shadowed bulge that spat expletives. "Mr. Ford's come to spy on us! Let's call the police and have him arrested for being so fat."

"No need, you little bastards! I'm off, I'm off," he bellowed as he unfolded upward. "I never hurt my wife," he boomed at us as he began to sob, gulping as if he were drowning. "My sweet wife! My little son. The loves of my life." He wailed, and then his voice cracked and he stumbled back through the hedge, mulching his words with the tears.

Alison stood quite still, her laughter caught short by the oddly touching scene. Billy strutted across the cropped grass, patrolling like a soldier, puffed up and proud of his fearlessness, his long tail feathers following like a rudder that might shift his direction this way and that. Then he spread his wings, hopped a few steps preparing for takeoff, and climbed into the air, returning to his post in the treetops with a final squawk to sound the end of battle. Slowly Alison slumped down beside me, one hand on my shoulder where I still lay on the hard ground, frozen by the unexpectedness of it all. "Maybe we should bring him a present tomorrow." She whispered so quietly I almost could not hear her. "Maybe ice cream, okay?"

W E   N E V E R   D I D bring anything to Mr. Ford; in fact, we never trod across his property again. Instead, Alison suggested we write him into our wills, with the promise that whichever one of us should die first would go find his Indian wife and his baby son in heaven and tell them he missed them badly. So the

wills were unrolled and amended and then secured once more
with the ribbons, and put away along with the Polaroids my father had made us pose for. Taunting the sad fat man for sport
was canceled indefinitely, and we turned our attention to fresh
pursuits, such as Miranda and her vain efforts to avoid us.

Labor Day came and the swimming pool was covered over,
the tennis court net was rolled and put away. Yellowed leaves
fell and matted down on the flagstone walkway that bordered
the house, making it slippery and lethal. Whole branches of rust
red leaves appeared seemingly overnight. In the evenings came
a damp coolness, forcing us into sweaters that had creased and
stiffened after months of inactivity. I hoped that something
might come to stave off autumn, keep me from having to return to England and school. Instead, Mr. Harris Sr. came one
afternoon, parked in my father's driveway with the radio
screaming that summer's song, and honked on his horn. His entire family and his three longhaired Alsatians were crammed
into the car, a station wagon with wood sides and rectangular
windows, and Alison in the back, lounging against the suitcases,
mouthing good-bye, waving at me. I stood barefoot on the leaf-
covered walkway that brooked the house from the gravel drive.
I waved at Alison and yelled good-bye and marshaled all my
self-control to fend off the tears.

Castle Cairngorm, 1987

It was Easter, last time we came to stay, six months ago, and yet lying here, I had the odd sensation that perhaps I had never left. I wondered if I had imagined my summer and had just awakened from an epic dream of travels to America and my father's house and Alison. Maybe I had invented them and I had been in Scotland all along, here in this room, sleeping. Gradually, as if to confirm fact over fiction, I remembered the nightmare of the drive last night. Ten hours of listening to Hamish and my mother fighting in that strange style of theirs, with Vivaldi's *Four Seasons* insinuating itself obliquely. I think Hamish bought his Audi with the cassette included, and I suppose it must have been stuck in the machine, because in four years I had never heard anything else. Midway through the sad strains of "Winter," my mother asked Hamish whether Charlie was expected for the weekend.

"What? What are you talking about?" Hamish said, acutely condescending. It had not always been this way, but recently he had only two visible emotions: one, a sort of weary compliance—a tight smirk, a shake of the head, and an immediate return to whatever he was busy with—the other, a disturbingly controlled temper, thinly disguised with sarcasm. "It's his bloody house!" Hamish continued, displaying the latter of his temperaments. "Where the hell do you expect him to be? On a safari?"

"He might be!" My mother sounded oddly amused. "You and Charlie may only be third cousins once removed, but as far as I'm concerned, you're all the same! Descendants of blood-thirsty Norse thugs! You thrive on murder! You kill for fun! Nothing is safe! Nothing except for your blasted dogs. That's all we'll be left with when you've killed everything. Men with guns. And your blasted dogs!"

"Why don't you sit behind that truck all the way to Aberdeen?" Hamish asked acidly. "Save me the trouble of making plans for Christmas."

"Don't speak to me that way in front of the children!" my mother said, glaring at Hamish, her little white hands gripping the steering wheel, her fingers flexing like inchworms.

"What? What?" Hamish replied, spitting the words up like phlegm. "Let me know if we ever get to York, and then perhaps you wouldn't mind relinquishing the wheel? I'd like to see the Highlands before I've gone completely gray." Drowning out my mother's response, Hamish bivouacked himself behind the pink pages of his *Financial Times,* rustling them meaningfully.

Perhaps to ease the tension, perhaps because it was our only form of communication, Miranda and I snapped at each other like territorial turtles, drawing a line down the center of the backseat, enforcing border controls with sharp swats to the head. "Ouch! Mama, she touched me!" we would exclaim pitiably if one of us so much as grazed against the other.

"One more word out of either of you," my mother hissed over her shoulder, "and I'm stopping the car, and you can bloody well walk to Scotland." This was not a threat to take lightly, as she had carried it out a few times in the past and left us, sometimes for a couple of hours—still bickering over whose fault it was that we had been abandoned—before she would return to collect us.

I awoke as Hamish gathered me in his arms and carried me to the house through a frigid mist that stung my nose so that I burrowed under his lapel for warmth. With my eyes closed I listened to the heavy front door creak open, to the tread of his shoes as we crossed the stone hallway and climbed the stairs to the top floor. Hamish propped me on the bed, unbuckled my shoes, and pulled my socks off. "Sleep tight, Maria," he whispered, tucking the blankets around me, kissing me lightly on the forehead. "Don't forget to bite the bedbugs back."

SLOW WITH HALF sleep, I pulled the blankets to one side and slid my bare feet to the drafty floor. The sharp cold bit at me, and I pulled the eiderdown around my shoulders, cape-like, fastening it beneath my chin with my hands, and dragged it so that it cleared a path across the dusty floor to where the dawn-lit curtains glowed. Marmalade velvet folds collected one against the other in a sluggish, ancient way as I pushed them aside, fixing them at either end behind pewter arms. The bright light hurt my eyes, and I slumped into the dense comfort of an armchair, a high-backed green-and-black tartan chair with the stuffing attempting an escape at the tips of the armrests. I tucked my chilled feet beneath me and cocooned myself in the eiderdown. My eyes adjusted, and the garden and the river, almost fully concealed by weeping willows, all came slowly into focus. It seemed impossible to believe, as I watched the wind-blown limbs of the willow trees, like streamers the day after a party, that less than a week ago I was at the beach in the hot sun, dancing in the ocean's waves with Alison.

At the foot of the bed, unclasped and yawning, lay my suitcase. An old, scuffed, brown leather box with a tartan lining that had once belonged to Hamish. It had been his when he was a child, to transport dirty linens home from boarding school on weekends, to be filled with sweets and chocolate biscuits and forbidden comics for the return journey on Sunday nights. I packed this little suitcase everywhere I went, despite its being too small to carry much. On summer trips to America it traveled, like a pilot fish, alongside a large kelly green vinyl case I shared with Miranda. Every trip, someone attempted to talk me out of traveling with Hamish's little beaten box, but I liked to keep my treasures separate, and Hamish's battered old case was home to these jewels. It sat, openmouthed, at the foot of my bed. Beneath the imbroglio of twisted, crumpled clothing was a Polaroid photograph and a roll of paper, a white pipe held together with ribbon. The will. I wondered whether we could include a memo specifying that Hamish and my mother would have to stop their quarreling. As soon as I was more awake, I would go downstairs and telephone Alison. I would go in a moment, but I was still so groggy. How I would love to bring Alison to Scotland one day. Would it ever be possible to draw together the threads I liked most from my separate lives and weave them into one? The thought made me smile, and like the flash of a bulb, it gradually faded away and Scotland reappeared before me.

Far away and almost imperceptible, like a painter's preliminary sketch, was the hazy outline of mountains. The garden rolled out like a picnic blanket, bright colors in a severe geometric design, sharply contrasted with the surrounding wilderness. A three-tier marble fountain at the epicenter of the pattern shot water upward, a stiff blue arc, before it trickled down from basin to basin, collecting in the lowest, where moss and fat koi floated.

Blackbirds slunk easily in the swell of the wind, and I was reminded of the many walks we had taken at Easter across the purple-heather hills, Hamish and my mother with walking sticks up ahead, in tweeds and caps and gloves and dark green Wellington boots up to their knees. I would try and befriend the birds that perched on the tops of fences, cawing at our ragged pilgrimage, offering them crumbled bread I kept in the fingers of my gloves, red-and-white gloves Hamish had bought me before we came up for Christmas last year. I would trot along, either far behind or far up front, lost in daydreams, collecting detritus that caught my eye, pocketing the treasure until I could haul no more.

Miranda was almost always sniveling and fussing on those walks, tiptoeing in hopelessly inappropriate shoes of suede or some other fragile leather. She had, occasionally, sat down on a low rock and exclaimed, "I can't go on! I'll die here, and then you'll be sorry!" But these declarations went unheeded, except for my mother giving in to a fit of giggles, and Miranda was obliged to continue, utterly miserable. Miranda hated the cold, hated discomfort of any sort, and although I won tremendous maternal approval for being rugged, it was this very sensitivity to luxury that made my father dote on Miranda. In that, as in most things, they were very much alike.

Easing out of the embracing armchair, I wedged my cold feet into a pair of brown leather shoes that gaped, laces sprawled on either side, tucked just beneath my bed. Tottering as I forced my way into the stiff shoes, I clattered out into the chilled corridor and padded down the carpeted staircase, silently descending the many high-ceilinged floors to the front hall, where a stained-glass window littered colored light like confetti. The lights bejeweled the medieval suits of armor that stood sentry by arched entrances that led to long, dark hallways.

With both hands I turned the bull nose ring of a door handle, creaked the heavy wooden door open, straining against it with my shoulder and my hip until I was face-to-face with the morning, crystalline cool like river water.

Garishly modern, contrasted with the opaque castle walls, were Hamish's Audi, Charlie's two Bentleys, his army-issue Land Rover, and a painted Gypsy caravan, where we were occasionally allowed to sleep, weather permitting. Dwarfing them all was a turquoise Cadillac with its taillights dressed up like a rocket ship ready for blastoff.

"Cripes!" I said aloud, mesmerized by the impressive machine, stamping my prints onto the polished sides as I peered in, breathing hot sticky clouds on the windows. "Gosh, it's as big as a house inside!"

"Lovely morning for a spin," Farquhar said from the front door, startling me slightly. Farquhar cut a smart figure, all in dark gray except for a starched white shirt with a wing collar, and a discreet silver fob chain across his waistcoat. From the bottom step of the thick stone staircase that lead to the front door, Farquhar collected a milk churn in his massive hands, and with a smile that crumpled his face as if it were paper, he said, "Kippers and eggs in the dining room, Miss Maria."

"Morning, Farquhar," I said.

"The motor belongs to Mr. Rupert Crandall," Farquhar said, heaving the churn up the stone steps to the front door. Then he added, whispering, with a wink, "Pedophile and Yankophile."

"Huh? Whato-phile?" I said, barely listening. I pressed the silver-button door handle with both thumbs. The door popped open and I clambered in to inspect this novel trove. It smelled of cigarettes and sickly sweet fake pine, which was oozing, green and sticky, from the base of a tiny plastic tree glued to the dashboard. On the floor, on the passenger side, it was two feet deep in cassette tapes and cigarettes and packets of chewing gum.

"I wouldn't advise tampering with Mr. Crandall's chewing gum," Farquhar informed me stiffly as I pulled a stick of gum from a pack and folded it into my mouth. Gripping the milk churn, he swung around and disappeared inside the castle. I emerged from the rocket ship car and leaned with all my weight on the heavy door to close it behind me. I listened to the vacant silence broken by wind wisps and jackdaw laughter. I turned slowly round, straining my eyes. I thought I heard the great gates to the park clank, and I swiveled quickly, grinding my unlaced shoes in the gravel. My eyes were hoodwinked every time tree limbs swayed, leaves rustled glitteringly. A dark bird flew out, up, up, and receded, flapping away into nothingness.

I entered one of the long dark corridors, which led to a small room and then a larger one, and finally arrived at a circular antechamber, a narrow cone of pistachio green cloth walls and ebony furnishings, the telephone room. Sliding the sweet, wet gum to one side of my mouth, I spoke into the heavy receiver, cradling the weight on my neck, propping it up with both hands. "Hello, Operator?" I said, mimicking my mother's intonation. "I'd like to place a transatlantic call. To New York. America."

In a manner I am confident is never used to address my mother, the operator asked, "My dear, do your parents know that you're making very expensive telephone calls?"

"Yes, of course!" I replied, checking about to be certain I was not under surveillance.

"And, my dear, have you taken into consideration that there is a six-hour time difference? That would make it, let me see, approximately two o'clock in the morning?"

I concealed my surprise while I considered delaying the call. But I could not wait, and I supplied the number despite minor reservations. I resumed chewing as I idly surveyed the dusty paintings clustered up the walls, all different sizes that seemed to fit next to one another like the pieces of a jigsaw puzzle. An etching of a couple lounging uncomfortably on a four-poster bed hung at eye level. They appeared to be distressed, clinging together with pitiful faces.

"Excuse me?" I said when the operator told me the line was disconnected. "Could you please try it again?" I spat out my gum and stuck it in a pocket before spelling out the numbers as slowly and clearly as possible. Securing the telephone receiver between my ear and my shoulder, I plucked the etching from the wall to examine it at close range. Yes, this was definitely bad news, as the couple appeared to be sobbing, clutching each other miserably.

Again the operator told me the line was no longer in service and suggested I check the number and try again later. Tucking the picture under my arm, I hung up, a strange disquiet muddling within me. Was it possible that Alison's family had moved? I stared at the telephone, as if an answer might spring up like some waking genie, but nothing happened. With a finger beneath the silken cord screwed into the back of the etching, I located the nail upon which it hung and replaced it on the wall. It crashed to the floor, splintering glass and bits of wood.

"Cripes!" I exclaimed, hopping out of the way of the explosion.

The picture landed facedown, exposing a handwritten letter closed into the back of the frame. I crouched down, gathering it gently in my hands, and attempted to read the faded scrawl, "in the event . . . my estate . . . witnessed by." But too many of the words were concealed for me to make any sense of it, and short of dismantling the elaborate pins and hooks and panels, I would never know any more. I removed the remaining glass from the front of the picture and rehung it, dropping the shards to the floor before easing them to the edge of the carpet with the tip of my shoe, praying the accident would go unnoticed. I retraced my steps to the front hall and raced up the stairs, wide stone steps with a worn dark red carpet down the center, like a spill.

I took a right at the landing and counted three doors to where my mother and Hamish stayed. I could feel eyes trailing me. I turned slowly to find myself confronted by the portrait of an ancestral Cairngorm hanging at the head of the stairs. The eyes twitched, tracking me if I took a step forward or backward. A wine red velvet cap sat flat above the contemptuous glance, smug with secrets and stolen knowledge. It seemed that the only thing preventing him from laughing out loud was the tremendous profusion of beard and artful, stiff whiskers. With his arms akimbo his torso looked square, swaddled in a gold-threaded jerkin and a burgundy cape trimmed with a polka-dotted pelt. From his neck hung a medallion with the crest of the Cairngorms: a dying stag shot through with arrows. Perhaps to prevent his departure, the artist had not provided his subject with feet, and a complicated gilt frame sliced across the man's stockinged legs. I knocked at the bedroom door.

"Mama?" I said, and knocked again. "Hamish? You awake?" I knocked once more and opened the door wide. The room appeared deserted. The bed was empty. Sheets and blankets poured over the sides, pillows with the deep prints of use rested up against the headboard. In a lightning jag, sunlight zigzagged the fringe where the curtains did not quite meet. "Mama? Anyone here?" I said, to no one. Suitcases lay open; a pastiche of colors and clothes poured out. I followed a trail, paved with socks and shirts and a turquoise satin robe, to the bathroom. A glow shimmered along the edge of the half-closed door, and there came the uneven sound of water burbling, the fount of the brook.

"Mama!" I called. "You in there?"

I was poised to announce myself, but something stopped me, caught my hand in midair; and as quietly and gently as I could, I pushed the door. The room was obscured in a dense, white steam that wrapped itself against me, confused my eyes.

Indistinctly, I could see my mother lying in the bathtub, her head back against the rim. Her eyes were closed, her mouth was open and moving as if she were trying to speak. But no words came out, only noises, moans. I wondered if she was hurt. A marigold yellow shirt lay on the floor, a man's shirt with oval silver cufflinks dangling loose from the cuffs. The sound of gurgling water drew my attention to my mother's hand, holding the showerhead at the end of its extension, between her legs. She was pressing it against herself, moving it slowly. And every now and again her body jerked and she moaned longer, deeper.

I retreated. I tiptoed across the scattered garments with my teeth clenched. I thought my heartbeat would deafen me, and I shut the bedroom door behind me. In the gloom of the corridor I leaned against a wall, let the coolness rush over me, clear my head. I felt like a thief, as if I had stolen something sacred from my mother and I did not know how to put it back.

Looking up, I encountered the stern eyes of the painted Cairngorm. I went up close, my hand outstretched to touch the cracking paint, and I thought I recognized an affinity between us. His gaze was not contemptuous as I had originally believed; it registered distaste. It was the unease one is left with, having witnessed more than one cared to. It was the rot you feel corroding your gut from storing too many secrets, other people's secrets.

Voices, women's high-clipped tones, signaled like a cavalry's bugler, and instinctively I looked about for somewhere to hide. I opened the nearest door and closed myself in.

The voices approached. Backing up toward an ornately carved cupboard, I unbolted the lock and folded myself onto the wooden floor, easing the doors back into place until the bolts clicked shut. Through a multitude of cracks, I could see the entire room as if I were in a box at the theater. Center stage, dark as a Highland lake, stood a canopy bed adorned with the Cairngorm crest of a dying stag. Silver frames sat in rows on the night tables. Pots of dry flowers topped stacks of books on little three-legged tables, like flags on mountain peaks. The stalks and the desiccated petals were brown, hanging down.

"Stop fussing, Nessie," Miranda said, striding in.

"This is Her Ladyship's private room!" Nessie said, rustling in behind Miranda. Nessie spoke rapidly and partly under her breath, as if the horror of the circumstances might be diluted this way. Nessie was not much over forty, but she walked with a stoop and the faintest trace of a limp that caused her bun of graying hair to bob like the pompom on a wool cap. "You really shouldn't even be in here, Miss Miranda!"

"I like it," Miranda said, with her hands on the hips of her milk white corduroy trousers. She stalked about like a dancer between rehearsals, turning the switches of every lamp. "Be a dear, Nessie. Run and fetch my things from that hole I had to sleep in last night."

"Och, it's not a good idea, Miss Miranda," Nessie said in an exasperated tone, vexed and powerless and wiping imaginary dirt onto the lap of her apron.

"Stop." Miranda raised one hand to halt the flow, evidently bored with this twittery display of nerves. She sat on the edge of the bed and bounced, once, twice, so that the stag lunged in death throes. "When you come back," Miranda said, pointing to the fireplace as if Nessie might not otherwise understand, "I'd love a fire."

Miranda pushed herself off the bed and drifted about, whistling. She paused in front of a chest with a display of stones. Her hand hovered like a bird of prey above a twig nest before her fingers swooped down and plundered. Examining a pair of pale yellow stones at close range, she smiled, closed them into her palm, and continued her tour.

Still whistling, she stopped in front of a standing mirror reclining at an angle on its upright wooden arms. She folded her arms across her chest and confused the pattern of red-and-white stripes on her billowy silk shirt. As she stared, a knowing, complicit look crossed her face, relaxed her eyes, softened her mouth.

Taking a yellow stone in each hand, she raised them to her ears. She scowled and dropped them to the floor. Miranda collected her long honey hair and piled it on the top of her head, so that it hung glossily and revealed her favorite strands of pearls wrapped twice around her neck, a luminescent collar with which the rough Highland stones could not hope to compete. She stood to one side, then the other, posed for a profile, and slid her faded blue eyes over to capture the angle. With a wink, she blew herself a kiss.

The door burst open. "Here you are!" said a man, shaking a mass of shaggy blond hair that was not so much long as it was full, like a mop. It began in one straight line across his forehead and traveled up and back, like a curling wave, flying off at the tips. His face was round and soft, and his eyes were small and intensely dark. He looked like a large cat. "You've got Nessie in quite a flap! What did you do to the poor girl?"

"It's polite to knock!" Miranda said, combing her hair with her fingers, obviously flustered by the intrusion. "But since you're here, can you build a fire?"

"I'm not getting covered in soot and ash, if that's what you mean." The shaggy man laughed through his nose, little sharp noises like an untuned trumpet. He took a few steps and threw himself onto the bed; the stag leapt in gamboling strides. In Levi's and a jeans shirt, he looked like a blue puddle against the wine-colored bed and the wine-and-gold brocade pillows. From a back pocket he produced a packet of Marlboros and a lighter, and he lit himself a cigarette. He exhaled the blue smoke in rough-edged rings, his mouth opening and closing like a guppy fish. "Come sit," he said with the last wisp of smoke, and patted the bedspread.

"I hate it here," Miranda said in a faraway, wistful way. She crossed her arms tight over her chest, so that the red-and-white stripes of her shirt met at right angles. She took a step toward the window and drowned herself in daylight. "I hate the cold."

"Where would you like to go . . . ?" the man asked, and he might have gone on, but Nessie backed into the room burdened with three suitcases, which she dropped to the floor.

"Be a dear, Nessie, and get the fire going," Miranda said, checking herself in the mirror with a sidelong look. "I'm going to freeze to death! This useless man has refused to help."

"His Lordship was asking after you, Mr. Rupert," Nessie said, kneeling before the grate, balling up pages of newspaper and shoving them under the logs. "I hardly knew what to say. It doesn't seem right, you two sitting in Her Ladyship's room like this. I told him I'd have a wee look around for you." Standing up, she wiped her hands on her apron, tucked a gray strand into her loose bobbing bun with one finger, leaving a hint of soot on her cheek, primitive makeup. "Who's been messing aboot with Her Ladyship's matches, then?" she said, opening boxes on the mantel with jittery movements, sending the bun into a furious jig. "How am I expected to light this fire?"

"Catch!" Rupert said, and tossed his lighter. "See, Miranda, I'm not entirely useless. Just out of curiosity, may I ask why you've chosen to set up camp in Lady Eleanor's personal room?"

"You'd never know she's married to Charlie. She's never here!" Miranda sulked. "She's off on some beach somewhere! I can't understand why Mama insists on dragging us up to this barbaric cold. Every winter I tell her, 'Let's go to the sun,' but it's always, 'We've got to go to Scotland and see Hamish's cousins!' Why? They're all ghastly!"

"Would you like to go to a beach with me?" Rupert said in what he must have hoped was a seductive voice.

"Dirt!" Miranda declared as she ran a finger like a plow across the surface of a table. "How revolting, Nessie, you'll have to fetch a duster. This place is a sty! And you'll have to get rid of all these hideous dead plants! I'm sure they're unhealthy! Probably carrying bubonic plague!" Miranda shook her finger vigorously to dislodge the dirt.

"I don't have the time, right now, Miss Miranda," Nessie said, uncharacteristically short of patience. "Besides, I don't know how long you'll be in here, once His Lordship gets wind of all this palaver." She banged the door closed as she left.

"Do you have any idea how beautiful you are?" Rupert asked. Rolling off the bed, he crossed the room and stood behind her, slid his arms around her waist, enveloping her. "Will you run away with me?" He breathed into her neck, his cigarette clamped between his teeth.

"Maybe," Miranda said, her voice thin and shrill. She forced a cough.

"What's your absolute favorite thing?" Rupert murmured hotly mixing his words with thick smoke. He wrapped himself tightly around her, as if he were a belt being cinched.

"Diamonds!" Miranda squeaked, and laughed. In a single graceful movement she thrust forward and escaped his clasp. "Diamonds and sunshine!"

"Let's go to South Africa," Rupert implored, walking slowly toward her, following her. "We'll make sand castles on the beach, out of diamonds. Do you like the sound of that?" He was on her again, near the bed; her back was jammed into a wooden upright. He removed the cigarette from his mouth and stubbed it into the dry earth of a dead plant. He ran his fingers through her hair, away from her face, while she gazed at the floor and wriggled her fingertips through the pearls at her neck.

"It doesn't make any sense to me." Miranda spoke rapidly. "All this! I can't imagine having all this and not living better. Eleanor has the sense to go off to some Caribbean island where she's waited on hand and foot! At least she knows how to live! You have to respect that. What's the point of money, after all, if you don't indulge yourself with luxuries?"

"Well, she has her reasons for making herself scarce when you lot come to visit," Rupert said. "Other than that, I quite agree with you."

"Do you have any with you?" Miranda asked falteringly. "Uh, diamonds, I mean."

Rupert cupped her face in his hands, his big catlike face staring down at her. Then he leaned forward and kissed her, though it did not last more than a second, since she pushed him away with both hands and scampered across the room.

"How dare you!" Miranda said, rubbing her mouth with the back of her hand. "Get out! Get out right this minute!"

"Silly girl!" Rupert said, laughing his strange, sharp laugh. He strolled casually to the door and then he turned and smiled, a sly, satisfied smile. "We'll have to talk some more." And he went out.

"Tommy Durban suits you better than that hairy creep," I said, pushing the cupboard doors open. One foot tingled with pins and needles, and when I tentatively placed it on the floor it crumpled beneath me so that I had to hobble.

"What on earth . . . ," Miranda said, mouth agape, pale eyes wide. She backed away from me as if I were emerging from a coffin. "How long have you—"

"D'you think he'll give you a diamond?" I asked as I hopped over to the discarded yellow stones, picked them up, tilted them until they caught the light. The soft yellow was striped with dark red, bled through like a sunset.

"He'll give me whatever I want, you nasty little spy!" Miranda said and slammed the door behind her, but it did not catch and it wobbled open. The emptiness descended around me, settling like the lingering vapors of Rupert's cigarette. The show was definitely over, and I did not like to stay in Her Ladyship's chambers by myself. There was something eerie in the emptiness. Limping on my sleeping foot, I stumbled crookedly toward the chest of drawers. Ungluing the drying wedge of chewing gum from my pocket, I pressed the stones into the viscous glob and stuck it to the inside of their twig berth, where a tiny note with *Cairngorms* scrawled faintly in brown ink pierced the edge of the nest like an explorer's flag. They were now secure against future theft, I hoped.

Skipping slowly down the wide stairs, my shoes sending up electric sparks against the wool of the red carpet, I looked up to catch the knowing eye of the painted Cairngorm. Big, bearded, solemn, and dense. I winked at him and vanished down the dark corridor.

• • •

HAMISH'S VOICE MET me before I reached the drawing room. "I've been on the phone all bloody morning organizing the shoot, only to find out that the odious Archibald Shell is staying with the Cochrans." Hamish stood beside Charlie in front of a spirited fire. Distracted, he chewed one end of a long cigar and spat the fragments directly into the chattering flames. As unobtrusively as possible, I sat myself on the arm of one the two huge high-backed sofas that sat opposite each other, my mother hunkered down the fireside end, Miranda melting languidly against her under a protective arm. "I'll be buggered if I'm going to shoot with him!"

"Careful what you wish for!" my mother said and immediately gripped the tip of her nose to stanch an explosion of laughter.

Despite the immensity of the grand drawing room, it was cozy, lit as it was by the soft glow of lamplight, with yolk yellow showering tables of stacked books and a haze from fizzing, popping logs and charring pinecones and the sweet pungency of cigar smoke and coffee.

"Shell, Shell, Shell," Charlie said, swirling an amber drink around the swollen base of a glass he held in long thin fingers that appeared ice white at the tips. "Do you mean that fat homosexual art dealer?"

"I mean that fat homosexual turncoat we tortured at Eton!" Hamish chuckled acidly. With a square of malachite in one hand, he lit his cigar and billowed out mouthfuls of dense smoke.

Charlie took a long swallow of his amber drink, tipping his dark red hair down his back. The men were dressed almost identically, in velvet slippers with their crests sewn in gold on the toe, long wool socks, Cairngorm tweed plus fours, and heavy Arran sweaters, thick and bland as oatmeal. The two men wore their clothes distinctively; Hamish was stylish, severe, and smart, where Charlie looked unkempt, battered almost, with

things not tucked in quite right and threads cascading dangerously where moth holes had developed. And then I noticed the
color of Charlie's shirt, piercing bright marigold yellow rearing
from beneath his sweater at the neck and the wrist, where oval
silver cufflinks hung loose, as if Charlie had dressed hurriedly,
or perhaps distractedly.

"You swine!" my mother said, pulling off her reading glasses
and tapping them impetuously on her blanketed legs. She was
sunk deep into the sofa, her legs propped on an embroidered
ottoman strewn with newspapers, a tray of blue-and-white
china cups, a glass coffeepot, and Oz, a blind black pug. A book,
opened to the middle and lying upside down, rested against her
chest.

"What's that, my dear?" Charlie muttered, stalling.

"You promised me no killing!" my mother cooed unhappily,
disturbing Miranda.

"Uh, right," Charlie said, his voice trailing indistinctly as he
shoved his velvet shoe into Hannibal, an old mustard-colored
Labrador splayed out fast asleep. "Hamish, old bean, I might
take the Greenpeace crowd for a walk."

"What? What?" Hamish said and cast my mother a furious
glare. Hamish had thick blond hair like flowering gorse and
dark hostile eyes that swept about like a searchlight in the night.
"Have you gone completely mad? I drove ten hours last night in
filthy weather, and you're going to go for a bloody walk?"

"No more murdering defenseless and perfectly harmless
fowl!" my mother implored sweetly. "You promised!"

"Did I?" Charlie said, smiling at some private reverie. "I did,
didn't I? What could I have meant by that, my dear? Heat of the
moment, if you know what I mean!"

"Can't someone remove this disgusting dog?" my mother
said angrily, pushing Oz's wet snuffling head away with her foot
so that he teetered over the edge of the ottoman before landing,
stiff legs flailing, onto Hannibal, who growled and snapped at

the air without so much as opening his eyes. "If you must shoot something—"

"What ho!" Rupert said, strolling in, one hand up in some form of salutation, a cross between a cowboy and an Indian and a proper country gentleman. He stopped to fix himself a drink at a table behind one of the high-backed sofas. Miranda sat up straight and with twitchy looks about the room ran a hand through her long honey hair, driving it back from her face. She adopted a bored, casual look, as if she had better things to do than sit and listen to the grown-ups squabble, but she had decided to stay just the same, as a favor.

"Rupert, my good man," Hamish said between puffs on his cigar, resting his elbows on the stone mantel, fairly leaning into the flames, "I'm expecting you on the shoot this afternoon."

"Natch, Squire!" Rupert said. He sat on the sofa across from my mother and Miranda, and placed an ankle on his right knee, so that one brown beaded moccasin pointed toward the ceiling. "I'll be a happy man if I snag a brace."

"*Poussin rôti* served up by a white-gloved French waiter is the only version of fowl I'll go near!" Miranda said, fingering her hair, wrapping strands in loops the way she did her pearls.

"Ah, yes, Miranda?" Charlie said as he wound his way over Hannibal and around the back of the sofa toward the drinks table. "Nessie says you've moved yourself into the wife's bedroom? I trust you'll be comfortable."

"What?" Hamish said, spitting flecks of cigar onto his fingers, flicking them into the hissing heat behind him. "What's this now?"

"Nothing to fret over, Hamish," Charlie said, splashing amber liquid into his glass from a rectangle of crystal with a silver chain around its neck and a carved plaque that read *Scotch*. Charlie wore round wire-rim glasses, beclouding the brilliant deep marine of his eyes. "The lovely wife is in Jamaica studying the teachings of Haile Selassie. Or black magic, or how to grow exportable ganja.

Eleanor will study just about anything if it can be taught outdoors
on a beach in the tropics! Easy to please, really!"

"Do take a look at this, darling, it's fascinating." My mother
sounded terse as she replaced her reading glasses and thrummed
the pages of her book. "It's written by a four-hundred-year-old
Indian ascetic! Teaches one how to live in harmony with nature.
How to communicate with animals. The part I'm reading now ex-
plains how you can reverse the aging process! Stay young forever!
Do give it a look, darling." She thrust the book onto Miranda's lap.

"But are you mad? Are you all completely mad?" Hamish
said. "Miranda, you'll go upstairs and remove your things from
Eleanor's room. Immediately!"

Miranda flared her nose and stared contemptuously at
Hamish. With an equine flick she resettled her long hair so that
it all fell down one side and bent studiously over the proffered
book.

"I said immediately!" Hamish thundered, his glossy eyes wide
with rage as he stabbed at the air with his cigar.

"Do stop all this yelling!" my mother said earnestly, gripping
her temples and batting her eyelashes so that her famous green
eyes teared. "I'm going to get a migraine!"

"How do you mean, Eleanor's gone off?" Hamish asked
Charlie, as if the gravity of the news had only just registered.
"Gone off where? Gone off for good, old boy? Splitsville?"

"No. Good Lord, no. On holiday, that's all," Charlie said
dispiritedly from behind the drinks table, where he seemed to
wish to stay. He stared thoughtfully out at the etiolated garden
and methodically polished his wire-rim glasses on the cuff of his
shirt. He stood framed by the expansive gray stone room, with
vast worn tapestries hung on the rock walls and dusty marble
tables heaped with ancestral memorabilia. And yet the only
thing I saw was the marigold of his shirt, the brightness stabbing
my memory in uneasy thrusts. I could not place it.

"Excuse me, sir." Farquhar was standing at the doorway of

the green circular telephone room, coughing politely into his hand to catch Charlie's attention. "Lunch is served, sir. Children's lunch is in the nursery," Farquhar continued from the doorway.

"I don't give a toss about the nursery," Miranda said, pouting, crossing her arms in an exaggerated way, sending the red stripes of her big soft shirt into a corruption of angles. "I want to eat with the grown-ups!"

"Too bloody bad, young lady," Hamish said, waving his cigar at her with a certain relish. "Now go on! Scat!"

My mother rose and stretched and tossed her reading glasses, hitting Oz square in the face, startling the little dog just as he had succeeded in clambering back to his position on the ottoman. The direct hit sent him hurtling off once again, landing beyond Hannibal and onto the marble hearth. He yelped as he struggled to his feet, and scurried first toward the flaming logs, then backed out into Hannibal, who greeted him with open jaws and a warning growl.

Hamish and Charlie strolled slowly, following my mother, Oz waddling alongside to keep up. Rupert yawned, stretching his arms up to the frescoed ceiling, so that his jeans shirt came free of his Levi's, displaying a healthy weave of blond hair descending in a pipeline into his waistband.

"I think I'm in love with you," Rupert said, approaching Miranda, sitting beside her. He looked at her with his big, soft, smiling eyes, creasing wrinkles like whiskers. "I'm going to take you shopping once we're back in London." He purred and painted an invisible *X* across his heart. "You can have anything you want."

Miranda had spread my mother's abandoned blanket across her legs. She and Rupert stared at each other until the clock on the mantelpiece, ticktocking in a sedate seductive way against a backdrop of flames thwacking up the flue, chimed once, announcing the hour.

"A fur coat?" Miranda asked slowly, watching him carefully.

"A floor-length chinchilla!" Rupert leaned toward her, took her hands in his, and kissed her open palms, his long blond hair falling forward. Then, deftly, he kissed her on the mouth. Miranda closed her eyes and permitted it.

"Yuck!" I said, giggling, and leaping up from my perch on the arm of the sofa. "Not in front of the children, if you don't mind!"

"She is such an idiot!" Miranda said, exasperated, looking up at Rupert. "Enough to drive anyone over the brink!" She stood up huffily, aligned with her knight, her arms crossed and poised for war.

"You two are so different." Rupert eyed the both of us with a contemplative look, calm and remote.

"How d'you know?" I asked, impressed.

"I'm fainting from hunger!" Miranda declared. "Rupert be a gentleman . . . " She wound an arm around Rupert's back and steered him away, whispering into his mass of hair.

I fell in a dead fall, tumbling into the thick cushions of the sofa and lay there looking up at the painted ceiling, constellations in a blackened universe with cherubs blowing on trumpets at the corners. I thought I heard the angel's breath hum through the horns and drift across the planets. And I tried to pick apart the sounds that filled the big room; discern my echoing laughter from the patter of the charring logs, that stuttered like an easy rainfall on a glass roof.

"SOMEBODY CALL FOR an ambulance!" Hamish and a fat man I did not recognize exploded into the drawing room carrying Charlie Cairngorm between them like a lumpy sack of coal, wrenching me from a deep sleep, a heap of orange coals hissing distantly beneath the grate. "Charlie's been shot! Call for an ambulance!"

Awakened by the commotion, I leapt up just in time to avoid receiving Charlie on top of me as Hamish and the stranger dropped his limp body onto the sofa. Hannibal and Oz lurched about, yapping and bounding. All at once the room filled with my mother and Miranda and Farquhar.

"No, no . . . ," Charlie began to say, weakly waving his hands in the air. "I'm quite all right, really I am . . ."

"I say, Farquhar, call for an ambulance at once!" said the fat man, whose long thin nose and sleepy brown eyes that sloped doglike down the sides of his narrow face were quite at odds with the generous girth of his middle and his stocky, ham-hock legs. He tugged on the cuffs of his sleeves as if he hoped he could trick his clothes into expanding at the same rate as himself, and glared knowingly at Hamish, who paced back and forth beside Charlie.

"It was an accident, Charlie! You realize that, don't you? It was a bloody accident!" Hamish's pacing quickened so that he stirred up a minor gust of wind, raging around in a tiny range of motion as if he were confined by a magnetic force.

"Of course, old bean! Of course!" Charlie said gently. "Don't think twice about it. Everyone should have a brush with death now and again. Gets the juices flowing!" He propped himself up, his ashen face searching for something, finally finding my mother, who shimmied toward him. He smiled faintly before allowing himself to recline, lacing his fingers across his chest.

"Accident!" The corpulent stranger spluttered, gripping his ample hips in thick pink fleshy hands. "My arse!"

"Spare us any mention of your arse!" Hamish spat out, still pacing.

"I'll make a statement to the police!" fired the fat man, wagging a chubby pink finger.

"No, no, no!" Charlie said, feebly waving his hands in the air again. "Don't like to involve the local constabulary for anything short of treason! Farquhar, can we have some tea around here, or a large glass of scotch? What do you say?"

"Right away, sir," Farquhar oozed, stooping slightly as he

shuffled flatfooted to the drinks table. His white gloves muffled all sound as if he were a player in a silent pantomime.

Hamish poked a stiff finger into the fat man's pigeon chest. "Charlie's bloody hat flew off in the wind, Shell, and I mistook it for a bird!"

"Then how is it that the hat is untouched and Charlie has a slug in his shoulder?" Archibald Shell said, pursing his mouth tight, screwing his entire narrow face into a twist of lips. "And there's no need to be rude, old boy!" he added, recoiling from Hamish as if he were on a listing deck.

"Don't bloody 'old boy' me, you bloody idiot!" Hamish snarled, quite out of control, jostling Farquhar as he feverishly began to mix tomato juice and Worcestershire sauce and vodka, jabbing it with a half-moon of lemon before sliding it between his teeth and, wincing, sucking the sour taste out of it.

"Hamish! You blistering fool!" my mother said, arching a sculpted brow, hovering protectively beside Charlie. "How could you fill your favorite cousin with gunpowder!"

"What?" Hamish snapped so violently that my mother fluttered a hand to her throat as her watery eyes registered effrontery and hurt.

"Charlie, did you see your life flash past?" my mother asked, one hand patting his chest as he gasped. "You know, a brilliant light at the end of a tunnel? A near death experience?"

"Death duties." Charlie said, the words emerging jerkingly, his supine face illumined by a gentle smile. "Far too expensive to die!"

"If you'd listened to me, you wouldn't have gone on the stupid shoot! I begged you, Charlie!" my mother said, tucking the ends of a blanket under Charlie's limbs, mummifying him. "It's all too depressing!"

"I'll tell you what's depressing!" Hamish said, gulping down a generous mouthful. "What's depressing is watching you flail about in your self-styled B-movie roles! Who do you think you're playing now, Mother bloody Teresa, or is it Florence bloody Nightmare? Huh?"

"Do stop bickering!" Charlie said, straining free of the tight blanket and raising the hand of a referee. He snatched a tumbler from Farquhar and downed his scotch in three quick swallows. "But that's about as likely as Farquhar singing us an aria. Is that right, Farquhar? Any chance you could sing us an aria, my good man?"

"No sir," Farquhar said, staring at the floor as if to look directly at Charlie might burn his eyeballs. "Unfortunately that would not be possible, sir."

"See nothing unfortunate about that, hah!" Charlie said, holding out his empty glass for Farquhar to replenish. "More scotch and then a kip, and I'll be right as rain."

A pinecone fizzled in the fireplace, the last gasp of a dying blaze. "May I suggest a visit to the doctor, sir?" Farquhar said as he slid silently across the room, wrapped his white-gloved hand around a poker and a fresh log, and jabbed the molten shards, expertly igniting flames, training them up and around the offering.

"Good idea. I think I'm going to get a migraine!" my mother said, clutching her temples with the tips of her fingers.

"For Charlie! A doctor for Charlie!" Hamish screamed.

"You shot him, you call the doctor!" My mother looked about with wild-eyed defiance, gathering nodding agreements all around.

"My beautiful Helena!" A man was standing in the doorway, dwarfed by the colossal archway flanked by stone walls hung with dour, fading tapestries. As he sauntered slowly in, his hard, square, blunt face and his cold, watery blue eyes were softened by a wide smile and a throaty chuckle. "Are you angry with Hamish because he hit, or because he missed?"

"Ah, Tino, hello," my mother said, evidently unhinged, her hands moving fast and nervously over Charlie's blanket, spreading it flat across his chest as though she were ironing it. "Do come in, sit down. Farquhar will get you a drink."

"My eyes must be playing tricks on me!" Tino said, blue eyes smiling, pouring himself a drink, dropping cubes of ice in. "I mistook you for a crazy princess I know, and yet you're behaving as if you're the lady of the manor! Or are you practicing?"

"How dare you!" my mother said, her dark green eyes engorged and livid. She glanced quickly back and forth between Charlie and the smiling man.

"Is Eleanor the next to catch a stray bullet?" Tino laughed as he crushed the ice between his teeth. "Let me make you an offer, Helena. What if we all chip in and buy you a country to play with? Will that make you happy?"

"I want you out of here right now!" my mother thundered ferociously, pointing toward the doorway. "Charlie, I'm quite serious. Throw him out!"

"Nothing fancy, Helena. How about a pretty atoll in the Scillies?"

"Fling him out!" my mother ordered, standing stiffly, her hands on her hips.

"There's really no need . . . " Charlie trailed off as he winced and grabbed his shoulder. "Oh, God, anything for peace."

"Get the man a doctor, for God's sake!" Tino said, his voice low and menacing. "Let me tell you this, Princess, I hold you fully responsible for what happened to Charlie."

"All right, let's go! I absolutely think it's time to go!" Archibald said, waddling backward toward the no-longer-smiling man, hooking his arm in his, and steering him out. "Just for the record, Charlie, if you're ever in the mood to sell, I particularly love the John Singer Sargent. But you really must get it cleaned!"

"Are you all mad?" Hamish huffed, still pacing in manic circles, threading his long fingers through his tight blond hair. "Or is it me? Maybe it's me! I don't know what to think anymore," Hamish said sadly. He held his head in both hands and slunk from the room, shoulders hunched forward in total defeat. "Wait, Tino, I'm coming with you," he called, and then he was gone.

"What a monstrous afternoon!" my mother declared. "I've never seen so many people storming in and out! When I'm in charge, we're going to tighten security around here!" And then my mother doubled over laughing, gripping the end of her nose with her fingers.

"Hurrah!" Miranda said, clapping her hands together. "I pray Hamish is gone forever! Ghastly common man! Mama, promise me you'll never make a mistake like that again." She ran to sit beside my mother, pressing against her, one arm draped across her back.

"You're too silly," my mother sang delightedly. Eyes sparkling and aflutter with the thrill of victory, she hugged Miranda tight. In their good humor, they inadvertently pressed in against the reposing lord, smothering him, so that he began to thrash against their laughing, pulsating bodies. Turning about, ready to swipe a dog off the sofa, my mother looked astonished to see Charlie lying there, airless and fading. " 'Farquhar, do call for an ambulance!"

IN THE DAYS that followed, Charlie returned from the hospital, relieved of pheasant shot and stitched closed, and was laid out in his bedroom, from where my mother delivered frequent reports on his recovering health.

Life was quiet without Charlie to guide us through the long afternoons on Highland romps or visits to the Cairngorm wool refineries, where vats of dyeing wool stank atrociously and I would dash about with my nostrils pinned between thumb and forefinger and skid exaggeratedly on the slick stone floor in borrowed, oversized boots. Miranda would accompany us only if we were headed for the mills, where with the minimum pleading we were permitted to choose from tidy shelves of tartan blankets and kilts and capes and every conceivable item of clothing, woven from the finest Cairngorm wool. My mother whiled away the week floating in a bathtub, turning the taps with her toes when the temperature cooled and a fresh insurgency of piping-hot water was required, reading or chatting on the telephone, all in the hopes of recreating the feel of the tropics by ignoring the chilly autumnal weather beyond the castle walls. Hamish's continued absence was treated with a similar disregard; his name remained eerily unspoken, and not so much as a word was breathed on his behalf.

Rupert begged my mother to allow him to drive Miranda down to Edinburgh for a few days to see the sights, catch a play, stay in a well-heated, comfortable hotel. For the sake of peace and so as to spare herself one of Miranda's strikingly persuasive tantrums, my mother agreed. Entertaining myself was routine since, had Miranda remained at Cairngorm, we would not have shared more than five minutes in a room together, steaming in war mode.

I converted a portion of Shank McKinty's meticulously groomed garden into a fabulous kingdom ruled by a small pile of rocks I had laboriously painted and named and imbued with specific duties and obscure powers. I would sit on the earth, my feet bare and muddied, and invent for hours, creating epic dramas with dire, drastic calamities that only the most exquisitely sophisticated diplomacy could avert—only, of course, at the very last minute, before dragons and gorgons wreaked unsalvageable havoc. But eventually this solitary sport would turn dull, and I would trot indoors and repeat the ritual of dialing the operator and attempting to place a call to Alison, although I always met with the same obstacle, that the number seemed no longer to be good. Despondent, I would return to my make-be-

lieve world and talk out loud to Alison, as if this might somehow encourage her to materialize. I would try to imagine the
adventures we would have if she came to visit. And though the
thought made me smile, it also made me miss her more
acutely, and I hoped there would be a letter waiting for me at
home in London explaining why the telephone number no
longer worked and providing me with one that did.

"Maria, darling," my mother called, finding me straddling
several warring armies of stone late one afternoon. There was
something in the way she stood in the arch of the open French
doors, unmoving and quiet, that made me uneasy.

"What's the matter?" I stood up slowly, so that we faced each
other, I rubbed my hands together, spinning the dirt off in a
dust storm.

"Maria, please come here," my mother said, extending a
hand. Dressed all in charcoal, she became a shadow in the shadows. The only visible color was the rectangle of fire-engine red,
her bright lipstick as vivid as a beacon in the night. "We need to
have a chat."

Slowly I crossed the garden, climbed the stone steps toward
her outstretched hand, reluctantly closing the safe distance between us, disquiet reverberating inside me like some as yet unseen train surging around a mountain bend. She looked quite
consumed with whatever was bothering her.

"Darling," my mother began soothingly as she took my hand.
I felt the coolness of her small soft fingers wrap themselves
around my own, felt them press gently into my skin, her thumb
rubbing almost imperceptibly against the bone of my wrist, and
I thought I heard the train whistle scream directly between my
ears. "Do you remember Alison?"

"She's coming to visit?" I said, thrilled. What a relief! The
train boomed by, shaking on its old iron tracks, gusting tremendous relief as it swept past, whisking away my macabre misgiv-
ings. "Mama, is she coming?" I asked excitedly, grinning crazily

at my mother's somber face as she led me inside to the huge velvet sofas.

"Alison died." My mother gripped my hand hard. I was staring up at my mother, and now I felt quite paralyzed, unable to breathe. I stared desperately into my mother's face. Inexplicably I began to record the infinitesimal details: the indent beneath her cheekbones, and how the skin molded over her bones as thickly and easily as cream, and the space between her famous green eyes, and each one of her long dark eyelashes, which curled up toward her eyebrows, which she plucked in arches. I felt nothing as I waited for her to retract her statement, nothing more than numbness. My heart thumped so violently that I began to gasp for air. I yanked my hand free and staggered back, knocking into an armchair.

"Calm down, darling. Mama's in no mood for theatrics." My mother clutched her rejected hand to her bosom as if it were a wounded bird. "It was all perfectly painless, no one felt a thing. There was a gas leak. The house exploded to bits. Don't worry, darling, everyone was fast asleep."

I turned and ran through the great room, down the flagstone hallway, and up the stairs, two at a time, up and around the endless sweep, until I reached the top floor and the long corridor ending in the door to my bedroom. I slammed it shut behind me and bolted it closed, jamming the old bolt shakily behind the iron loop. I set about plundering Hamish's tartan suitcase, tossing my clothes out so that they fell wherever until I found the tube of paper and the Polaroid. Shambling over to the window, clutching my treasures to my chest, I sank into the welcoming chair. Hot, briny water dashed my face, soaking my lap and the paper I crushed against me, spreading the carbon to graying shades.

"Darling, do come downstairs and eat something," my mother called, rattling the locked bedroom door. The sound of her voice raised my skin in goose bumps, and immediately I was seized with loathing. For all eternity she would be inextricably bound to Alison's death. I could not forgive her. "Darling, it's no good you sitting in there feeling sorry for yourself. Really, one would think you were the one who died! And the way you're behaving, you'd think I was responsible! Darling, are you listening?" I whistled faintly to myself, obscuring her words, hating her. "Darling, do answer Mama!" I pressed my hands to my ears and blocked out all sound of her, kept them there until I was certain she was gone. Darkness crept around, the hours introduced by the chimes of a grandfather clock in the hallway. I sat, slumped in the black-and-green-tartan armchair, picking distractedly at the stuffing that oozed from the ends of the armrests.

What if, in the middle of the night, I were to slip away with a small packed bag, slip off into the enveloping night? Wave down a passing taxi, boxy rumbling vehicle of freedom. Slam hard the door. "Heathrow Airport, please," I would say to the back of a man's head, cap sitting lopsided on his thinning hair.

And if I attached myself to a kindly stewardess, pleaded my case to her? "I need to go to America. I need to find Alison," I would say to the lady crouched before me, her gray uniform skirt hiked up so that her bare knees pressed together, rounded and smooth. I would look into her frowning, concerned face with the gentle blue eyes and the blond hair pulled back in a tidy ponytail. "My mother said my friend is dead. And it's not true. And, you see, I have to find her."

And if I arrived in New York, at the carousel, where the luggage tours the floor of the airport on that rickety belt that heaves and grinds? What then? Where would I go from there? Would I enlist another guardian to transport me to Alison? Come to think of it, I had no clue where she lived. I never visited her anywhere but her father's beach house, just a few houses along from my own father's pink-brick hacienda.

I sat quite still, too tired to cry, too scared to move, and traveled to America in my head, over and over, staring unseeing at
the picnic-blanket garden colored first by day, then by night,
and now by vague dawn light. I pushed the orange velvet curtains shut since my eyes were delicate from crying and the daylight stung. Undeterred, morning lit the rim of the orange
velvet curtains, so that they glowed like topaz.

With a jolt my neck collapsed onto my chest and I saw my
lap and the floor immediately beneath me covered completely
with white fluff, feathers and cotton I had pulled from the tips
of the armrests. Lying like rose petals on a fresh grave, they almost concealed the Polaroid of Miranda, Alison, and me smiling for the camera in my father's summer house on an August
afternoon. Alison's will had come unrolled from the ribbons
and lay open on the floor, and though my eyes could hardly focus, I could just make out our final amendment, whereby we
promised to pass a message along to Mr. Ford's wife and son. I
wondered if Alison would remember the pledge. Wondered if it
mattered.

"Maria? Maria dear, if you're still alive, just tap your foot
twice on the floor, so that I know you're in there and breathing."
Charlie's gentle murmur snuck through the cracks in the door.
"Maria, two taps. That's all I ask. Please, my dear, and I promise
not to bother you any further." I smiled, and gingerly I lowered
my left foot to the floor. My leg ached with the movement; my
hip joint felt as if I were snapping it like a wishbone as I dangled
it above the bare floorboards. "Maria, I'll make a bargain with
you. Listening?" I brushed the floor with the tips of my toes as
gently as I could, testing. "All right, my dear, here it is. You tap
twice on the floor for me, and I'll see if I can convince your
mother to let you stay here. Maybe I can get all of you to stay.
Would you like that? Maria?" I whacked the old wood boards
with the ball of my foot twice, and then twice more to be cer-

tain. "Very good," Charlie said, a sigh of relief slipping through. "I'll do my best to persuade the troops, and Ill be back with a report before sunup tomorrow."

I watched the darkening sky come claim the garden, smothering it with twilight, gradually obliterating it until there was nothing to see in the moonless night. In time, footsteps approached, the gradual steady step of someone climbing, and for the first time in two days I felt the unsettling stab of hunger. Anticipating Charlie, come to say an extended visit had been secured, I decided the time to end my vigil had arrived. Stiffly I rose and crossed the room, pulled the bolt from the iron clasp, and swung the door open.

"Hello, pouty!" my mother said, flicking a sconce on from a switch by my door, showering herself in a soft yellow. "Come give Mama a big hug, darling." She spread her arms wide and bent slightly, the fire-engine red lipstick coming down to meet me. I froze. I knew I ought to return the embrace, but the sight of her smiling face sent me scuttling backward. I could not make myself approach; I could not tolerate the sound of her voice. "What's the matter now?" she snapped, rising, planting her hands on her hips. "I can't stand all this pouting, darling; you really do have to pull yourself together! I'm very sorry about Alison, but—" I slammed the door hard in her face and jammed the bolt back in place as brutally as I could. "I hate you!" I shrieked, drowning whatever she was saying. I picked up the tartan suitcase and threw it at the bolted door, followed swiftly with a pair of shoes parked just beneath my bed.

WITHIN TWENTY-FOUR HOURS my mother was bustling Miranda and me into Hamish's Audi, Vivaldi's *Four Seasons* fiddling mournfully, intermingling with the sound of the warming engine. Miranda upgraded herself to the passenger seat, and I lay across the back, my leather case for a pillow, feigning sleep with exaggerated steady breaths until the insistent giggling from the front of the car became too tempting to ignore. I opened my eyes to mere slits to see Rupert, in jeans and T-shirt, lounging through the passenger window, murmuring into Miranda's ear, burying his head in her thick honey strands. He dove expertly and landed a kiss at the very tip of her nose. Tittering, she swatted his chest with a limp backhand.

"That's enough!" my mother declared and stamped on the accelerator, carrying Rupert with us a few feet before he extricated himself and pushed a hand through his leonine hair. I sat up. Only then did I see Charlie standing by the front door, at the top of the stone steps. He looked glum and ponderous with his arm in a sling and his free hand gripping the pommel of a dark wood walking stick. I had an impulse to burst from the car and cling to Charlie, beg him to let me stay, but my mother was revving down the driveway before I could muster the verve to act.

"I say! Wait a minute!" Rupert yelled, combing his hair with his fingers, as if a thought were hatching and needed encouragement to fly the coop. My mother sank the brakes to the floor, lurching us all forward, necks snapping perilously, my little case lunging to the floor. "How about Miranda goes with me? I'm leaving as soon as Nessie's finished putting my things together."

"Oh, Mama, please, can I?" Miranda implored sweetly, popping open the door before permission was granted. "We'll race you to London, and since you're in such an old heap, you get the head start!" Without waiting for an answer, Miranda slammed the door hard behind her and instructed Rupert to extract her suitcase from the trunk of the Audi and install it in the back of his enormous spaceship Cadillac. Typical, I thought, envy piercing my heart. I cast a last look at Cairngorm. Charlie was gone, the moss-covered castle looked sealed and impenetrable. Overcome with frustration and defeat, I flopped back, stretching out on the backseat. Folding my arms across my chest and pretending once again to be in a deep sleep, I was quite determined not to converse with my mother under any circumstances.

"It's a pigsty in here!" I heard my sister's shrill cry as my mother wended the car down the long driveway, toward the great gates. "And what's this disgusting green thing leaking on the dashboard?"

A B U R S T T I R E delayed us several hours under the protective overhang of a petrol station, where three scruffy young men took turns unbolting and plugging and reattaching the tire. Meanwhile I lay on the backseat and pretended to sleep, eavesdropping on the florid language of the attendants, planning to use all of the expletives in quick succession on my unsuspecting mother if she dared approach and attempt a conversation. Vivaldi's *Four Seasons* had rotated several years, and evening had long settled, prickly and damp, by the time we reached London. Without opening my eyes I knew we were nearing home from the telltale city sounds, the inimitable baritone rumble of the taxis, the surge of cars rushing by on either side, the occasional horn blasting into the night. I stretched my sore limbs aching from hours of immobility.

As soon as my mother pulled up on the hand brake, I flew out, hugging my little tartan case close to my side, and ran for the front door, pounding on the glossy painted panels, skewering the doorbell with a free finger until Jambi, the housekeeper, came to let me in.

"My oh my, Maria!" she said, tucking stray hair, thick like a horse's tail, into the loosening bun at the base of her neck. "I thought there was trouble! So much noise!"

I ran past her and pounded up the stairs. Arriving at my bedroom door, I pushed backward with my hip and my shoulder, but the door would not budge. Pausing to fortify myself and push once more at the stubborn door, I caught sight of colors, things of mine dumped in Hamish's dressing room, a room adjacent to the bedroom I shared with Miranda. Cautiously I approached. My clothes were heaped on Hamish's bed, still on their hangers, like so many flattened people lying atop one another—a narrow bed with tarnished brass encircling it on three sides, a bed he used to stack piles of books and old newspaper clippings he liked to save.

Standing in the doorway, hesitant to enter, I peered in. The leather-topped desk was cleared of Hamish's belongings, his pigskin-bound books for notes and telephone numbers and the dates and origination of wines he liked and bought and stored beneath the stairs in the kitchen. Instead, there were my bears and my teacups and saucers with the painted butterflies; my triptych of Beatrix Potter in a paisley-papered box; smaller, wine red leather-bound books of French and Russian fairy tales; my grandmother's hat pins, long, jabbing pins topped with crystal and semiprecious stones; a tiny silver tea set embossed with flowers. A porcelain tub lay fallen over, pens and pencils spilling out. Tears stung my eyes as I saw my most precious possessions strewn about as if they were pollen scattered by the wind.

"It was Rupert's idea!" Miranda said, appearing from what had until recently been our bedroom. "Now you can have your very own room! And you're not allowed into my room unless I'm there and I give you permission. Got it?"

"Same goes for you!" I said angrily, quickly wiping away a tear lest Miranda derive some sordid satisfaction from her direct hit. "You're never allowed into my room!"

"You couldn't pay me to go into that pigsty!" She smiled and was gone, skipping down the stairs.

Confounded, I picked up my suitcase and stepped across the threshold into Hamish's room. I sat on the bed and dangled my legs above the carpeted floor and eyed my new home. It was forlorn and drab and cold from a mean breeze that lisped in through a crack in a pane. Unease swept over me as I realized that Hamish was well and truly gone.

One by one I began to hang my clothes on the high railing in Hamish's cupboard, which I could reach only if I balanced on the very tips of my toes. The activity of finding homes for my possessions absorbed me, and soon I was consumed with sorting the rubble of treasures. A bear on the windowsill, my teacups along the back of the desk, the porcelain tub upright, the pens and pencils neatly organized like a bouquet, taller ones at the center, shorter near the rim. The Russian silver tea set, my most valuable trophy, passed down to me by my grandmother, was reverently granted the seat of honor, dead center on the desk. I fished Alison's will and the Polaroid from my leather case and moored them in a safe berth between the pages of a sturdy collection of Edward Lear, and sat them in the dark depths of the cupboard, behind my shoes, a cool mausoleum. Gradually the room was transformed, like makeup on an aging face, so that it looked pert and pretty and bright. I liked it. I sat on the bed, resplendent with bears and my favorite blanket, and admired the room from that angle. I went to sit by the window, artfully blocking the draught, to examine my handiwork from another view. I sat at the desk and pretended to write, bent over the way Hamish had sat, hunched and concentrating, and exercised an imaginary ink pen across imaginary paper. I closed the door to see how I felt about this room from the inside, as a sanctuary all my own. I liked it very much.

" W H O I S I T ? " I said to the knock at the door, hoping to sound like my own secretary, prepared to tell whoever it was that I was not sure if I was in, that I would check if he or she could just wait a minute. The door opened and Jambi's round face appeared.

"Maria?" Jambi said, rolling her *r*'s like a Spaniard. "Your Mama say you have to dress nicely and come downstairs."

"No." I shook my head. I had barely left my room in weeks, refusing to go to school, studiously ignoring my mother's efforts, which fluctuated between cajoling and haranguing as she attempted to penetrate my grumpy, stubborn silence.

Tugging open the creaky cupboard doors, Jambi selected a red wool dress with smocking across the chest, white wool knee socks, and patent leather shoes with a band that fastened with a button. She handed me each article singly, waiting as I zipped or buckled the previous item. "Am I going to a birthday party?" I asked, not unreasonably, for these were some of my smartest clothes. Jambi said nothing, just looked at me and smiled, and then she hugged me, so that for a moment I was suffocated, buried in the squashy, overripe peach of her bosom, richly scented with talcum powder.

"Come." Jambi held out a hand to me, one stiff arm extended in my direction, the fingers curling ever so slightly, beckoning. Jambi was my accomplice, bringing my meals on a tray so that I might eat in the privacy of my room.

"No." I said and wriggled across the bed until I was jammed up against the wall, pressing against the tarnished brass bars.

"Come with me, Maria, and I'll take you to buy candy afterwards."

"Chocolate?" I asked.

"As much as you like."

"Do you promise, promise, promise? Do you swear?"

She nodded and approached, and I slid to the floor and placed my hand in hers, the scent of talcum powder instantly detectable, soothing in its familiarity, and accompanied her downstairs and along the corridor that skirted one side of the patio, to the living room at the back of the house.

I arrived downstairs in time to feel the breeze as the front

door slammed shut behind Miranda. It felt gluttonously deca-
dent not to have to follow her to the bus stop and wait about for
the lumbering red bus come to gobble up the huddled gray-
faced Londoners cracking open another damp day.

"Darling!" my mother exclaimed when she found me lying
on my back on the floor of the sitting room, listening to a
record I had sent spinning on the turntable. "Your dress! Get up
off the floor and come and say hello to the good doctor. Why
are the curtains always closed! I must have said a thousand
times I want them open!" My mother pulled the brocade cord
that hung down one side of the heavy vermilion cloth. As daylight blinded the room, flattening the shadows, Cricklewood
sprang down from her peculiar perch above the rungs, flying
with the grace of a gust of wind, landing pertly on the back of
an armchair.

"Damn that cat!" my mother said, flustered by the aerialist.
"Look at the state of this," she said, grabbing at the claw-shred-
ded curtains that marked the route Cricklewood took to as-
cend. "One day I'll, well, I don't know! Dr. Jamison, may I
introduce my daughter Maria. Darling, do get up off the floor!"

I thought I saw my mother raise an eyebrow as I shook the
hand of this squat, snouted, compact man dressed entirely in
shades of mustard brown; he reminded me of Hannibal, the
Cairngorm Labrador. The only significant distinction between
the man and the dog was the cascade of limp whiskers forging
around the doctor's fleshy gray lips and merging in an extended
goatee as if they were a dirty river accommodating a midstream
island of shimmering teeth and darting tongue.

"Pleased to meet you, dearie," the doctor said, gripping my
hand with what felt like unnecessary force. Turning to my
mother without waiting for me to reply, he rubbed his hands
together. "I'd just love a cuppa tea, Princess. And if you have
some bickies, you know, to sort of fill the spot, as they say, that
would be absolutely scrumptious."

As if on cue, as if she had been waiting hidden right around the corner, Jambi padded in, laden with a tray and a teapot and cups and saucers and little silver spoons engraved with crests of a crown that looked vaguely like the outline of Mickey Mouse's head. The warmed scones oozed seductively, and Dr. Jamison snatched one before Jambi had set the tray down, and began to cram it into his mustache-curtained mouth. "Scrumptious!" he exclaimed, flouncing down into the comfort of a sofa, swallowing mouthfuls of scone, gulping as if he were a pelican downing a school of fish. "Absolutely scrumptious."

"Lemon and honey, doctor?" my mother asked, sitting beside him, tipping the beak of her yellow teapot, aiming the plume of steaming coppery water into a matching yellow teacup. It was a habit of my mother's to lift the teapot as she poured, so that the liquid descended from an ever higher point, the gushing gurgling increasing noisily, threateningly, until the cup brimmed and she would snap her wrist back and shut the flow.

"Milk and sugar, if it's not too much trouble. Very light and very sweet, thank you, Princess," the doctor said, patting his swollen stomach as if to explain how it came to be. "Lovely, lovely," he said, taking the cup and saucer with both his hands open and flat as if he were receiving Communion. My mother dropped a paper-thin slice of lemon into her cup and filled it, pulling up on the teapot until it was level with her face.

I knelt beside the low table, a rectangle of ivory squares, one elbow meeting with the spines of a stack of books, Cricklewood on my lap purring vibrantly into my legs. My mother and the doctor sat across from me, as if they were players on a stage and I the attentive audience.

"Dearie?" Dr. Jamison asked, slurping his tea over the rim of the cup. "Could you tell me how horses mate?" I looked quickly at my mother, certain she would laugh with me at the mad doctor's question, but she was grave and solemn, as if this were perfectly normal. Impatiently the doctor clicked down the sides of his yellow teacup with dirty, ridged fingernails. I could think of nothing appropriate to say and I shook my head.

"Well, dearie," the doctor said, punctuating his monologue by stuffing fingerfuls of scone into his mouth, pulling the little cakes apart so that his unappealing nails filled and he took to sucking them clean. "You have to imagine that the stallion, that's the male, has a very long penis, lucky for him, and what he does, you see, is he comes around the back of the mare, that's the female, and he climbs on top of her, well, just the front of him on the back of her, d'you see? Am I embarrassing you?"

To prevent myself from laughing, I stared at my hands, my fingers vanishing beneath the thick fur of Cricklewood's back. I felt the purring resonate into my legs. Her triangular ears twitched back and forth, collecting noises.

"Well, dearie, it's quite all right to be embarrassed, but it's nothing more than the birds and the bees I'm telling you about. One hundred percent organic behavior, certified by Mother Nature. So, where was I? The stallion stuffs his penis into the mare's vagina, and Bob's your uncle, voilà—the bun, as they say, is in the proverbial oven. That about right, Princess?"

"Yes, yes, of course," my mother said, inspecting the room, making the occasional trip to reposition flowers standing in a vase. I wondered what she thought she was agreeing with, since she did not appear to have heard a word Dr. Jamison had said. It was inconceivable that she should accept this ludicrous man with anything resembling sincerity, when all I wanted to do was scream with laughter and fall about pointing a finger at him. Instead I kept my eyes down, watched the ruffling of Cricklewood's calico coat as it separated into a thousand hairs, standing up, springing back down, flicking off onto the deep red of my dress. Cricklewood shot out a paw, smacking my hand, claws like tiny scimitars unsheathed, warning me.

"Darling, do look at the good doctor when you're being spoken to. The man's time is very valuable. He's doing us a great

honor by coming to see you. He comes very highly recommended!" my mother said, and I looked up at her beautiful angry face and wondered what had happened to her that she could
indulge a fool like this. Could one lose one's sense of humor
overnight?

"Do you see what I mean?" my mother asked, and I puzzled
over her words until, slowly, I realized she was not speaking to
me, but rather to the doctor. And suddenly all I wanted to do
was go upstairs to my room and sleep or play my music or talk
to myself, anything rather than reinforce the rapidly widening
gulch of differences between my mother and myself.

"Draw me a young man, dearie, would you please?" Dr. Jamison said as he pulled a spiral pad and a pen from the inside pocket
of his mustard tweed jacket. He tossed the pen and paper so that
they landed in a burst beneath my face. I hunched over the low
table, my knees securely tucked beneath, Cricklewood lounging
heavily, warmly, on my sloping lap, her claws piercing my wool
dress as a reminder not to jiggle about as I drew.

"How's he going to take a piss?" Dr. Jamison asked, holding
my sketch up in front of him as if it were a slide illumined by
some backlight. Throbbing with laughter, crumbs flying from
his mustache in a fireworks display, he jabbed at my drawing
with his thick fingers. "How do you expect him to take a leak?"
he repeated, his laughter shaking him recklessly so that the
teacup he held stumbled nervously on its saucer. Cricklewood
stirred and lurched herself off me, galloping away, her tail low
to the ground. I wished I could follow.

"Don't be difficult, darling!" my mother said, annoyance regis-
tering in the flash of her dark green eyes. I stared questioningly at
her for a moment before looking away, my cheeks flaring with indignation. Who was this strange woman with the earnest, eager
face who seemed ever more awestruck with each new absurdity
Dr. Jamison threw her way? She reached for the teapot, filling her
cup once again, except that this time she pulled up too fast and

drops leapt out like flying fish, landing in winking puddles all around. She did not seem to notice, and she sat back with one hand under the saucer and the other protectively around the cup. "Your moods! You can't expect Mama to know how to handle these things. I know you loved Alison, but it's very selfish of you to blame me! It's not my fault, you know!"

So that was it, was it? This was why we were gathered, to assuage any suffering my mother might be experiencing. I gazed at her and her keen, wounded eyes, dark and dangerous as a hawk. I exhaled noisily, expressing my sense of exasperation onomatopoeically, and looked down at my lap and picked at the calico hairs that clung to my dress, collecting them in the palm of my hand.

"Prockney Hall," the doctor said definitively as he crammed the last fragments of scone into his mouth. "That's the place for obstinacy. They won't put up with this sort of nonsense."

Brockney Hall, 1987

MY MOTHER AND I JOURNEYED IN SILENCE, our separate worlds overlapped only by the sounds of a crackling radio and the rain spinning off the tires and the steady complaint of the wipers building dirty arches on the windscreen of my mother's new, navy Jaguar. All attempts at conversation, amounting to little more than questions posed by my mother answered wearily and monosyllabically by me, had been abandoned before we were clear of Chelsea. All I could do was stare out the window at the cars whooshing by and hope to drown out the questions I could not answer that pelted me in an ever more irritated tone.

Beside me on the backseat sat my small leather suitcase with the tartan lining, and in amongst the clothes were my treasures, the will and the Polaroid. There was comfort in their proximity, and I pulled the case close, drumming my fingers over the taut scuffed leather, and smiled at the cars as they passed and sprayed rainwater against my window, further obscuring the view.

How I would like to obscure the view of the past month, I thought. Tumult seemingly without end—unless, of course, this drive to the Sussex coast on a rainy October day was an end of sorts.

"I'll make an appointment for her to visit next Monday," Dr.

Jamison had told my mother, feet firmly planted on the stone doorway of our London house, shaking her hand with both of his, smothering her little white fingers in his brown leather driving gloves with the airholes punched in a pattern.

Sitting here, in the back of my mother's dark blue car, I tried to force myself to watch the cars that passed and not think about the doctor. "They won't put up with this sort of nonsense," he had said, and for whatever reason I could not prevent the sound of his voice from ricocheting inside my head. I put my hands up to block my ears as if somehow this would shelter me. I shook my head, but Dr. Jamison had the tenacity of a barnacle. Disconsolately I saw his stringy mustache flicking a burst of crumbs as he laughed, head back, mouth open, black and wide.

I supposed that my mother must be motoring toward the appointment Dr. Jamison had obliged her by making on my behalf. I did not know anything more than this, and I lacked the courage to question, so instead I watched the cars pass the window, and the half-moon faces of the drivers with stern unblinking eyes staring ahead. I wondered how it was they were not all hypnotized by the wipers going back and forth, dismissing the rain as it aimed, in darts, at the windscreen.

The road came to a junction when we reached the coast. Ahead there was the sea, blackish green, merging indistinctly with a smudged horizon. I thought it would be awful to have to swim in that water. We turned left and I watched the cliffs approach and then recede in a jagged, untidy line alongside the straight macadam. Cliffs and gulls and a swollen black-green ocean. And facing them all, like some unimpressed, half-asleep audience, sat redbrick Victorian houses with witch's-hat turrets and octagonal observatories that jutted out to one side like an afterthought. As if anyone would want to sit and watch the empty coast road and the rough sea. The motion of the car was comforting, and I hoped we would continue indefinitely. When we slowed to better negotiate an oncoming car with its yellow headlights groping though the fog, I held my breath until it was certain that we were not about to stop.

But eventually I heard the ticking of the turn signal. I saw the green arrow flashing on the dashboard, and my heart sped up so fast I could feel the reverberations in my throat. My mother directed the car into a driveway, churning the gravel, and parked. A brick house with a slate roof sat slightly up a hill. I hated it on sight.

"Darling." My mother turned toward me, a comforting warmth in her voice as she reached and took my hand between hers. "I want you to do something for me. I want you to promise to be nice to the professor. If you aren't happy here, you won't have to stay. But you have to give her a chance." She squeezed my hand and then she let it drop. It fell into my lap, a dead weight. The car door thunked closed and she ran toward the house, one hand protecting her face from the rain. A young woman with a thick yellow braid circling her neck like a scarf emerged beneath a portico, and the two of them stood and motioned me to join. Gratefully I could not hear them, as their pantomime was silenced in the downpour.

My mother stamped her feet, in plastic boots, and gripped her arms, hugging herself. I could see her shiver from where I sat, one long snaking jolt that shook her whole body, and yet she was smiling and chatting with the young woman with the long braid. "Alison," I whispered. "Stay close. Over and out." Pulling my suitcase behind me, I exited the safe haven of the car and tramped across the rain-shined pebbles to join my mother.

"How do you do?" the young woman with the braid said, attempting to take my suitcase from me though I refused to relinquish it. "I'm Patty. If you'll follow me, I'll take you in to the professor. She's looking forward to meeting you."

We followed through an entrance hall, cavernous and damp. On one wall there was a corkboard pinned with a profusion of papers, curling and forlorn like loose shingles on a house. Chairs were stacked against another wall, three columns of orange and yellow plastic seats, stainless steel legs jutting out, buckteeth. "Professor," Patty said, opening a door wide for us to enter, "your guests have arrived."

A stout old lady with a fleshy overlapping face sat at a table by the windows at the far end of the long room, backlit by four white panes crying rain in snaky rivulets, through which I could see my mother's dark Jaguar parked at the edge of the garden. The woman struggled up from her seat, and I saw that she was cylindrical, tight like a full sack of flour. "Hello, hello, Princess!" she said, opening her mouth wide to smile. Repulsed by the display of gum that showed, pink wet flesh framing irregular stained teeth, I stopped, paralyzed. My mother had to take me by the arm and push me toward this woman who was reaching for me, trying to grab at my hand. I did not want to touch her.

"Hello, my dear," the professor said, smiling her hideous smile and breathing rancid oniony breath into my face. She patted the back of a chair as she spoke. "Come sit down, my child."

I could not move except to wipe the palm of my hand against my sweater, trying to remove the feel of the professor, a clinging oiliness I could feel seeping into the bones in my fingers. I felt my mother's hands on my shoulders, pressing down, until I collapsed into the chair.

"Can I ask you to draw something for me?" the professor said, shoving a blank sheet of paper and a pencil toward me. She wore several layers of thin, faded cardigans hanging off her like flaking paint. "Can I ask you to draw some nice kitties?" There was a definitive tone to her voice that suggested this was not a question she wanted answered. I wanted very much to leave. I wanted to feel the pneumatic pull of the car as it sped away. I looked at my mother, who sat across from me smiling happily, and lost my courage and began to draw.

My mother and the professor spoke as if I were not there,

except occasionally to recommend another animal for me to sketch. They sat no more than two feet from me, and yet I could not understand a word they said. I could barely hear them above the din of my heart beating with the rapidity of machine-gun fire, strafing my temples. My hand shook, and every line that marked the paper quavered slightly.

Patty returned and stood by the professor and they discussed my drawings, pointing at things and nodding their heads. I tried to listen to what they said, but I could not concentrate, because my pulse was deafening me. I had no doubt that the pounding was bruising my skin, and I began to worry that my heart would burst through my chest, splatter onto the table, and ruin my drawings. Could one die this way? At the least, I would have to do these pictures over again. I glanced at my mother, and the sight of her was confusingly reassuring. She smiled at me and winked one of her deep green eyes, but every time I tried to speak to her she put a finger across her fire-engine red lips and arched a finely plucked brow. So I would sit back and wear away my hands, rubbing them harder and harder against each other.

"Would you like to come with me?" Patty asked, swiftly picking up my little suitcase and reaching for my hand so that her fingers grappled with my balled-up fists, pulling them apart. I attempted to wrench away from her, but she yanked me from my chair, and the best I could do was clamp myself to my mother as I was dragged past her.

"Be a good girl, darling," my mother said soothingly, loosening my grip from herself. "Go with the nice lady and I'll be along in a minute." My mother unpinned me, stood me up in front of her, holding me by the arms. "Darling." She winked. "You promised Mama." And then she drew me forward and kissed me twice, once on either cheek, before thrusting me back to Patty.

Patty marched me out, steering me with one hand cupped at

my nape. Her grip was strong, her fingers dug into my neck. I had a tremendous urge to shrug her off and race away. But where? The entrance hall had been refashioned into a small theater and filled with people; children, really. The columns of plastic chairs had been dismantled and set about in a half-moon in the cavernous, dimly lit hall. The air was warmed with the heat of perhaps twenty bodies, the damp erased, replaced with an odor of soap and sweat and overworn woolens.

"Sit here," Patty instructed, pointing to a vacant chair, dropping my leather case alongside. "The professor will be right out."

I sat and stared at the floor, at the swirling pattern of the carpet, and listened to the violence of the wind battering the windows, rattling the wooden frames, and the odd quiet of many people breathing, and the hypnotic precision of a clock. I tried to pace my heart to the steady *tick-tock, tick-tock* until I noticed that I was not breathing at all.

"Good afternoon, my children," the professor said, moistening her gums with the tip of her tongue. I had not noticed her entrance, yet now she sat before us. She sat with her feet crossed at the ankle, with her calves squashed against each other, so that they looked as wide as thighs.

"Good afternoon, Professor," the gathering chanted.

"Today we meet a new student," the professor said and fixed me with her garish smile, wet gums glistening. Did she mean me? Did she mean that I was the new student? Here? I stared at the floor, at the dusty carpet with its swirling blues and greens and golds, worn bare in patches, hoping that if I did not look up she might lose me in the crowd.

"Maria, please come up here. Maria, come along so that I can introduce you to everyone."

Mechanically, I stood and crossed the room. It was with an odd detachment that I felt my legs moving beneath me, as if it were not really me doing this, for I would never have consented. And yet I felt I was weakening, as if my heart could take only so much and I had not the strength I needed to direct my feet toward the front door and run out and not stop until I reached home.

Standing by the professor, I clasped my hands behind my back so that she would not try to hold my hand. I could not bear the feel of her. There was something disarming in the scene, in this semicircle of faces of varying ages from young to old, and it took me a moment or two before I realized that they were not looking at me. Not one of them. They were gazing at the floor, at the wall, at nothing. They appeared captivated by private worlds, journeying deep and far away. I wondered how they managed this. I envied them their remoteness, their apparent calm. Their disinterest proved infectious and I felt my nerves relax, felt a hesitant thaw in my gut. I do not remember my mother leaving that day.

Major Darlington, the housemaster, declared me an insomniac and assigned me a complicated dose of sleeping pills that sometimes worked and sometimes had no effect at all. The quantity of little yellow pills I was to take, one after lunch, two at twilight, three directly before bed, was bewildering.

Most nights I would lie for hour after hour, afraid to close my eyes because of the nightmares that visited, recurrent scenes of soldiers come to mutilate my mother and my sister and me, come to cut off our hands and feet while we sat in a train carriage with no glass in the windows. I prayed it would start up and take us away before the soldiers came in their gray uniforms and their knee-high, glossy black boots, screaming orders. And then, of course, I would wake up, drenched in a clammy, cold sweat, my eyes wide. I would lie frozen awake until morning, unable and unwilling to go back to sleep.

I would speak to Alison during these long dark hours, whisper directly to her smiling face in the Polaroid, ask her questions she never answered out loud but that I believed I could interpret. She told me that Mama had made a mistake leaving me here, and if I just kept out of trouble and counted the days, I would be home soon enough. Twelve days so far. I believed I could feel her near me, and that was an incomparable comfort, and eventually the warmth of knowing her would wrap around me and I would fall asleep, curled on my side, hugging the blankets close to my face.

I shared my dormitory with Fiona, a pale wisp of a girl who would have gladly bent in the direction of the wind to accommodate it. Had she stood in a cornfield, she would have grown roots and turned golden before disturbing the soil with footprints. I did not like to tell Fiona about the nightmares. I was ashamed to tell her that at night I lay in a panic, terrified of sleep. The professor wanted Fiona and me to be friends and had made a point of introducing us when I first arrived, of rearranging the bedrooms so that we should room together.

Fiona was pretty, except that her eyes would cross at times and her teeth were crooked and it was better when she did not smile. She wore her brownish blond hair pulled back in a reed-thin tail, tied with ribbons. Fiona was very gentle, always smoothing out the creases in her skirt with her thin white fingers, and she preferred not to talk, shrank from noise of any kind. So I never asked her the thousand and one questions that buzzed around my head.

"Will you help me dress my girls?" Fiona asked me one day in the faintest trace of a whisper, introducing me to her world of dolls. I was fascinated by the distraction they offered and for the closeness they effected between us. Fiona and I would sit on her bed for hours playing with them, dressing them, and totally content, Fiona would murmur at the stiff, happy faces.

My quiet friend cared for me as if I were a doll, brushing my hair and advising me on what to wear. "Will you let me tie a pink ribbon in your hair?" she would say under her breath. "You can have it for keeps, if you like it. Do you like it, the pink rib-

bon? Do you like it in your hair?" There was a melody to the
way she spoke, like the singsong of wind rustling the boughs of
a willow.

Meals were served in the same room where I had first met
with the professor. It looked quite different with the lights lit
bright and filled with a noisy crowd. It was hard to imagine being menaced by it. Upon entering, you lined up beside the serving table and steadied a still-wet plastic plate in your hands.
Often it took several jerks of the serving ladle to shake free the
unidentifiable foods Cook doled out from stainless steel vats.
Lumps would hit the plate with a thud.

Breakfast was porridge that sat in the middle of the bowl, a
beige ball. Trying to force it apart with a spoon yielded nothing,
and to eat it was to chew on papier-mâché. Patty served us the
morning cup of tea from a steel trolley with an urn and a rattling
collection of chipped cups she wheeled down the center of the
room. The tea always smelled of cigarettes, and milk sat on the
top in shimmering coagulations. Perhaps it was overboiled, perhaps they made it with tobacco; I never knew. But you could not
drink it, and its only practical use was to set it down beneath your
face and allow the steam to warm you.

"Mmmm-mind if I sit?" Bunny would say, dropping his plate
onto the table, splattering his food like paint. Bone-rattling
thin, Bunny would scuttle around hunched forward, stiff like a
shepherd's crook, rubbing his hands in front of his concave
chest. When he sat, he would cross his legs to try and stay the
inclination to tap. But the twitch always got the better of him,
and what began as a gentle beat would invariably lead to a
manic swinging. Often his fork could not find his mouth, and he
would compromise by wiping his face with the food. His hand
would spasm from the effort of trying to locate his mouth, and
at times this caused whatever had been balanced on his fork to
flick around the room. I preferred not to watch because it sickened me. Once he caught me in the face, a forkful of beans

clinging to my forehead, my hair. I leapt up, wanting to vomit. I wanted to run out of the room and take a shower for a hundred years, but Patty restrained me, saying, "Well, I really . . . I want you to sit down like a good girl. We're all going to finish eating first, and then you can wash." I thought I was going to be violently ill. Instead, I closed my eyes and imagined I was with Alison, hurrying down a sandwich before heading back to the beach, and I tried to remind myself of her nightly promise. Just stay out of trouble and count the days, and I will be home before I know it. Twenty-two days so far.

On weekday mornings Patty took us for remedial reading in a classroom with posters of the alphabet decorated with faces and tails. We sat with textbooks in front of us and went around the room, each of us reading a segment in turn, except that we never got around the room, and there was nothing to do but watch the clock above the chalkboard and listen to the pitiful struggles. There were often hysterics. Fiona would cry when it was her turn to read. She never liked to raise her voice, and she would sob every time Patty asked her. "Give it a try, girl," Patty would say, playing with her thick yellow braid, and Fiona would, and then she would begin to cry again, weeping with her long thin fingers pressing against her face.

The classroom was at ground level, with windows that overlooked the kitchen garden, and kids would tumble out the open window, too bored and restless to sit and wait for Fiona to calm herself or to watch Bunny with his thick glasses and awkward stutter falter over sentence after sentence. I would sit, head down, hoping to be overlooked, and think about the day I would drive away from here forever.

Bunny had thick brown hair that splayed out in all directions like a thatched roof hit by a tornado, and he would sit with his face an inch from the page, his hair resting on the top of the book so that he was tented. We would wait in silence ten minutes while Bunny tried out every version of the print before him. "It's aw-aw-awl movin' around," he would say. "The words ke-ke-keep jumping."

When it was Mahad's turn he would announce, "I can't read a word of English!" and he would throw his head back and roar with laughter. "Want me to tell you about three-eyed Siva? Wouldn't you rather hear about the Lord of the Cosmic Dance?" Mahad would push his chair back, scrape the wood floorboards with a roar, and beat his open palms tambourine style on his desk. Mahad was tall and solid, and his hands sounded like slabs of lead as they thrummed the desktop. The noise was violent like thunder, and Mahad's wild eyes jeered at Patty, who would stand completely frozen in place, her little, serious face frowning at him. "I mean, really, Mahad, this is too much," she would tell him in a quiet voice, as if he could hear a word she said over his maniacal drumming. "Give it up, give it up now, or I'm going to have to talk to the professor."

Sometimes he would do as she asked; most times he would make a dramatic production of gathering his pencils and his reading book and stomp out of the room. Remarkably, these outbursts elicited no reaction from Fiona. And despite her natural timidity, she would watch Mahad's ranting and prancing as calmly as if she were watching the flit of a butterfly. The only time he made her jump was when, instead of barging out of the classroom, he started to spin, whirling faster and faster until he punched a fist right through the wall, cutting his hand and his arm all the way to the elbow, with deep gashes spitting blood. "Goddamn!" he yelled, clutching his bleeding forearm as if it were a trophy. "Goddamn, that feels good!"

There was little Mahad liked better than to be hauled off for a talk with the professor. Ten minutes or so later he would emerge, crashing through the doorway, and with the biggest smile on his face he would leap about the living room, jumping over furniture, whooping it up before he vanished out the back, through the kitchen, who knows where.

At the end of remedial, Patty would go and sit by tall, pretty Caroline and gently coax her into standing up. Caroline was almost six feet, and this height contrasted strangely with the fact that she looked like a child, like a floppy doll. Instead of limbs with bones at the center, it was as if her clothes were stuffed with rags. Propped up by Patty, Caroline would slowly coax her legs forward, wobbling slightly. A permanent thread of saliva fell over her lip and down her chin and collected in a stain on her blouse. She never moved her entire head, but her huge blue eyes would swivel slowly in their sockets, covering ground like dragnets, sucking in your stolen glances.

The professor claimed to have an ulcer or two that required the eating of steak everyday, for both lunch and dinner. On occasion, in a moment of goodwill, she would chose a favorite and let him or her eat the scraps off her plate. When it came to be my turn, I found out it was nothing to envy, since she left only the fatty gristle she did not want to eat. She insisted you eat it with her fork, which was disgusting. She wore sticky, balled-up, old-lady lipstick, and it clung to the tines with tenacity. I was embarrassed to be selected, called up before everyone else and forced to eat off her filthy silverware. She spoke to me while I chewed, calling me "my child" and breathing her hot rancid breath on me, and I would stare at her and think, This is all a mistake. Mama will take me away from here, and then I'll never have to see you and your nasty fork again. Meanwhile, the professor would natter on about goulash, this food she loved. She promised to make it for me one day. I just stared, saying nothing. I did not want to encourage her, but I did not want to contradict her, because she was swift with the punishments.

One time when I failed to appear sufficiently appreciative after the professor had force-fed me her leftovers, she sentenced me to my room, and I was to be given nothing to eat or drink for three days. I was also forbidden to talk to anyone, including

Fiona. By the end of the second day I was so hungry that I ate the petals of a tulip Fiona brought me. On the third day I gnawed on a bar of soap.

I developed the habit of writing Alison letters and posting them to heaven by wedging them into the cracks in the bedroom walls, or between rocks in the garden, so that the rains would come and melt the paper and integrate it with the organic world. To think of Alison made me feel safe. It became another world to visit, so as to ease out of this one. At night it was always cold because the one window did not lock into place, and it was continually harassed by a deranged wind thrashing over the Sussex Downs. I would listen to the wind and the surf rushing up the rocky beach at the foot of the cliffs, the very edge of England. Avoiding sleep and evil dreams, I would pitch the sheets and the blankets over my head and monitor Fiona's steady breathing and the incessant hectoring of the gales. I would whisper to Alison, smiling at me from the Polaroid, and ask her if my mother had forgotten about me. She would assure me, as she always did: just count the days till freedom, and you'll be home before you know it. Forty-seven days to date. I must be halfway home by now.

MAJOR DARLINGTON, THE housemaster, reeked permanently of tobacco smoke. If he opened his bedroom door on the landing at the top of the stairs, the smell of stale smoke billowed out like a lasso and snared anyone in its path. Major Darlington had no teeth of his own, and when he became irritable, his false set would hurtle precariously in his trembling jaw. It became a fascination with some of us to rile Major and watch the white half-moon shoot out the front of his mouth like an unbridled demon. Fiona would not consider joining in to torment Major Darlington, and I began very slowly to make other friends, new alliances with which to fill the monotonous days. "What do you think you're doing?" Major would roar, charging out onto the landing, scattering us. "Who do you think you are, to be making such a racket?" And then one hand would rise to catch the emerging teeth, and he would wedge them back in, and we would fall about laughing in an exaggerated way, just to pass the time.

Besides guarding the landing and keeping us all quiet after lights out, Major, as we called him, taught us about music on Sunday afternoons. He hoped to instill in us some basic appreciation for Liszt and Handel, to spot the difference between the various orchestral instruments. Why he thought he could do this I will never know. Silencing everyone long enough to play a prelude was impossible. Delinquency was not always willful. There were compulsive types like Bunny who could not stop the tapping of a foot; there were others who moaned and rocked in their seats. It was not uncommon for Caroline to start the thrashings of an epileptic fit. Without any sense of urgency, Major would pick up the needle coasting the vinyl grooves and fix it to one side of the record player. Then he would pin Caroline on the floor and ram his fist into her mouth.

THE ENTRANCE HALL was flanked on one side by the dining room and on the other by Noel's art class, a long room that ended in the same semicircle of windows as the dining room. The year before, Noel had instructed his class to paint the walls a fine shade of yellow, so the room was bright and cheerful, regardless of the howling gray gales outdoors.

"I've a project for you," Noel said one afternoon as he unrolled a pipe of paper. "I want each of you to design the perfect school." We were given pens, crayons, whatever we wanted. This project lasted most of that first semester. Noel often left us alone while we lolled around mapping out ways to imprison teachers in distant, uncomfortable towers while students slept in huge beds, ambled in and out of an overstocked kitchen at will, helping themselves to whatever they fancied.

Noel was in the habit of playing the radio during class. "Here's a bit of news," the disc jockey was saying. "London's sexiest, sauciest princess just got herself Lord Charlie Cairngorm, a really, really, really rich bloke! A Scottish lord with a castle, a fortune, good looks and . . . a wife! Yes, you heard right, a wife! Wink, wink, nudge, nudge, say no more, if you get my meaning. The rich and their curious ways! And now for sports . . ." I looked up at the radio, at the ivory plastic box sitting above the supplies cupboard. I wanted to ask the disc jockey if he was joking. Did he know for certain? I stared disbelieving, hoping there had been a mistake, but then Mahad began to sing, imitating the disc jockey's cockney accent. "Maria's mum is marrying a poofta! A really, really, really rich poofta!"

I ran out into the entrance hall and up the stairs to the professor's bedroom. Before I knocked, I closed my eyes and prayed to Alison to keep me strong. I deeply disliked going anywhere near the professor, hated catching a gust of that evil, oniony breath, hated seeing those pink gums and the smile that pressed her soft, fleshy cheeks into folds across her face like rumpled fabric. But mostly, I hated asking her for anything because it reminded me that I was her prisoner.

"Come in," she said from beyond the white wooden door. I took a deep breath and entered. The professor lay like a stuffed bear on her high bed, her legs sticking out in front of her, surrounded by pillows with frilly edges. "My little Maria," she said, sounding breathy and girlish. "I'm delighted you've come to pay me a visit. Come sit." Her fleshy hand wagged on the eiderdown. "Come and sit with your auntie Rayna."

My only inclination was to flee, and so as to prevent myself,

I gripped the edge of the door as if it were an anchor. "May I telephone my mother?" I asked, in a faltering voice. There was a long, deadening silence as she considered my request.

"No phone calls," she said, finally, the jauntiness gone from her voice. "You must write a letter if you have news."

Without answering I let go of the door and hammered down the stairs, the professor's squeaky voice pursuing me. I ran outside because I thought I would die of suffocation if I did not immediately inhale deep draughts of cold air. Without a particular plan I ran along the road awhile and scrabbled down a pebbly footpath cut into the side of the cliffs, down to the dark green water rising up and over the rocks. I flopped down, lying back on a boulder, and watched the gulls swirling on the edge of currents, and as they screeched at one another, I screamed at them. I lay there until night came and smothered the insipid light of a winter day, and my face was stiff with cold and the tips of my fingers were a bluish white. Count the days, Alison suggested. What was it by now, somewhere in the seventies? I was almost home. A fiercely cold wind heralded in the frigid night, and I watched the darkness encroach, moving in across the agitated sea.

The end of the semester approached. Counting down, I went about my days infected with a cheeriness I had virtually forgotten. I swear my head was cooled with the crisp scent of freedom. I could close my eyes and imagine being home, and instead of making me gloomy and claustrophobic, it made me smile. Mahad's rants held no menace that final week, and I could watch him impartially, unafraid for the first time since I arrived. When Bunny came to sit next to me at mealtime, I did not mind. In fact, I even offered to feed him.

On my last day I snuck into Noel's art room, where the yellow walls had been papered over with our architectural designs for the ideal school. Months ago I had thought no one would want to watch the dreary steel gray ocean, but here I sat at the window, looking at the water and the cliffs, where the seagulls circled. This pale gray day of clouds and rain spitting distractedly at the window was as radiant and welcome as a perfect summer day. Couples, like Noah's animals, arrived, and after slamming closed the car doors and vainly battling the wicked wind for control of scarves and hats, they trudged up the stone steps and entered the school building. Most times there were yelps of delight from the claimed child. But sometimes there was an eerie silence. Low, muffled sounds and then quiet, the heavy quiet of a cemetery.

Considering my time in this strange place, I realized there was no one thing that was particularly awful about it. My classmates were odd, there was no denying that, but their oddities were not a threat to me; they were not invasive in any way, except by accident. I would miss Fiona, I decided, but no one else. I would write to her from home, to thank her for being my friend while I was here. It was the least I could do, since the poor thing would likely be staying forever.

A flash of navy blue caught my eye and I saw the heavenly sight of my mother's Jaguar turning into the driveway, nosing between a metalic blue Ford and Peggy's boxy silver something. My mother emerged and I leapt up, on the verge of running out to her, when Charlie Cairngorm exited the passenger side. The sight of him was unexpected, and I sat down and pressed against the window. He wore a bright red coat that was startling against the dullness of the winter day. He stretched his arms up over his head and said something I could not hear. My mother was laughing, and as she turned to him, I saw flashes of brilliance, like clusters of crushed mirror, embedded into the collar of her fur coat, on her ears. She looked like a bear who had rolled in the snow. I could restrain myself no longer and I dashed out.

Apparently the professor had been waiting vigil at some other window, because we careened as we vied for first place by the door. "Welcome, Princess, welcome," she said, grabbing at my mother's hand, shaking it vigorously. "It's a pleasure to meet you, Lord Cairngorm," she said, in a treacle-sweet voice, reaching for Charlie's hand. "Please come in out of the cold."

My mother's entrance, in keeping with everything she did, was a perfectly ordinary event dressed up like a pageant. Noise filled every crevice of the entrance hall, ruffling the notices on the corkboard, captivating the attention of the huddles of parents bent over their offspring.

My mother crouched and wrapped me in an engulfing embrace. I submerged my face into the fur of her coat and rubbed my closed eyes against the velvet-soft tickle. I leaned in as close as I possibly could and inhaled the pungent sweetness of her gardenia perfume. Months of anxiety and fear frozen icy in my spine began to thaw, and I thought I might dissolve and become a liquid layer drenching my mother and her splendid new coat. She took me by the shoulders, holding me at arm's length, and I smiled my brightest, most believable smile. I so wanted to impress her with how much better I was. No more crying, no more moods, no more grumpy face. No mention of Alison ever again. I promise. Just take me home.

"Darling," my mother whispered, pointing at Caroline, who was leaning floppily against two adults I took to be her parents. "Look how that funny girl has put her makeup on! You can see the line along her chin! See? Two completely different colors!"

"Ha, ha!" I trilled, my whole body tense, my jaw setting in an uncomfortably stiff smile as I tried to humor my mother, at the same time hoping fervently that Caroline and her family had not overheard these observations.

"Hello, Maria," Charlie said, soothingly, distractingly. He bent down so that we were face-to-face, his bright red coat flaring out around him. On closer inspection I saw that it was frayed and worn, and there were stains, dark like muddy shores, lapping up the hem. I stared directly into the oily azure of his eyes, strangely engorged by the lenses of his wire-rim glasses. "Have you been well?"

I nodded. Inexplicably I wanted to throw my arms around this warm, gentle man, but I restrained myself, worried that any unscripted displays would provoke criticism from my mother. So, affecting a huge smile, as artificial as plastic fruit on a beach hat, I laughed and said, "Fine! I couldn't be better!"

"My dear Princess, Lord Cairngorm, will you join me for tea?" the professor said, flashing her frightful gums; the effort of smiling peeled her lips off her face. Clutching my mother's hand with both of mine, I followed the grown-ups into the dining room, to the professor's table, by the windows. My mother slung her coat over her shoulders so that it hung like a frame of downy moss. She wore a dark turtleneck and she kept her arms folded across her chest, leaning back against her chair. Her face was pale with powder, her lips stained her favorite red. The brilliant jewels on her ears seemed to absorb all the light in the room.

"Princess," the professor said unctuously as she passed her a china cup and saucer. "What an extravagant treat to look at your beautiful face!"

I hoped my mother would laugh at this absurdity, cut the professor down for her outrageous, transparent flattery, at the very least recoil from the rancid emanations I was certain must be wafting her way. But instead my mother gazed at the professor with what looked like adoration.

"I'll get straight to the point." The professor attempted a coy look, cocking her head to one side, flashing her awful gums. "I'm organizing a fund-raising event for Prockney Hall and I very much want the both of you involved. Please say you'll help! It would make all the difference to have names like yours on the committee."

"Of course we will!" my mother said, clearly delighted, and ran her fingers through Charlie's hair. "We'll do whatever you need. In fact, Charlie can write you a check this minute if you'd like. How much do you want?"

Charlie laughed and pulled my mother toward him, kissing her on her head and stroking her as if she were a child. Surprisingly I felt a vague twinge of envy, wished I could exchange seats with her.

"Thank you, thank you, that is too generous!" The professor began to pour tea, horse lips quivering over her offensive gums. "Princess, you are a delight to know. How will I ever thank you?"

"It's nothing," my mother said, beaming at Charlie as she pulled his checkbook from a pocket and thrust a pen his way, whispering to him until, with what looked like resignation, he scribbled, ripped the slip of paper from the flat gray booklet, and flicked it toward the professor. At last my mother trained her eyes on me, happy, playful orbs; her long eyelashes looked like a set of wings about to whisk her away. "Darling, are you taller?"

"Can we go home?" I exploded.

"Home?" the professor repeated. For some reason this was treated as an immense joke, and everyone, including the professor, broke up laughing.

"We are going home, aren't we?" I asked, panicked, pacing nervously.

"Charlie's invited us all up to Scotland for Christmas," my mother said, a frown disturbing her soft powdered brow. "Of course I'll freeze to death, but you'll have a wonderful time." Turning to the professor she added, "Maria doesn't seem to feel the cold."

"Professor's coming to Cairngorm with us?" I asked, stunned, sickened by the thought.

"No!" my mother said, tapping the end of her bony nose with her fingertips. "Maria, really, you are too silly for words!"

"My child," the professor said, a trace of annoyance in her

tremulous voice. "Go and get your things so that I might have a few minutes alone with your delightful mother and His Lordship."

In a sprint I was in my room, hugging Fiona good-bye, shaking hands with her parents, excitedly and a touch guiltily waving as I lugged my little leather suitcase, letting it bounce on every step until I reached the entrance hall, where suitcases were sat upon and snapped closed, followed by a symphony of farewells.

Charlie slowly backed my mother's Jaguar from alongside Patty's boxy silver car, amid a drumroll of trunks slamming, engines firing up. One family at a time, the school emptied, parents and students spilling out in one direction or another along the coast. Charlie pressed the accelerator, and I thought I was going to explode with happiness. I had been waiting for this precise moment for three months, and I wanted to experience each millisecond. I sat up and watched through the rear window until I was certain I could not see so much as the tip of the rooftop of the schoolhouse.

"I don't ever want to see that dump again!" I said, turning to face the backs of two heads and the windscreen view of dreary coast. I plopped down on the soft tan leather.

"I thought it was very cozy!" my mother said, glancing around. I smiled giddily, showing off my new, improved temperament, thrilled with everything.

"I want you to do Mama a big favor."

"Anything!" I said, exuberantly.

"I've arranged for the professor to take you for one more semester," my mother said, flaring her nostrils slightly.

The news chilled me, froze the smile on my face until it began to droop from the strain as I stared at my mother and her battle-ready eyes that dared me to defy her. As worry stirred the blood in my veins like storm winds come to whip up the surface of the ocean, I wormed a finger into the leather seat, the nail of my index finger burrowing like a pick.

"I haven't had a chance to find you another school," she continued, filling the silence. "Just one more semester and I promise I'll move you after that. Is that okay, darling?" she watched me, waiting for me to nod while I plucked at the loosening threads of the little leather canyon I had created. It all seemed so unreal, to be in a fast-moving car speeding away from Prockney Hall, and I realized I did not particularly care what she said; the feel of the car, the pull and the speed of it, were intoxicating. Nothing mattered anymore, so long as I was with my mother and heading home. Nothing mattered at all, and slowly I nodded, committing myself to Prockney Hall for another three months. "Good. Thank you, darling."

WALKING THROUGH THE front door of home, I was exhilarated by the familiar smells, the kitchen warmth that seeped up through the floors. A combination of coziness and cleanliness and the ever-present trace of coffee. If I had been blind I would have known where I was. I wanted to hug the air.

"Jambi, we'll take tea in the sitting room," my mother said, leaning into the cavity at the top of the kitchen stairs. "Maria, go wash your sticky paws. I have your favorite chocolate cake waiting for you! Then we're off to Cairngorm for the holidays."

The little suitcase knocked against my knees as I thumped up the stairs, past the landing with the casement window that overlooked the courtyard, a tiled square almost entirely covered with terra-cotta pots planted with baby orange trees and avocado shoots and my mother's prized gardenias, thick, fat white petals like cream filled with a dense nectar my mother invariably insisted we pay our respects to and inhale and admire. The initial sight of Hamish's old dressing room with a new lime

green carpet and pink, blue, and green striped wallpaper
stopped my breathing like a cork in a bottle. But in a glance I
saw that my things had not been disturbed, teacups along the
back of the desk, bears on the windowsill, favorite blanket
neatly folded at the foot of the brass-rail bed. I slung my little
case so that it landed on the new carpet and slid partially beneath the bed, a corner peaking out from a hem of fringe.
Revved with excitement, I dashed one flight up to the bathroom, newly painted a glossy turquoise, so that I felt I had entered the crest of a wave; I trickled a string of cold water on my
hands before surging down the stairs, two at a time, shaking my
hands dry, creating a tiny rainstorm all around me.

"Did you get my ring?" Miranda's voice hung in the corridor,
filling the little tunnel as I approached the sitting room. The sofas had been relocated to the center of the room, facing each
other over the low ivory table piled with books and a tray with
cups and saucers and a teapot and a plate of cakes. Fat red lamps
with corrugated shades illumined the corners of the square
room, sitting on zebra-striped columns. In my abundant good
mood I was delighted to see Miranda, and I ran to hug her. We
embraced awkwardly; she disengaged with a slithering move
and handed Charlie a glass tumbler filled with his requisite amber liquid. "Did you remember to get my ring?"

Without a word, Charlie, who sat beside my mother on the
sofa facing the patio doors, pulled a small crimson box from a
pocket and held it out on the palm of his hand. Miranda
grabbed it and unsnapped the tiny leather band so that the box
divided into two halves, opening like a flower, revealing a perfectly round ruby the size of a pea, submerged in a band of
gold. "It's divine!" she declared as she wedged it onto a finger—
she has the same blunt, squarish hands my mother and I have—
and splayed her fingers for viewing; then she forced it down
another, repeated the exercise.

"I hope I'm not horribly wrong, but I thought I detected a practical streak in you, Maria," Charlie said, revealing a long, slim packet with the stealth of a magician. "I have one myself, so of course I only mean this as the highest compliment!" I took the dark red satin box, pressed my fingernails into the crevice, and prized apart the panels. "Cripes!" I said to the round gold face with Roman numerals, a window for the date, a tiny sapphire to wind, and a glossy brown leather strap that ended in a bulge of gold like a rising tongue, the clasp. Charlie plucked the watch from its moorings, wound the sapphire, and fastened the leather strap to my wrist. "Do you like it?"

"I love it!" I said excitedly, thinking it the most beautiful watch I had ever seen and quite amazed that it belonged to me. I twisted the watch around like a bangle, feeling the strangeness of the weight, the stiffness of the leather against my skin.

"Charlie bought me the most heavenly diamond ring to go with these earrings, but I left it in the first-class loo on our flight back from Paris!" My mother giggled.

"Mama, why are you a princess and I'm not?" Miranda asked, fiddling with her new jewel, never taking her eyes away from the luminous mound. "It's not fair!"

"Life is not fair!" my mother said, sawing a silver knife through a dense, cloying chocolate cake. "Maria, darling, yummy cake?"

"Just a little." Glancing up, I noticed a paw and the sweep of a calico tail pouring down from above the rungs of the heavy vermilion curtains that hung open, a brilliant frame to the thick wintery dusk settled on the patio.

"But you love chocolate cake! Will you eat one fat slice for Mama?"

"Okay," I said, accepting the soft, weighty slab sitting beside a silver fork on the little yellow plate. Cricklewood flew down from her perch, landing on the back of the sofa.

"Damn that cat!" my mother said, flustered. Cricklewood

trotted to the end like a gymnast and neatly sprang to a nearby armchair, where she settled down to sucking the fur between her claws, reposing like a furry cushion, a cossack's hat. "Darling, it's very fattening!" my mother added, regaining her composure while she patted my stomach. "We don't want to become a rotunda now, do we?"

"Okay, Mama," I said smiling, and replaced the half-finished slice on the coffee table.

"If I gave you five pounds to eat two slices, would you do it?" Mama asked.

"Yup!" I said as I tapped the side of the little plate with my fork, uncertain if I should eat or not.

"How about the entire cake for ten pounds?" she questioned, studying me seriously.

"Of course!" I said, digging a hollow into the wall of chocolate, so that soft sections collapsed onto the silver fork.

"Darling!" my mother said, frowning. "You have the mind of a hooker!"

I let go of the fork entirely, and the dark crumbs splattered the low table in a fantastic spray. I wondered what it was my mother wanted me to do. Miranda would surely have known, and yet I could not get any further than the chattering muddle in my stomach. I barely noticed when Charlie set his emptied glass on the low table and reached for the silver knife. Carving the remaining cake in two, he forced one half on a small yellow plate, overflowing the sides with crumbling chocolate, the thick icing lurching heavily over the edge, and shoved the other half my way. "All right, Maria," he said, a forkful of cake poised beneath his chin. "Who ever gets sick first is a toad, and Mama has to clean it up!"

Unsure of what to do, scouring the faces of the grown-ups for clues, I was immensely relieved when my mother exclaimed, "You swine!" and dissolved in a fit of giggles, pinching the tip of her nose. Ecstatic with the change of direction this uncomfortable scene was taking, I followed Charlie's lead, and we raced our way through the shockingly sweet dessert, soon slowing down, until we allowed the plates and forks to drop and we collapsed on our backs on the floor, clutching our stomachs and groaning exaggeratedly. All the while, Miranda crossed and uncrossed her legs and expressed her disdain at our behavior with noisy sighs.

A light rain began, trickling down the mounting collection of suitcases that Jambi had hauled out to Charlie's waiting Bentley. My mother sat up front beside Charlie, while Miranda and I sprawled in the spacious cavern, where there was room enough to lounge without so much as brushing against each other, and a small television set to distract us from the interminable hours and our customary squabbling. Miranda had been the last to enter, arriving only after Jambi had been sent back in to summon her four or five times. "I will not be rushed!" she announced imperiously when she finally deigned to appear, wrapped from neck to toe in an enormous quantity of blue-and-white fur.

"You look like Cricklewood," I said, reaching out to feel the cascade of velvet-soft hairs.

"Get off! This was a present from Rupert," she said, swatting me away, so that I felt the weight of her ruby ring scrape the back of my hand. "It's chinchilla, and it's mine, so keep your hands to yourself."

"A hairy coat from a hairy creep," I said, hoping this sounded cutting, as I grabbed the remote control for the television, snaked it in Miranda's face a few times, and turned the volume up as far as it would go.

Fast asleep when we reached Cairngorm, I was transported to my bed in the little room on the top floor and laid out beneath the eiderdown.

"Night, Hamish," I mumbled. "Don't let the bugs in the bed."
"Night Maria," came an unexpected voice. I opened one eye
at the retreating figure, tall with lank auburn hair, and realized
too late that it was Charlie. But he was gone and I was asleep
again before I had a chance to apologize.

Castle Cairngorm, Christmas 1987

"MARIA!" A MEDLEY OF VOICES, ACCOMPA-
nied by bits splattering the windowpane, wrenched me from
my slumbers. More pebbles sprayed the glass. "Wake up,
sleepyhead!"

Struggling out of bed, sending the eiderdown to the floor, I
stumbled across the room and tugged on the window sash until
it loosened and rattled upward. The frigid morning slugged me
in the stomach with the strength of a battering ram. I tightened
my grip on the frame and leaned gently forward. Charlie and
my mother stood beside the frozen fountain at the center of the
garden, swaddled in hats and gloves and heavy coats. For the
first time in a week, there was a thick white quilt of snow with
footprints polka-dotting the walkways like battalions of march-
ing ants.

"Merry Christmas!" Charlie called, his face tilted up, one
hand like a visor across his brow so that the pale morning sunlight winked on the lenses of his glasses. "Get your coat on and
come down as quick as you can."

"We're going to go fetch the milk churn before we open the
presents!" my mother said, covering her face with her mittens
between words.

"Hurry down, Maria! We'll wait for you on the back steps,"
Charlie said, burrowing his hands into the pockets of his dark

green jacket. He and my mother strode toward the castle, so that I had to edge further to keep them in sight. "Don't fall out the window, lassie. Be a clever one and take the stairs," Charlie called up as the two of them vanished from view.

Grabbing my blue wool coat, I dashed into the corridor, which was lit from high windows at either end, most of it in a gloomy darkness. Rows of closed doors and shadows cast from craven ghosts gave me the shivers, and I ran down the stairs, one hand lightly tripping over the handrail, dizzying myself from the wide, sweeping arc as I worked my way into the sleeves of the coat, fingered the buttons closed. From the great hall I sprinted down a hallway, through the dark red sitting room that no one ever used, across the book-lined study, frequented on occasion by a retiring guest, crossed the circular turret of a room with walls of green cloth, pale like a sugared almond, where a three-legged table served up the heavy telephone. "Ouch!" I yipped and tumbled to the floor as I seized my foot. Turning my sole toward me to survey the damage, I saw a stab of glass piercing the underside of my big toe. "What idiot . . . ?" I began as I plucked the shard and stanched the drop of blood with my thumb. "What idiot dropped glass all over the place?" I muttered to myself. On closer inspection, I noticed a wealth of shattered fragments in a dusty heap by the wall. A recollection stirred and, guiltily, I looked up at the unprotected etching hanging tellingly above me. "Cripes! Doesn't anybody clean this place?"

Limping, I reached the enormous drawing room that faced the garden. The bowed wall of French doors invited a shallow gray light, which hung about the huge room like some reposing cloud, lounging like gaseous finials on the tops of the worn velvet sofas, spiraling in swirls of ash in a column up the fireplace. The curled, sleeping dogs barely acknowledged my entrance. Standing in the shadowed room was a fir tree festooned with silver bows and glass figurines of angels and trumpets, and a moat of wrapped and ribboned parcels of every imaginable size swimming darkly beneath the lowest branches. Since our arrival at Cairngorm, decorating the tree had become a daily event—enhancing the stately limbs, securing a ball-gowned angel to the highest twig, cutting and wrapping and taping and tying up boxes and setting them just so under the tree.

"Where are your shoes?" Charlie asked, laughing, as I emerged, shaking the handles of the two middle doors until they pushed open so that I met, face-to-face, with the stark wintry air. "Go get something on your feet before those Yankee toes start fussing about the cold."

"I'm okay," I blurted, looking down at the moss-hemmed flagstones beneath my blue-white feet. I felt the cold penetrating deeply, freezing into the hollow of my fresh wound.

"Typical! You'll freeze to death, darling! You're in pajamas!" my mother said, not unkindly. Rolling her famous green eyes in a grand slow way, she closed my face in her gloved hands and kissed me on the cheek.

"I'll be fine!" I said, suddenly self-conscious about my outfit, one I would most likely never have noticed. "It's not even cold!"

"No. It's not too bad at all," Charlie said distractedly. "Where's Miranda?"

"Hah!" my mother exclaimed, stamping her feet, blowing white clouds against her gloves as she slapped them together. "I tried to bribe her, but she's too expensive for me!"

"Let's get you booted up at Shank's." Charlie said. Grabbing me around the knees, he hoisted me onto his shoulder in a fireman's lift and carried me down the steps into the garden.

"I need sun," my mother said, sinking onto a stone bench, her eyes closed in anticipation. "I'll wait here."

For no particular reason I began to laugh, little bursts shooting into the quilted green cloth of Charlie's jacket, disjointed chortles like a car backfiring, as I bobbed with his shoulder blade gouging my stomach. Crossing the kitchen garden, where the vegetable rows were buried under drifts, we arrived at Shank McKinty's toolshed, where I was unloaded onto the saw-dust-covered floor. The wooden walls were hung with hoes and rakes and mallets and Shank's famous saws in a thousand different sizes and a thousand different stages of decay. Some were new but most were useless, with their teeth blunted and bro-ken. Shank called them hummers and used them to play his ver-sion of the Highland fiddle on nights when he took his cider rather too seriously. Charlie rummaged through a collapsing stack of Wellington boots under a shelf of scraps and shavings and coffee tins stuffed full with nails.

"Try these for size," he said, handing me a pair of cracked rubber boots with molded handles to pull them on. "What's this blood?" Charlie asked, grabbing my foot and scrutinizing the puncture in my toe. He pressed the flesh together until I let out a yelp. "How did you do this?"

"I didn't!" I protested, jamming the boots on.

"Maria, my dear," Charlie said, crouching down before me, speaking in low, soothing tones. "Whatever happened, I'm not going to be upset with you. I'd rather you just told the truth. Besides, it's Christmas Day, and all transgressions are void on religious holidays. That means, short of murder, you're off the hook."

By the time I was finished recounting the chain of events that led to the piece of glass lodging itself in my foot, Charlie and I had returned to the scene of the crime, the telephone room. I pointed at the uncovered etching and Charlie took it down, swept a hand across the surface, turned the picture over and ex-claimed, "What the devil!"

"What's the matter? What did I do?" I whined gratuitously. Something in his manner made me realize I was not about to meet with a stiff sentence, if any at all, yet I felt obliged to at least appear penitent and concerned. Charlie was not a frightening man. Charlie did not answer me; he stared transfixed at the back of the little picture. Gently he encouraged the letter out from the pins and staples holding the frame together. It emerged slowly, two folded pages of the stiffest cream-colored paper scrawled over with looping letters. Before it came completely free I heard it tear like a sigh, and then it was loose, and Charlie sank into the hard-backed chair beside the little table with the telephone and began to read, stopping occasionally to let out a laugh. Shaking his head, he folded it up, took me by the hand, and led me outside.

"Where's Hannibal?" Charlie said, searching the room with his eyes as Oz, the little pug, wisely darted for shelter under the sofa. "Come along, you lazy hound! Hup, hup! Hannibal, let's go!" Charlie said, ushering the waddling Labrador through the French doors. The wind had abated somewhat, and my mother was sitting quite still, her eyes closed tight, facing the faint, faraway sun. "Helena, I think I just found your Christmas present!"

"What is it?" she asked, intrigued, trotting alongside the tall man, her thick fur coat round and wide like a bear. "Tell me immediately!" They were both laughing, peels like church bells slicing the huge white silence, and I fell back a pace or two so as to watch and not to intrude on their peculiar union, Hannibal padding beside me unfazed from the sharp drop in temperature. Charlie handed my mother the letter, which she read as she walked, emitting trills of merriment. "I'd completely forgotten about this!" she said, laughing, linking her arm through Charlie's.

Excluded from the joke, I busied myself trying to fit my boots into Charlie's footprints, but his gait was too wide and I almost lost my balance several times. Frost clung to the stone statues, where a shallow sun had begun its thaw, relaxing the grip of the crystals. Willows bent over the river like the vaulted ceilings of a cloister, and all that could be heard was muffled, earnest whisperings as dangling boughs brushed the ice-topped river, as if nuns were gathered for a gossip.

"Free at last," Charlie said as he stepped to one side, allowing my mother and then myself and Hannibal to pass through a low gate set in the rock wall that divided the formal garden from the feral moors.

I tramped unsteadily in my spacious boots to the top of the nearest hill, squelching the snow-packed earth, Hannibal loping alongside, his four paws drilling holes in the snow. There appeared an undulating valley of whites and shadows tumbling endlessly, rising from the banks of the river, which meandered in arching loops through the scraggy hills.

A wind spun up, snuck between the layers of my clothes, made my skin pucker. My eyes watered, and the view melted into variegated greens and beams of light, and then I saw Alison under the oaks at the foot of the garden of my father's summer house. I saw her in her white bathing suit, dappled in shadows right before she would duck into the hedge and vanish across the border into Mr. Ford's terrain. I blinked until the scenery returned bold and sharp, and America seemed impossibly far away, unreal. Like a dream.

The path sloped down toward the river, through a field of Castle Cairngorm sheep, recognizable by the rare yellow hue of their fleece. Shank McKinty was of the opinion that the color was a result of the sheeps' tremendous ingestion of cairngorms, lustrous yellow semiprecious stones that, once polished, could pass for diamonds. He also believed that their wool glowed at night if the moon was full, so that the field looked inhabited by low-lying, grass-nibbling clouds. Much as I wished to see this vision, I had never visited there at night. I did not like the dark, and without Alison to talk the monsters away, I doubted I could gather the courage. Perhaps one day, when I was much older, I would have a lover to accompany me and we would walk arm in arm the way my mother and Charlie did. We could watch the ghostly sheep in this perfect romantic setting, and he would profess undying love for me. I could see us, standing against the fence, the moonlight picking out an eye, the hollow of a cheek, the white of teeth. He would place an arm around my shoulders; I might withdraw slightly; he would pull me toward him gently, firmly, lower his face to mine, hover above me for a while, brushing my lips with the warmth of his breath, never quite touching me . . .

"Come on, lassie!" Charlie called, glancing back, his arm entwined in my mother's, the two of them receding in the distance. "Don't dillydally, don't make me call you Sally!" I scaled a wooden split-rail fence. Hannibal wedged his stiff mustard body beneath, and we set about disturbing the timorous beasts, sending them shambling off in tight packs, their long mud-encrusted wool shaking on their backs like cheap toupees. I wanted to tell Charlie and my mother about Dad's tennis partner Swifty Durban, who liked to wear a hairpiece for a hat, but it seemed too much to explain, too far away and irrelevant. Instead, I watched and laughed as Hannibal sent the sheep into a frenzy of bleating and snorting as they straggled away to the depths of the field.

When there were no more sheep close enough to torment, I chased Hannibal down the slick path with my arms stretched out, gathering the cold wind against my chest, listening to the slap of my too-big boots against the solid, squeaky snow.

"Here," Charlie said, laughing softly, pulling off his gloves when I caught up to him and my mother. "I've got bread crumbs stuffed down the end of each finger! It's a silly habit, I know, but you can feed the jackdaws with it."

"I do that too!" I said, amazed to have found a comrade who shared this quirk, and for a moment Charlie and I stared at each other, a fraternal smile binding us in our private cult. "But I forgot my gloves!"

"D'you know about fossils, Maria?" Charlie said, bending to pick up a brownish rock, prying it from its setting, never looking away from the stone cradled in the palm of his hand. With his fingertips he dusted away the ice and earth, and then he rubbed the stone hard against the front of his quilted jacket, as if he were bringing out the shine on an apple, leaving healthy streaks of mud on his chest. I watched as, gradually, there appeared the striations of half an antique worm embedded in the stone. Charlie held it out in front of him, a hint of a smile on his face. "Fossils are one of nature's ways of teaching us history. Little clues that explain how certain things came to be." He dropped the fossil into the breast pocket of my pajama top before buttoning closed my wool coat. He took me by the hand and walked on, towing me. "Old people are like fossils. If you look closely, you begin to see things about yourself. You should make a habit of examining fogies. Never know what you might find out." He gave my hand a squeeze. "Now, make yourself useful, lassie, and pick me some berries, and I'll fix you a breakfast fit for a king. Or a princess!" he added, laughing, catching my mother by the back of her bonneted head and kissing her flush on the mouth.

"I think I have frostbite!" my mother declared sadly, stamping her feet as she walked. "I'm becoming delicate in my old age. All I want to do is lie on a hot beach and never have to think about clothes again!"

"Like Eleanor!" I said, quite pleased with myself, until my mother's glowering face silenced me.

A whorl of winterberries grew beside the path, and as we ambled we plucked at the shiny dark fruit crouching in huddles amongst the thorns, and tumbled them into pockets, the juice staining like tannin. I watched my fingers as they dug in between the spikes and gathered the succulent berries, watched the thorns etch white lines across my skin. Hannibal loped, his tongue hanging gloriously.

At the foot of the hill sat the Mackenzie Dairy truck, driving white clouds of exhaust into the frosty morning. Mr. Mackenzie coaxed a milk churn from out of the back, wheeled it to the wood fence, and leaned it against the open gate. With a wave and a "Merry Christmas to you all," he beat his gloved hands together and leapt back into the chuffing truck. "Thanks, Mr. Mackenzie! Merry Christmas to you too!" we yelled as we hastened down the slope. The silver missile, the milk churn we had come to fetch, was smartly emblazoned with *Mackenzie Dairy* along one side. Charlie tackled the heavy lid, twisting it open, and placed it on the ground a foot away. Hugging the shiny torpedo, he gently tipped it forward until the thick, slow cream dropped into the upturned lid.

"Toss your haul in," he instructed, turning his pockets inside out and dumping his catch. We watched as the winterberries sank and vanished, enveloped in the whiteness. "Tuck in, everyone, before the jackdaws come steal this out from under us," Charlie said as he withdrew three large silver spoons from the inside of his jacket.

The sun was faint, sheltered behind a shroud of clouds, but I could detect the scent of heather and Highland wildflowers as they stretched through the melting snow. Lying on my side on the icy heather, Hannibal for a cushion behind me, I slid the berries and cream into my mouth and let them sit for a second on my tongue. "Dee-licious!" I said as the delicate fragrant flavor overwhelmed me, and I closed my eyes. I sucked on the tart sweetness, rolling the smoothly rounded shapes, flattening them against the roof of my mouth, pressing the juice out.

"I can't bear this blasted cold! Wouldn't everyone prefer to go to Madagascar next winter? I've heard it's spectacular." My mother was still standing, hugging herself in her fur coat, thick and dark against the stark scenery. I wondered how it was that she could even feel the temperature. "I'm going to freeze to death if we don't get home right away."

"Off we go then!" Charlie said, pulling himself up with one hand on the gatepost. He fit the lid to the top of the milk churn, polished the spoons on a dock leaf, and returned them to a pocket.

"I'm not bothered by the cold," I said half under my breath as Hannibal licked the cream from my fingers.

"Me neither," Charlie replied just as quietly, winking at me. Like a windblown tree, Charlie walked leaning sideways, his free arm out, balancing the weight of the churn, Hannibal panting, exhausted from the journey and his extreme seniority. The tarmac disappeared into a forest of fir trees, where jackdaws *flack-flack*ed from branch to branch, barking in their private dialect. The high gate of cast iron and brass pushed open easily, and there the eerie forest ended and we entered the grounds of Shank's neatly kept park. The castle was wrapped in mist, and the lead-latticed windows blackly reflected a shy morning. As we trudged, Charlie whistled, barely disturbing the stillness with the unnatural hollow sound.

"It's time to open presents! Everyone to the sitting room! Right away!" my mother said, sprinting up the stone steps, heaving open the studded front door. "Damn that blasted dog!" she yelled as Hannibal rushed her, knocking her to one side.

"Last one there's a toad!" Charlie challenged, and after depositing the heavy churn beside the front door, he too disappeared inside the cold, dark castle. I entered and wedged my heel against a half-moon of iron, worked my legs out of the boots. Ice and mud flew about, and I rubbed my sodden feet, inspected where the glass had cut me. It was white and ruffled, like the underbelly of a mushroom. Barefoot, I followed the noise to the sitting room, transformed by lamplight and a surging fire and the tiny white lights on the Christmas tree, which flickered on and off. And there beside the tree, sitting amid an eruption of torn paper, was Miranda, with a smile brightening her angelic face. "Mama, Charlie, little sister, Merry Christmas!" she pronounced confidently.

"You little wretch!" my mother said, shaking free of her dark fur coat, tossing her hat and gloves onto the sofa so that flakes of snow began to melt in puddles, staining the worn velvet in patches. "You've opened everything!"

"Nothing had a name on it." Miranda explained sweetly. "So how was I to know which of them were mine?"

I stopped in the doorway and waited for the hand of God to strike my sister. Hannibal was flopped in front of the fire, licking himself in noisy slurps, Oz tucked in a tight ball nearby, shaking and jolting from some deep, dream-filled sleep. I watched my mother closely, wondering what swift, cruel punishment she would indulge in. But instead of wrath she was struck with the giggles, and a gush of laughter consumed her.

"You really are too much!" my mother said sinking to her knees beside Miranda, stroking her daughter's long honey hair. "Where do you get this ghastly selfishness from? Of course you can have anything you want if it makes my baby happy!" And she kissed her on her head.

"Thanks, Mama!" Miranda said, picking a camera out from the confusion of wrapping paper. "I love this! Can I have it? Mama, please?"

"Of course, darling!" my mother said, laughing.

Thrilled by my mother's response, I ran across the room and skidded into the mound of paper.

"Careful!" Miranda snipped, drawing various items toward herself as I landed in the heap.

As if it were water, I tossed the empty paper in the air, thrusting it up above my head so that it knocked against the glass ornaments, sent them tinkling in a spray of chimes. Hannibal bounded across the room, as boisterous as I, and pounced into the thick of wrappings and loose ribbons, and gripping an

emptied cardboard box in his jaws, he swung it this way and
that, snarling in a benign manner. Oz, intrigued by the activity,
neared snuffling along the ground, inhaling dust and clues on
his approach.

"Look what I got for Christmas." my mother said, extracting
the letter from her pocket, at the same time shoving Oz off
course with her foot.

"It's a will!" Miranda said, reading the pages quickly. "Well,
half a will. Where's the rest?" Genuinely intrigued, she looked
between my mother and Charlie. "where's the other half?"

"In my solicitor's vaults." Charlie said.

"Why?" Miranda demanded.

"The idea was that whoever produced the other portion of
the will could claim Cairngorm. When I'm dead, of course."

"I completely forgot about it!" my mother said proudly,
laughing, kicking Oz away again so that he tumbled backward,
legs flailing like a beetle before he righted himself. "It was all a
joke, late one night after a lot of drinks!"

"Who is something-or-other Brooks?" Miranda asked, holding the second page up close to her face.

"Yes, well, he's a former friend," my mother explained vaguely.

"But what about Eleanor?" Miranda asked, her words measured and slow, as if to mention the name at all might upset
things. Charlie gulped back the last of his amber drink and studiously began to replenish the tumbler, transferring cubes of ice
from a silver bucket, rolling them down the palm of his hand,
splashing scotch over them, settling them.

"What's that?" he asked, sipping his drink, patting the silver-
topped cork into the mouth of the decanter. A charred log tumbled off the andirons into the soot and sent a cloud up the
chimney; the raging flames turned black for a millisecond.

"El-ea-nor." Miranda said, chopping the word up so that it
sounded like a long sentence.

"Eleanor?" Charlie repeated, sucking on his scotch. "Dear

Eleanor wants a divorce, which is not hugely surprising. And under the circumstances, it's not altogether unwelcome. I'm told she's fallen in love with the chief Rastafarian from Montego Bay, and although I never thought I'd say this, I can't help feeling relieved that the poor dear's infertile. Kilts and dreadlocks are not the best combination."

"Mama!" Miranda said breathlessly, rising from the Christmas wrappings, clutching the will with outstretched arms. "You realize what this means, don't you? When Charlie dies, you get Cairngorm! Then you sell it for a fortune and I go shopping!"

"Uh, hello, the heart is still ticking, if you don't mind!" Charlie said, laughing as he strolled toward the telephone room. He returned with the dismantled etching, and taking the pages from Miranda, he slid them back behind the lip of the frame and passed it to my mother. "Keep this safely. I'd hate to think of it falling into the wrong hands!"

Fingers worked their way toward my breast pocket, feeling over the reverberations of my beating heart until they located the stone Charlie had dropped there. Moving slowly, they worked the fossil up behind the fabric until it fell freely into the palm of my hand. Brown and gray, the half worm lay wound in a coil, little ridges like tiny walls dividing it into shallow chambers.

"Alison and I wrote wills this summer," I said, half under my breath, wondering why I was saying this at all. "And then she died."

Brockney Hall, 1988

A FEW WEEKS INTO THE WINTER SEMESTER, a meeting was called in the hall. Under Major Darlington's supervision, we pulled chairs down from the stack against the wall, formed a semicircle, and awaited the arrival of the professor.

"Do not make a sound until you're spoken to," Major wheezed, waddling around in a mercilessly tight waistcoat of grubby brown paisley. The tobacco stench vibrated around him in waves, and as he passed by me I pinched my nose and grimaced until Fiona glanced my way. All I could incite in her was a timid gasp before she returned to the administration of the doll in her lap. Major flicked my hand away from my face as though he were swatting a fly. "There's no need to behave like an imbecile, Maria," he said, his false teeth flying out on the turbulence of his heavy breath. He caught them with his fingertips and jammed them back in. I had perfected the feat.

The professor emerged from the dining room with Patty and a sour-faced boy with blue-black, shoulder-length hair and tiny, dark, marble eyes set at the edges of an unusually narrow face. Like a shark.

"Good morning, my children," the professor said as she sat down, hooking her ankles and squashing her fat calves together. I hated to look at her worn bulldog face with the faded, colorless skin sagging in jowls.

"Good morning, Professor," we said dutifully, a lifeless chant. "I want you to meet our new student. His name is Roland Saunders. Please say hello."

We did the professor's bidding as Roland stamped from foot to foot like an enraged bull pawing the ground. He kept his arms crossed, and when the professor asked him to greet us, he stared at the floor and snorted. I remembered how excruciating it was to stand up there in front of a roomful of strangers, and I supposed he was as shy as I had been on my first day.

ONE AFTERNOON IN Noel's art room, I was lying on my stomach on the floor, attempting to reproduce the contents of a fruit bowl Noel had provided for a still life, when Roland threw himself off of his chair and onto me.

"I've got a hostage! Don't try to move!" Roland yelled into my face. He put a hand over my mouth, and with his other hand around my waist, he pulled me into a sitting position, on his lap, as if I were a ventriloquist's doll. I could feel his heart thumping, could feel it beating through my back, it tickled. When I tried to wriggle against his hold, he clamped me tighter. "I don't let my hostage go till I get what I want. You listening, Teach?"

Noel stood very still, his face nervous and twitching. The seriousness of it all made me heave with laughter until Roland squeezed the air out of me and I gasped. "Yes, Roland," Noel said, looking worriedly at me. "I'm listening."

"I don't like drawing fruit," Roland shouted, locking his arm around my neck. He jerked it tight so that I had to suck air through his sticky hand flattened across my mouth. But somehow I could not stop the giggles that bubbled up and through his fingers as I checked from one frozen face to the next.

"Okay."

"No one else likes drawing fruit, neither."

"Okay, Roland." Noel, whose general coloring was gray, wore only gray baggy clothes on his lanky frame. He looked like a pile of faded laundry. Noel never smiled; he never had any expression on his face at all, other than a trace of sorrow. A tiny crease appeared between his eyes. "What would you like?"

"Frogs," Roland said and shoved me away, so that I tumbled face-first into the carpet. I was not sure whether or not to move, and I glanced at Roland for direction. He was scowling profoundly, etching lines into his face as deep as canyons. And then he winked at me, and I lay on the floor laughing excitedly, thrilled to have had this agitator join the ranks. Now there might be some comic relief from the monotony of spasming, stuttering children, whose company could, after a while, seriously lower morale.

In less than a week Noel had located a selection of local frogs, from small green ones to larger brown frogs with huge, bulging eyes. Noel provided a glass tank, which we filled with grass and pebbles torn from the sodden garden.

"No one's to touch this 'ere frog," Roland said, grabbing the widest, darkest frog. "He's Jack the Ripper, and he's private property. I'm warning you, there'll be trouble if anyone messes with my Jack! Most likely there will be trouble anyways!" he added, guffawing to himself as he tossed his frog in the air.

Bunny developed an affection for a large brown that he liked to pet at close range to his face, partially hidden by his thatch of hair. Mahad chose a pair with olive green and black splotches, who he maintained were rival warriors who needed to be subdued at all times by his own particular brand of diplomacy. My favorite was the smallest pale green one with toes so fine they were practically transparent, the green bled away to a scallion white. I christened him Oliver Cromwell on account of his round head and impassive, doleful gaze and the fact that Patty was steering us through the history of this man in remedial. Fiona preferred not to touch the slimy creatures but managed, nevertheless, to affect a certain affinity with the loner frog, a medium-sized grayish brown who seemed to have no friends and squatted in a corner of the tank on his own. Fiona would sit by the tank and draw her frog from this position so that she would not have to handle him. The rest of us would place our frog of choice in an upturned glass at the edge of our sketch pads and draw the little prisoners until their cages fogged. It was a coveted daily exercise to feed the frogs with flies and garden dregs and, if Noel had his back turned, the occasional baked bean.

"You in love with 'im, then?" Roland asked me one day, accidentally knocking Oliver's glass over, so that the frog hopped about in search of shelter.

"Careful, clod foot!" I said as I caught Oliver with both hands and returned his thrusting body to the confines of the upturned glass, glad for the minor conflict, anything to break away from the boredom. "You're going to squish him one of these days."

Roland could not seem to cross the room without tipping over Oliver's glass or stepping on my drawing and splitting the paper, smearing the pencil lines. It was annoying, but even the annoyance was a welcome distraction from the solemn routine of life at Prockney Hall, and in my own way I would encourage him.

OLIVER LOST AN eye. In place of a swiveling black orb, there was a vacant cavity, a little empty hollow. The frogs appeared entirely passive, but it was agreed that at night, when no one was looking, they must be attacking one another.

"You realize, don't you, that frogs don't do this sort of thing?" Noel asked us one dreary afternoon. He sat on the window seat, by the frog tank, with a crestfallen look in his gray eyes and his mouth pinched as if he wanted to tell us more, but he could not quite bring himself to. "Frogs are not cannibals."

"I think they're unha-ha-happy," Bunny said very sadly, with his frog held at eye level, one leg dangling loose from a severed muscle.

"It's their revenge," Roland explained, staring at Noel with his arms crossed, and an odd smile on his narrow face. And then he winked at me and I laughed, automatically. I was quickly learning that to oppose Roland was as good as a signal to battle, battles I was not always inclined to fight. "They don't like being locked up any more than we do."

One frog at a time, they were mutilated. Sometimes it was just the one dislocated limb, other times it was both eyes gouged. But they would die, no matter how small the surgery. Roland assumed the role of undertaker and made a big fuss over proper burial procedure, telling us where to stand and what to say, and we would troop out to the kitchen garden and watch as Roland dug a berth in the frozen mud, dumped the frog in, and stamped the earth with his boots. "Our Father, who art in heaven," Roland would say, making the sign of the cross on his chest, "bless this our frog and send him fast up to the scummiest pond you got."

The only frog never to meet with disaster was Jack the Ripper, Roland's pet. A vote was taken and Jack the Ripper was charged with frogocide, but before he could be exiled to the Sussex Downs, he met with a fistful of sewing needles, and we found him gasping his last breaths, trussed like a hedgehog.

Passive and incident-free studies of flora were resumed, and to the surprise of us all, Roland was forbidden to attend class for the rest of the semester. "Mind your own business," was all Noel would volunteer on the matter.

O N A R A R E , rainless day, an opaque pallor wrapped around the clouds, I slid down a path of smoothed chalk worn into the face of the cliff. The descent was treacherous with no rail to grip, but I did not like to lounge about the schoolhouse day after day, and the ragged beach, although heavily outlawed by the professor, was one of the few destinations that usually afforded a respite from the goings-on of Prockney Hall. Wild winds tore up the surface of the ocean and tossed the seagulls in midflight as casually as if they were dust, sucked the cries right from their orange beaks and muffled them. The dark green surf crashed on the seaweed-topped rocks, licking up the sides of the cliffs at high tide, luring anything it could back into the water so that an ugly collection of flotsam bobbed eternally by the shore. I loped along, jumping from one wet rock to the next, arms out for balance, occasionally pushing back the clammy strands of hair that whipped across my eyes. The professor did not approve of girls wearing trousers, and my bare legs alternately stung and ached as I was sprayed with seawater and then blown dry by the numbing wind.

Meeting with a ferocious smell, I stopped and wobbled atop a slanted rock, my feet pitched at right angles, my school skirt snapping against my legs. Just ahead appeared an odd-shaped rowboat abandoned on its side, a half-moon. As I approached, the lines of the boat redefined themselves into a cow. It was an odd sight lying there, alone on the beach, flecked with spume and a throb of flies. Despite the strength of the wind, the stench of rot was overwhelming, sickening, and I pressed the collar of my sweater against my nose. I circled the waterlogged animal and disturbed the aggressive flies from its swollen belly, stretched pink and hairless. Only one eye was visible, gray, vacant, with flies shuddering over it, sucking on the oleaginous delicacy. There was something infinitely sad about this beast, and I was almost embarrassed at my revulsion at the putrid smell, as if somehow I ought not to hold that against the unlucky cow.

"It's time you had a good walloping!" Roland said, coming up behind me.

"Go ahead. I won't even feel it," I said, not taking my eyes from the cow, a vague tremor of worry igniting in my stomach. Roland's threats had become habitual, his customary greeting, and I had learned, over the weeks, that the best defense was to appear quite unconcerned and never to look him directly in the face. He did lash out on occasion, but the less attention one paid him, the sooner he lost interest and rumbled off to fresh pursuits.

"You want it?" Roland said, stamping from foot to foot. He slammed a fist into my arm, so that I toppled back a step, losing my balance. I fell clumsily on the uneven boulders, scraping my knees on the rough surface. Out of the corner of my eye I could see Roland's mean, narrow face so contorted that his eyes seemed to have vanished to slits, the muscles contracting into a grimace. I glanced around to see what chance I had to run, but there was always the danger that this would encourage him. He liked nothing better than the sight of fear. I saw him pull his arm back, saw the anger twisting his surly mouth. Standing up, I prepared myself. I tightened every muscle in my body, clenched my jaw, held my breath. I stared at him contemptuously as he sank his fist just below my collarbone. It did not hurt immediately.

"Wh-wh-what've you got there?" Bunny said, approaching gingerly. I had never seen him venture beyond the schoolhouse, and it was worrisome to see him shaking slowly over the rocks, with his crazy thatch of hair zipping around his head. I could not speak to Bunny, because if I had let out any sound at all, I would have begun to cry. So I stood as still as I possibly could and tried to will away the pain in my shoulder, tried to imagine it dissipating into the rest of my body, melting to nothingness.

"An airplane," Roland said. "What's it look like, you stupid pillock!"

Bunny continued, his sandaled feet steadily finding footholds as one leg after the other jerked forward. He wore no socks and his exposed toes were a lifeless white.

"No need to be—to be—to be nasty," Bunny said, squatting

down by the cow's face. His stick-thin limbs folded easily in his
billowy red overalls, like a deck chair. He seemed quite unconcerned with the greedy water lapping him, soaking the hem of
his overalls a deep crimson. "Can't you b-b-bury it? Like you
did the frogs?"

"Get away, old man," Roland said and kicked Bunny with a
sideways jab, launching him against the dead animal. "Who
asked you to come bother me?"

Grabbing at the sodden cow, digging his long thin fingers
into disintegrating tufts, Bunny crumpled, panic sweeping
across his face. Roland kicked him again, on the side of the
head, and it looked as if Bunny's eyes spun in their sockets, as if
they might tip out.

"Stop it!" I yelled, and I sprang at Roland. I wanted to push
him away, but I found that I could not lift my arm, and instead I
landed against him crudely. In one firm move he grabbed me
and flung me away as easily as if I were a scrap of cotton. I fell
down bumpily on the slimy, seaweed-strewn boulders.

"Don't let him know he's hurting you, Bunny," I whispered,
afraid to help, afraid not to, hoping my voice would carry only
to Bunny. "That's all he wants to see."

"Keep out of this!" Roland snarled, shaking a fist at me. There
was a wild look in his tiny dark eyes, a glazed intensity that paralyzed me, and I stayed crouched on the cold boulder. I could
still feel the weight of Roland's fist embedded beneath my collarbone, and I pulled my useless arm across my chest, hugging
it close.

Bunny's whole body shook so that he could not stand himself
up, and desperate to flee, he began to crawl, whimpering.
Amassing smallish rocks, Roland pelted them at Bunny. "Who
asked you to come bother me?" he yelled, laughing.

"Enough!" Bunny sobbed, protecting himself with one hand
over his head as he tried to haul himself away.

"Coward!" Roland yelled, hurling his ammunition at the scrabbling figure. "Stupid coward!" Roland hopped deftly over the rocks, pursuing Bunny, pausing only to collect more to lob.

"Enough!" Bunny screeched, waving his arms around, the words coming out fainter and fainter. "Enough, enough, enough!" At first I thought Bunny was bobbing his head to avoid Roland's assault, but then I saw that he was bashing his head against the sharp rock he crouched on. He was doing it himself. Blood spurted out, drenching his face instantly. His body began to spasm, his arms and legs flicked around, rebounding against the jagged rocks beneath him as if he were bouncing on a trampoline. And then he stopped, and he lay perfectly still.

"Don'tcha love the sight of blood?" Roland said, chucking down the last of his missiles onto Bunny's immobile back. "That stupid pillock got what he deserved. I would've done him in myself, if I'd known he wanted out like that."

Roland skipped toward me, and, automatically, I recoiled.

"Let's go see what else is down the beach." Roland said, holding a hand out for me. Against the massive white chalk wall of the cliffs Roland looked very small, nothing to be afraid of, a dark wisp with mad, wind-shagged hair and a smile on his narrow impassive face.

"Suit yourself. But . . . ," Roland said, bending down in front of me, tipping my head up with a finger under my chin. He lowered his face into mine. "I was never 'ere. Understand? Tell anyone anythin' and I'll kill you." I nodded slowly and watched the mixture of sweat and saltwater drip from the tips of his eyelashes, landing like rain, running down his cheeks between the flecks of dirt. I smelled his hot breath on me. I felt my heart stammering against my chest, felt the throb right through the bone of my bad arm pressed against me. And then he was up and off, prancing over the boulders as surefooted as a dancer. I heard the seagulls scream and the howls of the wind, and it occurred to me that not five minutes had passed since I had first found the cow. As Roland faded out of sight, I made my way over to Bunny. I tugged on his sleeve, but Bunny would not turn around, would not speak one word to me. He lay facedown, a mess of blood and limp limbs.

"Okay, okay," I said, as much to calm myself as to comfort Bunny. "I'm going to get someone. I'm going to get someone to help you." As I ran across the rocks and up the cliff path, clutching my arm, I chattered incessantly, transmitting soothing messages to the boy resting on the beach near the fly-smothered cow.

PATTY AND THE professor ordered everyone to wait in the remedial classroom, which overlooked the kitchen garden, so that we would not watch while Bunny was gathered and loaded into the ambulance. The room was as full as I had ever seen it, with huddles of children whispering and idling. Fiona engaged in deep deliberations with two smartly dressed dolls she hosted on her lap. Mahad trilled a tuneless tune and rocked his chair, so that it creaked. Noel sat, spiritless, at Patty's desk while Major patrolled, pacing up and down in his broad-checked tweed suit with loose threads that trailed at the seams. Back and forth he marched, slapping a wooden ruler against his open hand, and I wondered if stale smoke exploded from his skin each time he smacked himself, like dust from a rug.

The door opened and the professor's large head appeared, a helmet of stiff gray curls. "Maria, my dear," she said, exposing her pink gums as she curled a fat finger at me, like a worm searching for dry land. "Come with me."

Bedraggled from my escapade, I tried to pacify my hair, wending my fingers through the matted tussles, wipe the brine from my face. Obediently, I followed the professor to her table by the window in the dining room and tried to decide whether this might be a good time to implicate Roland, to tell the professor of his threats and beatings, of how he had intimidated Bunny on the beach. We sat beside each other, which spared me the effrontery of seeing her frightful mouth, and looked out at the cliffs, at the seagulls dueling with the wind, and I pulled my sleeping arm onto my lap and shrank into the furthest corner of my chair. We sat in silence for a while in the gloomy room that smelled of boiled cabbage and vinegar. Across the street, at the top of the cliffs, Roland appeared. My heart seized and I was grateful, as I calmed myself, that the professor had not seen my face tense up and that she could not hear the argument in my head. Watching Roland skulk across the road, kicking at stones, I knew it was too risky to inform on him.

"That's what I wish to talk to you about," the professor said, pointing a fat, bent finger at the window. Roland ambled up the driveway, his hands jammed into the pockets of his jeans, entirely unconcerned with anything around him, unaware, presumably, of the whirligig of activity he had caused.

"Is Bunny going to be okay?" I asked, not wishing to discuss Roland, remembering his threats to kill me if I did. The professor reached for my hand, grabbing it from my lap. I thought I was going to be sick from the pain of disturbing my inflamed shoulder. I hated for her to touch me, but I had no power in my arm and I could not stop her.

"Patty tells me you spend a lot of time with Roland," the professor said. It was hard to think clearly; my head was dizzy, and I was rocked with nausea each time she yanked on my hand. I thought my arm was going to come free from the joint. Very vaguely I noticed that it took this amount of pain for the professor's vile breath to hold no menace over me; it could not compete. "There's something you ought to know about your friend. Roland stabbed his little brother to death. He killed him with a kitchen knife. I don't want you to discuss this with him.

I'm only telling you so that you will keep away from him. My child, you are forbidden to play with him from now on. Now, please go to your room."

"Is Bunny going to be all right?" I asked, my throat dry and cracking, trying not to think about what she had just told me.

"Bunny is dead," the professor said evenly, not taking her eyes from the window. "He was very weak, my little Bunny. It was inevitable. I don't want you to concern yourself with him, Maria. Now go to your room."

I LAY ON my bed facing the wall and clutched my pillow, pressing it against my stomach as if it could somehow fill the holes my nerves were drilling. "I know, I know," I whispered to Alison. "If I just count the days I'll be home, right? I don't think I can wait that long."

Overwhelmed with a desire to get as far away as possible, I organized myself, harvesting the necessary supplies: a box of Twigglets, some coins, a sweater, and of course the Polaroid and the will, and chattered to Alison until long after I heard Fiona's light tread shift from the washbasin to her bed. I lay in bed fully dressed and waited until Fiona's breathing steadied to deep, rhythmic expirations. With clenched teeth, moving as carefully as I could, I padded down the stairs to freedom.

The dark always frightened me, and standing on the threshold of a black blustery night was terrifying. I made myself go on, walking down the driveway to the road that hugged the Dover cliffs. The cliffs were high, but sea spray strafed the road, puddles reflecting whitely in the moonlight. Walking along, I stared hard into the blackness, hoping to see the danger before it saw me, seeing scary faces in the shadows, hearing sounds in the ocean's moan, scaring myself half to death. I walked along talking away the fear, talking to Alison, and soon enough it occurred to me that I had nowhere to go. How could I go home?

My mother might be momentarily impressed with my daring, but then I could imagine a stay of maybe half an hour before being hustled back to school, and to be returned in such a manner would be a disgrace. What if I ran to Scotland, begged Charlie to hide me in one of the many rooms of his castle? I thought of all the times my mother had shooed Miranda and me out of the car, dumped us on the side of the motorway, when we bickered too much, threatening to leave us there for the vultures to come pick clean. I shuddered at the memory, and I sat myself on a low mossy rock wall that hugged the road and allowed my thoughts to travel much further than I would ever have reached on foot. Rampant thoughts of saviors clambering out of bed in the cold of the night, come to find me, to rescue me, finding me fallen asleep by the side of the road, soaked through with rain, gathering me up in strong arms, carrying me gently, close to the warmth of a beating heart, taking me home.

Eventually I had to concede that there was nowhere to run, that the only truly safe place was in the confines of my mind, where I could trip about as carelessly as I pleased without disturbing anyone's peace. Maybe as late as dawn, when the hollow morning light picked up off the ocean's back, I returned, crawled between the sheets of my bed, and fell into some jagged-edged sleep.

EVERY MORNING, GOVERNOR Gordon, the postman, would play a quick tune with the doorbell, announcing the arrival of the daily mail, and then the slot would open and vomit a proliferation of letters and rolled magazines onto the carpet. Patty would collect them and pin any letters destined for students to the corkboard in the front room, alongside the curling notices that never seemed to be cleared or edited as their relevance grew dim. Use of the telephone was strictly forbidden by the professor, which forced all and sundry to rely on communicating by post, raising the status of missives to unnatural heights. They would be pored over and reread until they were worn thin from the sticky fingers that mangled the pages, the edges frayed and ripped, the seams of the envelopes burst from the many removals and reinsertions.

A week before school broke for the Easter holidays, a thin blue airmail envelope addressed to me was pinned to the corkboard. I snatched it down, tugging against the feeble hold of the plastic pin that impaled it, and carried it away to examine in private. As I walked with it I read my name and the address of the school scripted in my mother's loopy scrawl and tried to temper the excitement that burbled in the wellspring of my stomach, but it got the better of me, and impatiently I ripped the letter open. Tumbling out with the letter came a handful of dry rice, scattering on the floor by my feet. "Ha!" I laughed, elated with the very feel of the paper in my hands. "That's Mama!" As I began to read I sank slowly to the floor, landing cross-legged in a corner of the front room. She explained that she was touring Thailand with Charlie. Today she had walked in a rice paddy, "actually sank my feet into the watery field and thought of Jambi cooking her fish soup and rice!" Unfortunately, Charlie and Mama would not be home to see me for the holidays, but she hoped I was healthy and happy and she missed me terribly and thought of me all the time. She hoped I didn't mind too much getting myself down to London by train at the end of the semester. Jambi would have money for the taxi from Victoria Station when I arrived at the house. She loved me and sent me "a hundred kisses and bone-crushing hugs, Mama."

The news set me on edge. This did not bode well with my plans to leave here, never to return. Had my mother found another school for me? Surely she did not mean for me to come back to Prockney Hall, did she? Had she forgotten her promise? The only thing I felt confident about was that the color of my bedroom walls at home would most likely have been painted another shade. This odd mania of my mother's amused me, everything forever changing. She was predictable only in her unpredictability. But surely she did not intend to send me back to Prockney Hall?

London, Easter 1988

"THAT'LL BE PLATFORM TWO, POPPET,"
said a whiskered gentleman behind a grill at the station. "Mind
you don't miss your train; there's not another one until tomorrow morning."Thrilled with the sensation of independence, I
waited on the windy platform, my little leather case by my feet,
my school skirt slapping my cold legs. Well, I thought, if she
tries to send me back here, I will run away. I will vanish into
England without a trace. After she has had time to stew, I will
call and demand she move me to another school, once I have
some bargaining power. Strengthened with resolve, I boarded
the rattletrap train, sat myself beside a window, and rumbled
through dreary, soggy fields dotted with rain-bedraggled sheep
feeding incessantly. A book, open and uninviting, lay in my hand
on the scratchy wool seat, but it was unable to hold my attention for more than a few lines at a time. The train shook me
from side to side, freeing the book from my grip until I let it
drop to the floor, where it vibrated its way under the seat in
front of me, into the recesses of a dusty corner. At Haywood's
Heath, halfway to London, a light rain spattered, dribbling dirt
down the windows. The water took my reflection with it in its
descent, so that I watched my own eyes twitch and shake an
inch from me. The station manager's voice boomed out on the
loudspeakers, inaudible and fuzzed, spinning out a list of future

stops before our intended arrival at Victoria, at five-fifty-five in the evening.

"No need to ring the doorbell like that! I'm not deaf!" Jambi said, poking a finger into the base of her bun. She sailed out to the awaiting taxi, navigating loose-fitting slippers with the balls of her feet, and leaned so deeply through the driver's side window the man was forced to slope sideways. "Daylight robberies!" Jambi said, extricating herself and the folds of her long pink nightgown from the narrow chute of the window. "You've fiddled the meter, you devil! I'm not giving you a penny over five quid! If you don't like that, you can go and lump it!" She continued hollering as the chugging cab merged into the traffic, blending with the anonymity of the flow. "Call the police, why don't you, I'm not afraid of the likes of you!"

I had never known home empty. The rooms seemed larger in the silence, the ceilings higher. The walls pulsed with a peculiar sense of self-importance, as if without the competition of life force they could dance to a beat of their own. It was intimidating, and I found it hard to linger long in, or even venture far into, any room, backing out through doorways, scurrying down corridors, checking over my shoulder when I thought I felt a coolness following me. I stood for a while by the entrance to the sitting room, taking stock of the changes. New high-backed dusty brown sofas with dark red pillows of rough silk, the floor covered with a rush matting in geometric designs, all the paintings gone, replaced with huge mirrors with ornate, swirling gold frames. I was glad of the changes, if only as a sign that if change itself was the constant, everything had, in fact, remained the same. But in the quiet the room was unwelcoming and drafty, and even Cricklewood had abandoned her favorite perch above the curtain rungs, opting instead for a basket beneath the kitchen stairs where Hamish used to store his wine collection.

"Fish soup and rice for dinner," Jambi said, scraping hardened rice from the bottom of an orange iron pot, clanking the ladle on the metal sides of the sink, creating an oddly effective tintinnabulation. "Rice your Mama sent me from Thailand. She picked it herself. She very thoughtful, your Mama. She think about you all the time, you know? She love you very much."

"Did Mama find another school for me?"

"Handpicked rice!" Jambi said, filling the scraped pot with water and placing it on the lit stove. "But if little lady muck wants fasty food, I have a couple of quid, and you can go buy chicken pies. Please yourself."

"What about school, Jambi?" I asked impatiently, unable to conceal my annoyance. "Am I home for good? I mean, do I get to stay here when the holidays end?"

"Well . . . I don't think so. Noooo, I don't think so," Jambi said softly, shaking her head and staring intently into the heating water. "Maybe we should ask your Mama to send more rice. This going to be very delicious!"

I trekked upstairs, hauling myself up by the wood banister. "Why, why, why?" I whined feebly. "Everybody's forgotten about me! I've been abandoned!" I passed my own room, the door wide and gaping in a toothless way; it looked horribly uninviting. I eyed it with slit-eyed loathing. "I hate you!" I snarled at the dismal room and kicked my shoes off so that they sailed up and in, thunking against the eggshell-colored wall behind my bed, staining a dark scar into it. "Oh bloody hell! That'll give her a good reason to repaint; she repaints the whole bloody house every time I turn around anyway . . . What?"

I yanked on Miranda's door. It was locked. My old bedroom bolted shut. I slumped weakly against the wood frame. "You're not even bloody using the bloody room! It's so bloody unfair!" I whispered, cautious in case there was in fact somebody home. I held my breath for a second and scanned for stray sounds, but all I heard was the cars chugging up and down the street, the occasional blast of a horn. The longer I listened to these faraway, abstract signs of life, the more wretched the deserted house felt. "I can't believe this!" I said passionlessly and trailed up the stairs with my head hanging listlessly, and watched my socked feet, toes emerging from holes at the seam.

The door to my mother's bedroom shuddered on its loose hinges as I approached, a ghost footman ushering me into the lady's chambers. I flopped down on the wide white bed with its linen cover and rows of stacked pillows, and smaller, squashy, lace-trimmed cushions. I lay quite still, the traffic sounds jabbing the silence intermittently. Three tall windows lit up one wall, pertly dressed with new, pale pink cotton curtains hung on bars of black iron. The three remaining walls were a pale pink, and I wondered if they were pink when I was here last. I could not remember. Had they been green? No, that was my room. But wait, was it still green, or had I seen an eggshell white? It was all too confusing, and I slammed my arms down on the linen bedspread, leaving visible prints in the thick cotton. "Hah!" I hissed vehemently. "You going to punish me for messing up your bed? You going to trace my fingerprints? Well, see if I care! I don't care one bit about any of you! Not the least bit!" I whimpered, gradually losing momentum. Rain stabbed the windows, darkening the room, and I slid under the covers and pulled the butter-soft sheets up to my chin. I rolled over and hugged the profusion of pillows, prepared to weep and soak the stiffly ironed linens, when unexpectedly a stack of books piled on the bedside table caught my eye.

I pulled on the two chains that winked just beneath the lamp shade, and light spread, dispelling the pall. Sitting up, I crammed pillows behind me, smoothed the bedspread flat over my legs for a table, and hoisted the books onto my lap. *The Autumn of the Patriarch* by Gabriel García Márquez. The title made no sense to me, and the man's name was unpronounceable. However, it looked appealing enough, with a fat man in army clothes lying on a silver serving platter, surrounded by a flourish of vegetables. I flipped it open and read the first line three times before letting the book fall by my side. I examined the exterior of a big blue book titled *Whales and the Cosmic Universe* by Baba Vita Rajneesh. No thanks, that sounded just like the kind of book my mother was always pressing into people's hands, imploring them earnestly, "Read it, I promise you it will change your life!" I tossed it aside without so much as a glance between the covers. Next was a pale brown notebook. I flicked quickly through, fanning it with the tips of my fingers. It was filled with my mother's inimitable scrawl. Big loopy letters, all straight up and rounded out.

The very first page was headed "Dinner with Edwin S." I sat up and leaned in toward the lamp.

> *Frightful dinner at La Cocina. Drank too much. Frightful unfunny comedy in Soho. Fool sitting behind me coughing throughout. Sick people ought not to be allowed to infect others.* Remember to call Prince Charles and discuss possibilities of introducing as law. *Eddie drove me home and insisted on a nightcap. Gave him glass of brandy left over from Hamish's collection. Quite sure it's turned to vinegar, hoped it might encourage Eddie to leave. Totally unexpected—Eddie squashes me up against the curtains in sitting room, kisses me and rams his hand up inside me! Could feel his signet ring—v. cold! Cricklewood flew out from the top of the curtain and poor Eddie almost had a heart attack!*

Reaching the end of the page woke me slightly, and I looked about guiltily, my heart racing, sick at the thought of being caught, yet unable to put the notebook down. I slithered under the sheets, pulling the incriminating book with me, raised a corner of the sheet just enough to permit light to enter the tent. Better positioned for covert action, I flipped the page.

Weekend jaunt with Jonty P.——sex in the back of his Rolls-
Royce, which I ruined because I forgot I had the damn curse.
Bled all over the salmon-colored leather. Destroyed! Told him to
say he was attacked by virtually extinct wildcat. Jonty so agi-
tated his hairpiece flew off and when he tried to stick it back on
it was the wrong way around. Cried real tears from laughing so
hard.

My pulse sped, my whole body on red alert. Every now and
then I would stop, hold my breath, and listen for the sounds of
someone approaching. Footsteps on the stairs. The slam of a
door. But it was never anything more than the pounding of my
own heart. Serves her right, I thought, cocky each time the
imaginary dangers passed. If she was here, I wouldn't be reading her bloody secrets.

Snickering at the entries, rereading the raciest of them several
times, I was embarrassed and fascinated all at once. Halfway
through I came across a page with just one simple line, "Charlie
says he's Maria's father." I read it again. "Charlie says he's Maria's
father." I sat bolt upright and shoved the page directly under the
light, and frowning so hard I could feel the creases in deep folds
on my forehead, I read it again. "Charlie says he's Maria's father."
Charlie who, I thought? Charlie Cairngorm? And who's Maria?
Not me, surely. Right? My heart began to thump wildly, and I
leaned rigidly back into the pillows. Me?

Shakily, I replaced the notebook on the side table. The very
feel of it suddenly disgusting me. Reconstructing the books on
the little night table in the order I had found them, I wriggled
out of the bed and scampered downstairs, bounding down as
many as three or four steps at a time, all the way to the kitchen
in the basement, where Jambi was stirring the contents of the
orange pot on the stove. The air was thick with the smell of fish
and onions, and Cricklewood was carving figure eights around
Jambi's legs.

"Hungry?" Jambi asked, never glancing at me, tucking the long dark strands back into the bun they fled. "You want fish soup and Mama's rice, or some money for chicken pies?"

"Fish soup, please," I said sullenly, flouncing onto the bench moored beside the kitchen table, while Jambi padded back and forth from the sink to the stove, apparently lost in the machinations of her broth. I considered questioning her knowledge of the notebook. Had she seen it? Had she read it? Had she read the part about Charlie? Steam ascended thickly, wrapped itself against her, dissolving her features until, if I closed one eye, she resembled my mother, with my mother's famous green eyes, hawklike and menacing, and her fire-engine red lipsticked mouth open, teeth showing, laughing eerily. And then the steam dispersed and Jambi reappeared, tucking loose strands into a bun of glossy dark hair, and I knew for certain that I ought not to confide in her; they were allies, these two. "Soup only," I said, shuddering. "Definitely no rice."

T W O   W E E K S   I D L E D by uneventfully, my daily routine reduced to obtaining money from Jambi in the morning, followed by a visit to the record shop, where I would finger through the secondhand 45s in a white wood tray by the front door, selecting graphically pleasing square paper envelopes, making a quick check to be sure the clerk was looking elsewhere before scraping a fingernail across the ridges of the oily black disk, listen to the clicking. After choosing with painstaking uncertainty, exchanging fifty pence in heavy, solid coins, I would steal home with my prize, pressing the flat paper package against the front of my navy wool coat with the velvet collar. I walked with eyes down, occasionally catching the covetous sidelong glances of strangers, so that I clutched my haul all the tighter and quickened the pace. Once home, I would barricade myself in my room and send my latest purchase spinning under the diamond-headed needle that bobbed gently, like a squirrel's tail, as it drove the lanes round and round. Lying on my back, one leg crossed over the other, I would close my eyes and fuse with the music, feel my whole body fill and lift up, lost in space for as long as the song lasted. Unceremoniously jolted by the crackling as the needle skidded toward the spindle, I would roll off the bed and trudge, light-headed, to the machine and send the record spinning once again. I would happily listen to the same tune a hundred times, halting only when Jambi came and knocked sharply on the door, summoning me for meals.

In the afternoons, after lunch, Jambi would walk with me down to the river, where we would hang over the thick stone balustrade and watch the tugs and barges stirring the steely gray surface into thick peaks that lunged up the sludgy banks. Seafaring birds swooped about, idly pursuing the boats, occasionally attacking decks for stray fare or attaching themselves to masts when they tired of flying. With stolen glances at Jambi, warmly wrapped in a fur coat passed on to her by my mother, I would construct imaginary conversations whereby I quizzed Jambi as to what she knew about Charlie being my father. I looked for signs everywhere. If four boats with their names painted in red went by, Charlie was definitely my father. If gulls flew in twos, not threes, then he was not. If, however, Jambi interrupted my ruminations just as I was concluding one way or another, then he was Miranda's father and the conspiracy was murkier than anyone suspected.

On my last day of freedom I decided I ought to find a permanent and safe haven for Alison's will and the badly cracking Polaroid. After staring closely at our smiling, suntanned faces until a stab caught me in the heart, I wedged my treasures between two pairs of boots and pushed them deep into the recesses of the floor of the cupboard. And only when I felt certain that their identity was sufficiently concealed by strategically placed shoes and stout piles of books did I trot downstairs to sit in the front hall and wait for the taxi to arrive. Crouched on the bottom step, I examined the quiet I had found so intimidating two weeks ago. We had made peace, the spectral solitude and I. It no longer overwhelmed me with its denseness threaded through with sonic thrums, Mother Nature's Morse code. I felt a comfort in the silence, someplace to gather strength when I thought of having to return to Prockney Hall. Interrupting my communion, I heard the sound of a car pulling to a stop, a door slapped shut, and assuming it was the taxi come to take me to the gallows, I went out to meet it.

Miranda and my mother emerged, laughing and chattering as the chauffeur pulled a thousand packages and boxes from the back of Charlie's silver Bentley. Seeing Miranda shocked me. I do not know where I had thought she was, had not in fact given it any thought at all, but seeing her now I brimmed with self-pity, fairly felt myself heat up like a rocket preparing to launch.

"Darling! Give Mama a big hug!" my mother said as I buried myself in her embrace and every ounce of anger flowed directly out, replaced instead with the relief of being near her again. "That's so extraordinary; I was just thinking about you! Isn't that remarkable, darling? I was just thinking about you, and here you are! Oh, it's so good to see you. Did you have a good holiday, darling? Did you get my rice? I was in the field, you know, picked it up out of the water myself! I bought you mountains of presents. I do hope you like them, I spent hours choosing things for you."

"They're hideous!" Miranda laughed, fixing her hair with her fingertips, catching the eye of a well-dressed gentleman passing between us on the sidewalk. "How is it possible that you have such bad taste, Mama, when I have such good taste?"

"They're not hideous, you little monster! They're exquisite!" my mother said, chuckling.

"Yuck!" Miranda said, wrinkling her nose. With one hand she closed herself into her long chinchilla coat and swished off to-

ward the house. "I'm embarrassed to be related to you!" she
called over her shoulder.

"Impertinent brat!" my mother said, laughing, lobbing a
glove at Miranda's back. "Unfortunately for you, you always
know who you're mother is; it's your father you can never be
sure of!"

"What?" I said with the velocity of a bullet slicing through its
target. "What did you say?" I demanded, my voice scratchy and
faltering as I attempted a recovery. "I mean, wouldn't that be
wonderful, you know, I mean, to find out that one's father was
not one's father. You know, wouldn't that be fabulous?"

"Why would it be fabulous?" my mother asked, eyeing me
suspiciously, her face a storybook of information, drastically
contradicting her casual tone. A bus whistled by in a screech of
noise, collecting all the street dirt in its huge wheels, spinning
it up to eye level, allowing me a second more to compose an argument.

"Well, because Dad's so difficult with me. It would be an explanation. You know, it would be an easier reason to believe
than that he just doesn't like me." My heart thumped so hard I
thought I might choke, but I put on a carefree face, tried to affect a look of happy indifference. "Why, Mama, could it be?" I
coaxed. I felt as if I had taken the last step before going over a
cliff. I could feel my toes curled over the loose earth edge, felt
myself teetering vertiginously, worried, in fact, that I might
faint. Instead, I smiled eagerly, encouragingly, and waited for
my mother to speak.

"How would you feel if I told you Sammy Moses was not
your father?" she asked, watching me closely.

"I would be thrilled," I lied, smiling widely—believably, I
hoped—though I felt quite sick. My heart raced to dangerous
speeds, my whole body rigid, and yet I smiled at my mother
and tried to appear overjoyed.

"Would you really, darling?" She looked very relieved, her dark green eyes fluttering excitedly as she filled with confidence, preparing to reward me with the full story.

I nodded enthusiastically and clapped my hands together. "Yes, Mama," I said, hoping she would spit it out before I had a heart attack. "Who is?"

"This really isn't a good time for all this," my mother said, frowning suddenly. Speaking earnestly, she held me close to her. "There's been an accident. Charlie went missing somewhere up near the border of Burma. Mama's very unhappy, darling. Can you understand that? Let me sort this out, and then we'll discuss everything some other time."

A taxi pulled up alongside Charlie's Bentley, jolting me. "Mama, please!" I said, panicked. "Jambi says I have to go back to Prockney Hall, but you promised! Please don't send me back, Mama, let me stay here with you!"

"Darling, it's just one more semester," my mother said as she hugged me and bundled me into the chugging cab. "I'll find you another school after the summer holidays. I promise. I mean, after we've found Charlie. Can you imagine, darling! He simply vanished!"

NEWS OF CHARLIE'S DISAPPEARANCE FIL-
tered in via the ivory radio sitting atop the supplies cupboard in
Noel's art room. Those first few weeks back at Prockney Hall I
was accosted daily with nerve-racking updates, weepy, staticky
statements by my mother claiming he was "the love of my life,"
her "soul mate," until one weekend at Balmoral Castle, the
Queen Mother broke her hip and gradually the reports on
Charlie diminished, one item at a time, until no more than once
a fortnight did we hear mention of his continued invisibility.
News grew dim, as easily as if Charlie had only ever been a
handful of sand that could slip irretrievably through one's fingers. The professor maintained her rule regarding use of the
telephone, cutting us all off from any possible link to the world,
and in order to keep my anxieties from short-circuiting completely, my imagination took over like ivy surging up a tree
trunk, meaning only to reach the sunlight, inadvertently stran-
gling the oak in the process.

Soon I was consumed with visions of Charlie having run away,
in disguise, made off in the middle of the night, just as I would if
only I had the courage. I realized, as my mullings took form, that
I ought to join him, somehow find him and travel the earth hand
in hand with him. But how? My nights were devoted to long,
drawn-out, detailed planning with Alison, who promised to act as

guide. Frequently I would repeat the act of gathering supplies, wooly sweaters, little paper bags filled with crumbling biscuits and boiled sweets, and as late as I could wait, when Fiona's even breaths signaled it was safe to flee, I would creep, jaw clenched, down the steps and out the kitchen door. For a moment I would stand quite still, talking myself down from the fear as I faced the frozen night so dense I could not make out the hem of the cliffs that seemed to have melted blackly into a coal sky. Easing gingerly down the driveway, too scared to draw breath, I would reach the rock wall that bordered the road. Settling on the achingly cold stone, my knees tucked into a snug embrace, I would listen to the waves as they lurched sloppily, drunkenly onto the shore below. And then it would occur to me that maybe Charlie was traveling to me, to save me, and if I left now we would never find each other. Eventually the morning light would come flood the land, exposing me and my threadbare plans, and I would concede, defeated and exhausted, and return to the school, crying as much from fear as from frustration.

Roland began to stalk me, appearing like a recurrent nightmare from behind the doors of an empty room I might have entered to hide from the turbulence of the school. He loomed from shadows in the corridors, sprang at me from within a concealing crowd, until gradually my nerves thinned. If he thought we were alone and unobserved, he would command me to kiss him, or to touch him, or to permit him to touch me. He would pinch at my chest viciously while he held my arms imprisoned behind my back, a look of mocking triumph glittering in his tiny, mean, dark eyes. In time he grew bolder, and he began to force a hand down between my legs, hurting me. Roland would jab at me, pinch at me, dig his fingernails into my skin, and I would stare, biting my lip, an inch from his face, breathing in the peculiar stale smell of him, hating him, never uttering a word. I never ran away from Roland, never pleaded for clemency when he would announce he was going to hit me. I could not allow him the satisfaction of believing he had broken me. I could not allow him to win. For courage I would make my thoughts fly away to a time in the future when I would be free and I would answer to no one. My mantra was "This has to come to an end; one day this has to end." As I saw that to appear unfussed in the face of danger, to laugh at his threats, to always appear unafraid, was a weapon available to me, I employed it more and more often, learning, slowly, a self-styled Zen. This did little to protect me physically, but mentally I would remain indomitable.

Toward the end of the semester the gales abated, and on clement afternoons when the rain ceased long enough to allow for a game of field hockey, Patty and Noel led rival teams in a fallow section of the kitchen garden, with disinterred vegetables marking the goalposts and squares of paper pinned to our chests for team colors. Late to take up my position, I was changing hurriedly in the musty locker room that backed onto the kitchen, a long corridor of a room, more like a hallway, with a metal rack down the center where we hung our muddied gray gym shorts and maroon T-shirts. The room was lit by narrow windows near the top of the wall, where it met with a slanted roof of beams and cobwebs. But today was relatively bright, and the cement floor was brushed with dusty sunlight and the fragrant scent of warmed spring air. Patty's authoritative voice rose above the staccato of shrieks and apologetic yelps. I pulled my navy blue tunic over my head and dropped it to the floor, unbuttoned my shirt and flung it aside. I reached for a maroon T-shirt when, startling me, Roland yanked the shirt from my hand.

"Get away from me!" I yelled. I backed away, staring at him. Watched his face closely as it searched mine, scanning like radar for the fear in my eyes. That was all he was ever looking for.

"Whatcha going to do about it?" Roland asked, dangling the maroon shirt like a taunt.

I heard Patty call a foul, heard the groaning lamentations that followed. It sounded like Mahad's exaggerated protests. I stared at Roland and his mad eyes, small and furious, filling with hatred and rage. A breeze pressed against the windows, forcing through the cracks, shaking shadows like darting minnows across Roland's face. I threw myself at him, rammed into him headfirst. It was a tussle until he overwhelmed me, throwing us both down to the cold floor. I knocked my head so hard that for a moment my eyes went out of focus, and all I saw was blackness. Pinioning me with his face on mine, he kissed me roughly, and I thought I would die of suffocation and the noxious ache in the back of my head. He tugged down my underwear and jammed a hand between my legs. I screamed from the pain. I thought it must be his hand inside me, but then I saw that both were free, supporting his weight on either side of me. I thought he had ripped me apart. I had the feeling that consciousness was rushing out, like water whirling down a drain, and then, just as I thought I would faint forever, I heard the frenzied cheers of a goal, accompanied by Mahad singing the refrain of his football club's victory chant. Roland leapt up, one hand tucking his shirt down the front of his trousers. He picked up my T-shirt and hurled it at me. "Get yourself dressed." He pranced toward the door. "One word and I'll kill you. I'll fucking strangle you with my bare hands. And don't ever forget that. Don't ever forget it."

I sat for a while with my heart pounding and a strange sense of guilt wrapping around me. Slowly I stood and continued dressing as if nothing had happened, except that my hands trembled as I pulled on the shirt and a pair of gray gym shorts, shakily tried to fasten the clasp. My hands shook so violently I broke two elastics before tying my hair in a ponytail. Pulling my hockey stick from a wooden tub by the door, I walked, a little unsteady, out of the changing room.

"Maria, where have you been?" Patty demanded sternly,

handing me a square of red paper and a safety pin to attach to the front of my shirt. The kitchen garden was transformed, covered over with kids shrieking and jousting with one another. "Go stand over there and guard Fiona, please. All right, children, one good game and we'll go in for tea."

THREE YEARS PASSED and my mother remained too distracted by the intricacies of her own life to place me in another school. Though my entreaties to be rescued never ceased, their impact was reduced to that of a low-lying daisy in a field of flowers trying to catch a bee's attention. During holidays spent with my father I would lay my appeal at his feet, but it was immediately swept away with shirking disclaimers and the exasperating suggestion that I take it up with my mother.

In the middle of the summer semester of that third year, at the venerable age of fourteen, I arrived home from Prockney Hall. Clattering into the front hall of home, I kicked the door closed behind me with a resounding boom and dropped my suitcase to the floor. "Mama!" I called, shaking free of my coat, slipping my keys into a pocket. Three small children playing beside the dining room table gazed up at me, transfixed. I did not recognize them. Nor did I recognize the carpet upon which they sat, legs sprawled, plastic toys tumbling about like ice floes. As my eyes inched about the room, I saw that almost everything was new. But it was not the newness or the children that perplexed me. "Mama!" I called, less loudly, pressing my coat over my arm. Something I could not identify nagged at me, and I searched about for clues.

"Hello," a blonde lady said from the top of the stairs. Her questioning tone snapped me to attention. She was tall and narrow, and her straight skirt stopped at the knee, flicking forward slightly with every step she took. She stopped midway down, resting a hand limply on the banister. "Who are you?" she asked sternly, her silhouette lit by the window behind her at the top of the stairs.

"Maria." I was indignant at her curt tone. "Who are you?"

The blonde lady frowned, pursed her small lipsticked mouth together, raised a finger to cup her chin. "Are you Helena's daughter?" she asked, recommencing her descent, one long leg at a time, her plum wool skirt winking at the cusp of her knees.

"Yes," I said, challenging her. "Where is she?"

The blonde lady stopped a few feet away, a look of curious wonderment on her face, and I noticed how tall she was, looming over me, shadowing me. She swept one long bare arm in the direction of her brood, still silent on the carpet. "We bought the house a month ago. Didn't your mother tell you?"

I stared, unmoving, afraid even to breathe, survival instincts shrieking for me to slam on the brakes, freeze the moment, and prevent any further disaster. I stared blankly, seeing nothing, understanding nothing, muddling this strange lady's words over and over in my head.

"I believe your mother moved to America," the blonde lady continued, crossing her arms in a gently definitive way. She shifted uncomfortably from one foot to the other, and I had the distinct impression that she expected me to leave. Where did she want me to go?

"Where's my mother?" I mumbled, wishing I could just sit down for a moment, catch my breath, and start this madness over again. Vaguely, I could hear the gurgling of the three children on the carpet, no longer bothered by the intruder, returning to the intensity of their games.

"I think she said New York," the blonde lady said, embarrassed, tightening her long bare arms across her flat chest, where gold medallions hung in the folds of a silky camisole. "But I really don't know for certain."

"What about my things?" I exhaled, sickened by the memory of

Alison's will and that photograph still lodged in the cupboard in my bedroom. I felt my body chill as nausea overwhelmed me.

"I don't know," she said, her gray eyes gathering at the sides in pleats of consternation. "Everything was gone when we moved in."

The blonde lady stood in front of me, planted firmly, proprietorially. She said nothing more, offered me nothing. No option but to leave. But where to? What should I do with myself? Why couldn't I stay here? Achingly slowly I slid into my heavy winter coat, hating the portentousness of every tiny movement, the gross significance of it all. I moved haltingly, hoping against hope that some manic clown would come crashing into the foreground, claim credit for the prank, put everything back the way it had been.

Feeling my key in a pocket, I wondered what I should do with it. Was it still mine? I toyed with the cold metal, pressed the fleshy tips of my fingers into the jagged teeth, and then, as if it were someone other than myself, I watched as I handed the key to the blonde lady, placing it in the palm of her hand, all the while waiting for the clown. If he could just come soon enough.

And yet there remained that indefinable something that had nagged me since I entered, something beyond the blonde lady and her children and their toys. I searched the furniture, the paintings, the curtains, taking in the details as if I were a video camera, and finally it struck me. There was no scent of coffee in the air. There was no scent of anything familiar, and then I knew that this blonde lady was not deceiving me, that my mother was well and truly gone. I felt very cold inside. With small shaky moves I collected my leather case from the floor, padded silently to the front door, and let myself out for the last time, taking nothing with me because there was nothing to take.

At school, the initial effects already dimming, I regaled my few friends with the hilarity of my mother's actions, the unique eccentricity of her crazy ways, and it was only their distressed expressions that gave me cause to question if this was in fact an unusual act. Gradually, directly as a result of their reaction, a strong sense of indignation replaced my joviality, settling deep inside me, building another layer of resentment on the ever-growing strata of perceived injustices.

And when, a few months later, I asked my mother why she had failed to tell me that she had sold the house and moved away, she said, stopping as she crossed the room of her new home in Manhattan, dressed in nothing more than a towel and a bra, with a filled and sloshing watering can in one hand, "I didn't think it would interest you."

"Where did Jambi go?" I asked quietly, wondering if I even wanted to know.

"Back to Jakarta." my mother said and proceeded to drown a series of potted gardenias lined up on a deep windowsill. "Aren't these extraordinary, darling! Come and smell the nectar; they're simply divine!"

Automatically, I rose and approached the plants, leaned forward to inhale the scent, and as I did so I asked, "Mama, who's my father?"

"I really don't know!" she said, smiling at me, a tad contrite. She tossed the emptied can aside and embraced me, patting my head with long intense strokes. "I'm awfully sorry, darling. I just don't know. Try not to hate me for it."

When I pass by the house, as I have done now and again over the years, I never stare for too long. I prefer to look away. I think I noticed once that the curtains were different in the bedroom I used to share with Miranda. But I would not know for certain, because I never entered that house again.

PART THREE

Côte d'Azur, 1996

CARRYING MY SMALL SUITCASE, A BEATEN leather box with a tartan lining that was virtually shredded with age, I walked out of the provincial airport to see Tino driving a dark green Jensen convertible. He held the polished wood steering wheel with one hand and waved wildly at me with the other. "You're here!" he yelled as he maneuvered the shiny auto toward me. "I've broken up a tennis game to come pick you up. I had to see for myself that you'd actually arrived." The car lurched to a stop. Hoisting himself up by the top of the windscreen, he leapt over the low door. In khakis, a pale pink oxford shirt, espadrilles, and tortoiseshell sunglasses, he looked very much at home.

He held me at arm's length, staring at me with the look of a child who has just been allowed to go mad in a candy store. A gust of soft, warm, honeysuckle air swept around us. The intensity of his stare was so comforting that any concerns that had begun to build on the long plane journey eroded away.

"I think you'll like the house," he said. "It's quite grand. It's not a palace, like you're used to, but I trust you'll find it's adequate."

"Not a palace! This is an outrage!" I said, laughing. "What you don't know is that, right at this sorry moment, I'd have to accept shelter in a tin shack. Madeleine asked me to move on."

199

"Why, did you cross the Maginot Line?"

"The what?"

"She's French, isn't she?"Tino frowned at me when I made no reply. "Don't you know anything? My God, were you asleep all through school?"Tino collected my suitcase and threw it on the backseat of the sports car, so that he never noticed the wry smile creep across my face, come and gone as swiftly as the shadow of a cloud passes over land. "Where does she want you to go?"

"To hell, no doubt! Although she didn't quite put it that way." I fell gently onto the deep leather seat. Tino nudged the Jensen past the idling taxicabs to the coast road. "Doesn't really matter though," I told him. "It's time for a change. I might go to Tahiti for a year, make mats and unearth Gauguins. Maybe I'll go to the Himalayas. I'd love to—"

"What's all this nonsense?"Tino drove with one hand on the wheel and an arm resting on the window ledge. He looked like a movie star from the fifties. That was the first time it occurred to me that, in fact, he was from the fifties. He was more than twice my age. "You're not to go anywhere before you consult with me. I won't have you gallivanting around the world un-chaperoned and without a penny in your pocket! It'll be a mir-acle if you come back alive!"

"Not really," I said, more to myself than to Tino. "The mira-cle will be if I come back. Period."

A low, fat sun had begun to melt into the horizon, bleeding its golden color onto the sea; a serrated sword lying flat on the water. Swallows outlined arcs with stiff-winged dips. I closed my eyes and let the afternoon sun warm my winter-white face. I hoped we would never arrive wherever we were going. I wanted this moment to last forever.

"Don't go to sleep, little dummy,"Tino ordered. "We're al-most there. Don't you want to take a dip in the water? I was in this morning. It's a bit brisk but quite divine."

Tino turned the Jensen off the main road, and we jostled down a long driveway through a dense forest of pine trees. The only sound was the crackling twigs beneath the tires. When the trees cleared we arrived at a brick-paved courtyard with a stone fountain burbling at the center. Through an archway in a wall of trellised ivy appeared the house, a two-story stone affair with a tile roof.

"Emil!" Tino yelled as he led the way through the ivy arch, bounding up a semicircle of flagstone steps to the front door. "Emil, *viens chercher les valises!*" Two huge wood doors with metal studs stood open, welcoming. "Where is that imbecile?" Tino asked the empty hallway. The entrance was cool and elegant with stone walls, a high cupola ceiling with stained glass windows, and stone floors occasionally covered with the muted reds of Turkish kilims.

Tino took me by the hand. "Come. I want to show you around." We walked through the house, through huge, silent rooms with oversized sofas and dark leather armchairs and great wood tables piled high with leather photograph albums and open backgammon boards. Vases of irises and yellow roses. The air was sweet.

We pushed through lead-latticed doors and came out on a terrace, a wide stone patio. Huge pots of baby orange trees reminded me of home in London years ago; my mother used to grow the same little trees in a courtyard behind the house. A table had been laid for two with endless silver forks and knives lined up on either side of the porcelain plates. Bunches of white roses and blue forget-me-nots sat in diminutive silver jugs. The house was on a promontory, overlooking a bay of the deepest cobalt blue. Sandstone cliffs rose out from the water, prehistoric and colossal.

"What do you think?" Tino asked, just as a flock of doves took off from nowhere like a fast-moving cloud, flapping toward the sun so that they became black against the light and quickly vanished into the distance. "You'll be happy here, won't you?"

"I don't know," I told him. "I'm used to so much better." I linked my arm in his. "Are you crazy?" I said, laughing. "This is perfect. How did you find this place? Have you been here before?"

"Of course!" Tino told me. "I've been coming every summer for fifteen years. Last year Julia came to stay and almost drowned. She forgot to tell me she couldn't swim, the silly thing."

The news rankled. I looked away at one of the baby orange trees imprisoned in a terra-cotta pot. A beetle with green spots clung to a leaf, falling backward with each attempt to haul itself up. I wanted to rescue it, but just then it thrust too hard and went tumbling to the ground, landing on its many feet. I watched it scuttle away, and I wished for a second that I could go with it.

"Who's Julia?" I asked, keeping my voice as light and disinterested as I could manage.

"Jealous, are we?" he said. "I'll take that as a good sign. What do you expect when you ignore my every effort to get your attention? I've only been trying to get you to open your eyes for two years! Most men would have given up a long time ago."

"But then, you're not most men." I said. The leaf the beetle had clung to with such tenacity still shook slightly. "They'd be happy with a few gold coins, whereas you want the entire cargo of the Armada on its way back from plundering South America."

"Very clever," Tino said, with a hint of annoyance. "Are you going to be ridiculous all the time?"

"Probably," I said. "Let's go for a swim. I can't talk underwater."

Shooting directly down toward the shell-carpeted seabed, I closed my eyes and imagined the liquid was a zero-gravity planet and I a gill-less fish, tumbling and spinning weightlessly. Then I kicked myself up to the surface for air, a new supply of oxygen before sinking down again. Unreal, dreamlike moments where up is down and there are no sides, no barriers, no rules.

"You're quite a little fish," Tino said as he wrapped me in a huge towel. "I thought I'd lost you a few times there." We sat on the beach, the cliffs behind us, the house only partially visible at the top of a steep flight of steps cut into the cliff wall. An evening breeze blew casually about, and my skin puckered in goose bumps. The sun was gone, but still a subtle light remained, a reflection of the day. The sea-salt air mingled with blossom-scented currents. A feast to inspire. I dug my toes into the sand, working the soft grains against my skin.

"I love the water," I said, staring out to sea, watching it fade into the twilight. "It's total freedom, isn't it? I don't suppose it would feel like that to a fish, though, because then it's just your home. We've the benefit of contrast. Unless, of course, you're Julia and you thrash about swallowing seaweed."

"Enough about Julia," Tino said, laughing. He put an arm around my shoulders and drew me near him. I felt a knot in my stomach. Suddenly I was unsure of how I felt. Of why I had come. I tried to ignore his move, continued staring out to sea. I knew I must keep the conversation from anything remotely provocative. But the more my head filled with tactical thoughts, the more panicky I became. I leapt up.

"I'll race you back." I said. "Last one up's—"

"Don't be afraid of me," Tino said, lying back, propped on his elbows. "I want you to trust me."

Feeling like a fool, I crumpled back down beside him, and we lay side by side listening to the water trickle up the flat beach, watched it bubble back into the black, diamond-sparkled water. We stayed until a crescent moon was the only light, snaking a shaky tail across the water, igniting the phosphorescence. From high above in the pine-tree forest an owl trumpeted, a nocturnal call to arms.

Not until the chilled evening wind came and scooped tiny

gusts of sand against us did Tino breathe a sound. Turning on one side, resting his head on the palm of a hand he said, "Why did you come?"

"I came because . . . " I looked at him, searching for a way out of this. What was I to say? "I came because of what you told me that day in New York. The thing you swear you never said."

"You are ridiculous." A flicker of a smile tempered the admonishment. "Still harping on about your imaginary conversations! Tell me, honestly, why did you come?"

I knew he wanted me to say that I had come because my heart had told me to, but that was not true. I did not know what I felt for him. All I knew was that the fear of losing him had seen me across the Atlantic and all the way to Cap d'Antibes.

"You don't have to say it if you don't want to. I know why." He took one of my hands in his, and I felt a coldness swirl around inside my stomach, and somehow, perhaps in the limpness of his grip, I knew for certain that he could feel my unease. "Maria, do you know that I'm in love with you?"

I was caught completely off guard. I was grateful for the shroud of night so as to hide the heat I felt for certain had rouged my cheeks a deep crimson.

"Do you believe me?" Tino asked, squeezing my hand.

I thought it over. Could he love me? Did he love me? Or was I as much a fantasy to him as he was to me? Was it what I represented to him, whatever that was, that he loved?

"No," I told him slowly, staring at my hand in his, lying on the cooling sand. "I don't think you're in love with me. But I believe that you think you are." I looked up at him, at the unclear outline of his face, at the moonlight caught on the surface of his eyes. "No man has ever said he loved me before."

"Don't talk nonsense," Tino scolded. "You've heard it a hundred times. Flattery will get you nowhere."

"I don't see what's so flattering about that. And in any case, it's true."

"Don't perjure yourself." Tino ran a finger down the side of my face, like a sculptor learning the details. "Maria, I want to make you an offer, but I don't want you to give me an answer until next Friday, when you leave for New York. I know you, you'll tell me no before you've even thought about it." He stared at me, his mouth tense. "I want to look after you. I want to get you an apartment and give you an allowance, something you can live on so that you aren't dependent on your friends and your useless family. We'll have to work out how much and how you get it, but we can deal with that later. I hope you'll be sensible and accept this. No strings attached."

"No strings attached!" I pulled my hand away from his. Those were my words! From my fantasy! The one where I look longingly into a storefront of jewels and wait to be noticed by some caring type who promised me everything, "no strings attached." How could Tino know? "You are bizarre," I told him, stalling for time. "Have you forgotten that you're married?"

"We have an arrangement," he told me, brusquely. "I'm not discussing my wife with you."

"But—"

"No." He put his fingers to my lips. "Not a word before Friday. Think about it, seriously." He stood up and offered me a hand, an innocent gesture. "Now let's go in. I'm famished."

I rose. I was a foot away. He was a darkness in the already dark night. I could feel the warmth of him, and suddenly I wanted nothing more than for him to embrace me, perhaps because I felt certain he would not. He seemed to be fully aware of the effect he had on me, and purposely, he kept his distance. The sound of his breath was steady, calming, and I wanted so much to reach and touch him, but I was afraid. I do not know what of. I wished I had the courage to lean forward, to kiss him

on the lips, but if I had been on the other side of the planet instead of inches away, it would have been equally impossible. Instead I followed him up the many stone steps, feeling the
rough-worn rock against my feet.

Dinner was served on the patio by Emil's wife, Amalie. Pure
white hair shimmering from beneath a fortress of pins. She ambled heavily, burdened by her dense, bell-shaped dress, so that
she looked like a medieval nun. She rocked around, talking
more to herself than to us. *"Monsieur Tino, encore un peu de vin?"*
she would solicit, in between muttering hotly to herself in a
heavy southern dialect. *"Mademoiselle, un doigt?"*

Crickets and night noises and the sound of the crackling wax
candles on their silver stems accompanied the melodic bass of
Tino's voice. He told me about his early years in New York. I
drifted away. I watched his face as he spoke. His bright eyes
shone, animated and vivid, catching candlelight.

The little bouquets of flowers in their rounded crystal vases
surrounded the silver candlesticks, a floral moat. The white
rose petals were bluish in the dim light; the forget-me-nots had
darkened to a Tyrian purple. The colors matched the dress I
wore, borrowed from Madeleine, and I wondered if that was in
some way providential. I wondered if coincidences amounted
to anything more than the sum of their parts, or if they were
manna scattered randomly to entertain us mortals.

" . . . hard to believe, but I've known your mother twenty
years!" Tino was saying. His manicured hands fingered the stem
of a wineglass, turning the base around and around, letting the
thick potent liquid swirl up the sides.

"Twenty?" I said, feigning a look of horror. "That's my age!
Perhaps you're my father!"

"You are ridiculous!" Tino said with a short laugh. "I've
known your mother since I was up at Cambridge with Charlie
Cairngorm and the gang."

"Did you know Charlie well?" I asked, the rarely spoken name flooding me with memories.

"Your mother knew him better!" Tino exclaimed. "Up at Cambridge!"

"Mama never went to University!"

"Not technically, but she spent a good deal of time visiting."

"Why?"

Tino sat back, and the stillness of the night filled the silence between us as I waited for him to continue. But instead he merely smiled at me, and I wondered if perhaps he thought he should protect me from unpleasant truths or florid memories not fit for troubled offspring to hear.

"And?" I said, impatiently battering the table with my fingertips.

"Quiet, little dummy," Tino said, dismissing my entreaty. "You loved Charlie, didn't you?"

His words pierced me, and pursing my mouth tightly, I nodded.

"For a long time I suspected your mother—you know, thought she'd done away with him. If not actually killed him, then at least been involved in his disappearance. You know, it was all just a bit too convenient, the way he vanished into thin air. But the more I've mulled it over, the more convinced I am that she isn't nearly clever enough to pull it off and not get herself discovered," Tino said, fiddling with his napkin.

"You can't seriously think that my mother . . . " I laughed at the implications, gradually remembering how I had always secretly harbored doubts about Alison's demise, always wondered privately if my mother had somehow been responsible, and that was why she had been so irritated with my all-consuming collapse. But that was so long ago, and I was a child then, just overreacting. But what if . . . ?

"I think Charlie'll turn up one day," Tino continued, seemingly amused by my puzzled expression. "I think he's just waiting to see the whores come out of the closet and try to carve his fortune up.

Can you imagine the embarrassment of whoever tries to claim, and on the last day of reckoning old Charlie saunters in, tanned from so many years in Rio, and sends them all packing with their tails between their legs!" Tino leaned in, placed his elbows on the table. "You know that if anyone but Eleanor winds up with Cairngorm, under Scottish law it will be razed and divided up into tiny lots for council houses, and in less than a few years there won't be so much as a memory of it?"

"That's terrible!" I said, profoundly agitated by the ugly picture Tino painted.

"I know," he said. "I'm glad you agree with me. You realize your mother has some sort of phony will, and she means to use it when the time comes?"

"What will, what time?"

"After a certain number of years from when Charlie disappeared, he will be declared legally dead. If he doesn't show up by then, and we don't do something, Cairngorm will be destroyed."

"But what can we do?"

"I don't know. I'll have to give it some thought," Tino said softly, staring down at the table as his voice cracked with emotion. He brushed a drop from his eyes and then he sat back and shook his head slightly. "Enough about that!"

"Want to play backgammon?" I suggested, a surge of awe and admiration rushing my insides. I knew then and there that Tino and I were inextricably bound together for all time, that we were allies, and that we would fight evil side by side, an indomitable force. "Ten thousand dollars a point. I bet I win your whole inheritance off you!"

"You're such a little fool," Tino said, stretching his legs beneath the table as he lit a cigar, puffing gray ghosts into the heavy warm air. "I don't gamble with children."

"But you go on holiday with them?" I chuckled and immediately slammed a hand across my mouth.

"If you keep this up it's going be more like work than a holiday."

I slept alone in a room at the other end of the house from Tino's. I had so prepared myself for the scene—the one where Tino begs me to come sleep with him and I get coy and afraid and tell him, "No, I can't. Tomorrow night, maybe"—that when it did not happen, I wondered if perhaps he had had a change of heart. It worried me, and I thought of Madeleine's favorite summation of the male species, that you do not even like them until they fail to telephone, then instantly they become marriage material.

I lay in the huge four-poster bed of wrought iron uprights with a tapestry canopy, and as the night hours ticked by I lost courage in myself and in Tino and in all my new, fanciful ideas. I should pack my things and leave now when I could. If memory served me correctly, there was just the one road, and I could surely walk the distance to the airport. And in the morning I could take the first flight home. The ticket Tino had bought for me was quite conveniently an open return. I listened to the sea rustling against the cliffs below, and I thought of England and Prockney Hall and the crazy storms that battered at my bedroom window at night, when I would imagine running away. I never got very far, never much farther than the course of my imagination. A long time had passed since then, and yet here I was doing the same thing. I thought of all the times I had dreamed of freedom, and yet the only time I have ever felt it was in a moving car or a hurtling train or experiencing that wonderful sensation as the plane pitches up into the air, sucking you back into your seat, taking you away.

I awoke to find Tino sitting on my bed, watching me. I blinked him into focus. White morning light wafted in on the edges of the thin curtains, which fluttered with the breeze. The sound of a bird clearing his throat, readying himself for a day of screeching, punctured the stillness.

Tino pulled the sheets away from me so that I lay naked, propped up against huge, square pillows with embroidered edges. I was still too heavily drugged with dreams and sleep to be afraid as I watched him lean down toward me, felt his mouth on mine. I closed my eyes and slid my arms around him, pulled him closer, felt the cold, soft, springy hair on his chest against my bare skin. I wanted so much for this to be right. With every move he made, I was that much more awake, and an odd fear seeped into me, reminding me of something I could not place.

I watched Tino and I worried he was trying to trick me into needing him, trying to pry open my heart, expose feelings I had buried out of harm's way years ago. I watched him, with his eyes screwed shut, transporting himself who knows where. And then I saw Roland in the locker room, forcing me into the cement floor, and immediately I hated Tino, hated him for confusing me, so that I no longer knew what, if anything, was honest and what was manipulative fiction. Fat tears sidled cautiously, gathered in puddles on my chest, proletariat picketers furtively demanding justice, ready to capitulate at the merest acknowledgment.

"Maria." Tino kissed me, whispering directly into my face. With his fingertips he swept loose strands of hair from my face, ran his fingers through the wet tangles. "I've wanted to make love to you since the first time I met you. Since that dinner party. Do I sound like a crazy person?" He was laughing as he said this. "I don't care if I do. I love you so much. You must believe me. Please say you do."

Breathing in short, quick breaths, trying to compose my flustered, pounding heart, I stared at Tino and said nothing. I looked at his eager, questioning eyes, and I thought I felt his neediness. His need of assurance made me feel corruptly powerful. It appeared that he had noticed nothing of my delirium. Was it possible to have a fit inches from someone's face and go unnoticed? "Tino," I said, adjusting myself so that I lay on my side, facing him, lacing my feet between his ankles. "I don't know what I think, because I'm as fickle as the wind. I change my mind practically every day. Whatever I might believe today I won't believe tomorrow."

"How can you live your life like that?" he asked, still training strands away from my eyes, fixing them behind my ear, the way I used to as a child.

"It's exhausting," I said.

As the days turned over, day into night, night to day, I was reassured to discover that Tino and I were quite compatible. Most of our time together was spent reading on the beach, if I was not off on some long swim, exploring caves along the hem of the cliffs, diving into grottoes with emerald walls and odd, hollow, aching sounds. There were friends of Tino's who would come for lunch, a game of tennis, a swim. And they would treat me with an odd regard. It seemed that they had elected to avoid me, and yet no one of them could have been accused of being unfriendly. No one ever made it perceptibly clear that the child and the married man were in any way offensive to their notions of propriety. Perhaps they had none. Most likely they were afraid of angering Tino. He was, without fail, treated with extreme consideration, as if he were an unpinned hand grenade about to blow.

I could never decide if I liked being with him or not. Every day I changed my mind. I loved him, I thought. I had come to depend on his affections, and yet I was revulsed by the charade of a man and a woman pretending to be enamored with each other, which I firmly believed we were not. He would come into my room in the mornings, sit on the side of the bed, and slowly work his way toward me, indefatigable and predictable as the tides. And though I wished I could relax and return a favor or two, I was grateful for his continued tolerance of my nervy reserve. My feelings would swing violently from one end of the spectrum to the other. I would find myself watching him, watching his mouth move when he spoke, watching his square, blunt fingers, browned from the sun, a white band where his wedding ring ought to be. His stomach barreled out, hard, taut, obscured by graying hair that covered like a warrior's breast-plate. The skin at his elbows and his knees was gray from age, wrinkled from time; his hands were a palomino of brown spots, thick-knuckled, misshapen from street fights, and yet smooth and uncallused from a life of servants. I would examine his hard but aging body as he strode down to the water's edge, and I would hear the criticisms rebounding in my head until I leashed them and forcibly restrained them. Most often, I found him wonderfully good looking, smooth and sculpted, and with those entrancing liquid eyes. I never knew what I thought. My mind changed as surely as the hours of the day.

Friday morning came and Tino asked me for my verdict on his offer. As with every morning, Amalie had cooked us hard-boiled eggs. I took one of the warm ovoids from its shelter in a basket and decapitated it, one clean slice with a knife. "I've thought it through," I told him as I dipped the tip of a spoon into the orange center. "Believe me, no one is more disappointed than me." I looked up at him, at his expectant, eager face. I put the spoon back down on the side of the plate and picked up a napkin to fiddle with. "But I can't take you up on it."

"I knew you'd say that!" he said. "I'm not taking no for an an-swer. Go back to New York and find yourself a place to live. You can't traipse around like a Gypsy for the rest of your life! You won't even be invited anywhere for the weekend, at this rate, if you've got nowhere to go, come Sunday night! Listen, little dummy, I inherited all my money. Easy come, you know? I've got more than enough for a couple of extra homes, for God's sake! I'm not offering to buy you a palace!"

I imagined myself in an apartment, light streaming in on me

from big bay windows as I whiled away the time reading, in peace. And then there would be a knock at the door—no, the door would open and Tino would enter, brandishing his set of keys like a jailer. No strings attached. I didn't believe the rules would be upheld.

"The thing I didn't realize when I used to mope around wishing for everything you've promised is that I'd be a prisoner. You'd own my time."

"Why do you have to be so dramatic?" He crossed his arms and shoved his chair back, a look of disdain on his otherwise untroubled face. "Why won't you let me look after you!"

"I just can't," I said, wishing I could say quite the opposite. Dew sat on the petals of flowers Amalie had left in bowls on the table. I wanted to wend the tip of my fingers along the tiny petals, dry the glint of water with my skin. I wished I could stay and be taken care of forever and see these flowers every morning, breathe in the gentle sea air. Never go back. It was so desperately important to me that Tino never so much as consider I was with him because of greed. I was with him because I loved him, loved him for wanting to take care of me, and I did not wish to spoil anything by accepting some ugly transfer of things. I despised things. Things could not be relied upon. "I can't. I'd feel suffocated."

"I only want to make your life a little more comfortable. I'm not looking to buy you," he said, sipping his coffee. "How about if we trade? Knowing you, that's probably the only way you'll accept anything, if you think there's less in it for you than for me. Am I right?" He paused until I nodded. "Maria, you said you'd do anything to help save Cairngorm. You remember what I told you about the council housing? Unless you work with me to stop your mother, Cairngorm will vanish forever and be replaced by hundreds of hideous shacks."

"What do you want me to do?" I asked, unsure if I should

proceed. I could see the trap clearly before me, and yet I could not see how to avoid it, or even if I should. "You don't have to bribe me, you know? I'd be happy to do you a favor, especially if it has something to do with Cairngorm."

"No! Agree to trade, or you can forget the whole deal!" he said hotly, as if I had offended him. His strange blue eyes were menacing in their intensity, and I thought they made the breeze cooler as it passed idly by.

"What do you need?" I said, capitulating.

"Your mother has a piece of paper, a will signed by her and Charlie and me, that permits the bearer of the document to legally claim the Cairngorm estate. It's half of a twin document that I believe Charlie kept in a bank in Scotland, or with his lawyers, I don't know exactly. As soon as Scottish law declares Charlie legally dead, Eleanor will be invited to a meeting with the executors of Cairngorm, and unless anyone can prove otherwise, everything will be handed over to her. I suspect that birdbrain mother of yours is waiting until that time to thrust her ugly childish joke of a claim under Eleanor's nose, which will probably give the old dear a heart attack and reduce her to abject poverty and a draughty old-peoples' home, where she'll spend the last few miserable years of her life. Help me do the right thing, Maria! Would you do me that favor? Would you find that document for me?" he asked, grinning infectiously.

"I know exactly what you're talking about," I said, memories overwhelming me so that I was once more at Cairngorm, in the pale green circular telephone room, eye level to the picture that I dropped to the floor, smashing the glass that would later cut me on Christmas morning. I watched Tino's childishly happy face beaming with excitement, and like brushfire, I felt it come devour me.

"If you help me, you help save Cairngorm. Do it for Charlie! I know he loved you very much."

As I listened to Tino, I filled with a moral fervor for the worthy crusade, Tino's earnest righteous concern boring deep into my heart until I could see nothing but my mother standing in front of Cairngorm with a massive chain saw, carving it up into tiny pieces, laughing demonically, her famous green eyes flashing dangerously as she reduced the beautiful moss-covered castle to rubble. "Absolutely!" I declared, laughing, as I flung my napkin on the table and pledged my allegiance. "I'll do anything I can to help!"

MADELEINE BUCKLED AND EXTENDED MY
stay in her guest room another six months. Part-time jobs kept
my pockets from emptying entirely, but September loomed,
and soon I would need to pack and move on. Tino continued to
call every day, ten o'clock sharp, and every now and again he
would remind me of the offer. Then August came, bringing his
family to Cap d'Antibes, and I was returned to the shadows of
his life. The loss of contact allowed my imagination to run rampant. Daily, my feelings for Tino grew. I was left alone to fanta-
size, to imagine he was telling his wife about me, telling her he
could no longer be married to her. He must surely miss me. I
missed him. He was in my every conscious moment, and it
warmed me to the core to own this secret, this private cham-
pion who had come to save me from a life that was neither good
nor bad, just one I could not seem to manage, one I could not
seem to manipulate in my favor. And now there was no need,
because Tino was going to take care of everything. He had
promised—urged me, in fact, to allow him—to take care of
me. And by handing over the etching with the letter stuck down
the back, I would be helping Tino battle my mother's efforts to
destroy Cairngorm. I had to do this for Charlie, and for the
preservation of a once proud Scottish dynasty. The more I
thought about it, the more it seemed like an honorable plan.

I arranged to visit my mother one afternoon, brought cakes and pastries from a fussy, frilly shop on Madison Avenue, and while she had her back to me as she occupied herself filling the teapot with boiling water, I plucked the etching from the nail it hung on, quickly checked to see the stiff pages still tucked into the back, and, my heart thumping, substituted a small picture hanging three frames farther up. Quickly I shoved the etching into the folds of my jacket lying on the sofa, and with only a second to spare I moved beside my mother in time to assist her with the tray. Carefully I carried it to the coffee table and set it gently on the top of a pile of large glossy books.

"Darling, do you know I'm flat broke? I don't know what I'll do! I've got nothing left to sell! I've lost all my jewelry, and what I didn't lose I've given away, so I've got nothing! Absolutely nothing! Hold that steady for me, would you?" My mother picked up a long serrated knife, preparing to stab the top of a squat loaf of bread. "I'm waiting to hear back from Icy Pïk about importing herring Caviar to the States! It's divine, and half the price. Isn't that a good idea, darling?"

"Do you mean Pïkasta, queen of Finland?" I said as I steadied the loaf, mildly amused at the sight of our busy square little hands.

"Of course, cousin Pïk!" My mother continued to slice inch-thick slabs that fell weightily one against the other, the fresh cozy odor escaping upward. "I've also had a chat with a divine woman who organizes celebrity lecture tours around the country; you know, to universities and things. People are paid a lot of money for this, and all they have to do is warble on for an hour of so! And if Ivana can, why not me?"

"Lectures on what?" I asked, guiltily eyeing my jacket. I thought I could see the corner of the etching peeking out, and my heart skipped a beat. "Crown polishing?"

"Cheeky brat!" my mother said, jauntily impaling the long

knife into the unsliced half so that it stood at attention. "I don't know! Whatever the peasants wish to hear about!"

"Ouch!" I screeched as the bread knife neatly sliced an opening just beneath the knuckle of my thumb.

"Oh my God!" my mother said. She grabbed a napkin lying on the tray beside the little cups and saucers and squeezed my thumb to stanch the blood. "Darling, I'm so sorry! Are you all right? Tell Mama you're all right!"

"Yes, of course," I said as she continued to pat the small gash with the napkin. "But I think it would feel better if you'd stop jabbing! I'm fine, Mama, don't worry about it. Let's have tea."

As soon as I could leave without causing suspicion, I made my excuses, accepted my mother's extravagant apologies for wounding me, studiously ignored the nagging feeling that I was in breach of acceptable conduct, and skipped home to Madeleine's, electrified by the heist.

I DEVOTED ALL of September, my last month's tenure at Madeleine's, to scouring the city for a home. My roommate vigorously disapproved of my decision to allow Tino such a permanent foothold in my life, but I was resolute and summarily ignored her protests as I ventured off to inspect a kaleidoscope of apartments in every conceivable shape and size, always something wrong, until, at last, I found the perfect one. A floor of a brownstone in the West Twenties. I thought it was charming, and relatively inexpensive for a tycoon.

I waited for Tino's return to New York, and we agreed to meet for breakfast at Leo's, a coffee shop near his home on the Upper East Side.

"You know I don't approve of what you're doing," Madeleine declared the morning of the talk. "But if you insist on going, you can't turn up in jeans and a T-shirt!" She stood riffling

through one of her many overstuffed closets, dressed impecca-
bly in Saint Laurent and ready for work at the French Fashion
Institute, where she was highly paid to advise on matters of
taste. "Wear this," she said, presenting me with a blue-and-
white Chanel suit with matching accessories. "And for good-
ness' sake, brush your hair!"

"I can't be dressed like that for breakfast!" I told her, frowning at the outfit, holding it up on its hanger for scrutiny as if it
were a dead and putrid pheasant. "He'll think I've lost my
mind."

"Tell him you've got a lunch to go to," she said, encasing herself in a sand-colored mink. "Good luck!"

"You are invited to stay with me permanently if you ever
need to!" I called to Madeleine as the door shut behind her, and
immediately I was engulfed with the marvel of it all. I could just
imagine closing a front door behind me, locking it, and standing inside my own home, where I could not be asked to leave,
or tossed from one room to another, or ever suffer the iniquity
of returning to discover this home was no longer mine, sold
presumptuously to a new owner.

I arrived early at Leo's and chose a booth at the back of the
narrow, steamy room. Red vinyl banquettes, Formica tables, a
counter with stacks of sticky buns and stainless steel pots of
green relish. Bottles of coagulated ketchup fenced in the team
of dark-haired cooks screaming orders at one another. A wind-
storm of commotion. I felt absurdly overdressed and I placed
my contraband, the etching, wrapped in rumpled, recycled
Christmas paper, beside me on the seat and eyed it with a certain curiosity. It was, after all, the key to my security. It represented the end of the struggle, and a surge of excitement spread
up inside me, one I had not previously wished to encourage,
just in case things were not what they appeared. But by now, all
doubts had been laid to rest, and I began to smile.

I was well into my second cup of coffee when I looked up to

see Tino swaggering in. Still tanned, he approached me with a big smile. "Hi there, little dummy," he said, leaning down to kiss me. "What's this all about then? I don't think I've heard you so agitated on the phone since I invited you to the south of France." Ripping open a packet of sugar, he reached for my coffee, tipped the granules in, and drank the last of it. "And what is this outfit you've got on?"

"I'm going to lunch." I said, too fast. My stomach constricted at the thought of what I was here to do. Suddenly my little offering of stolen goods seemed horribly insignificant, and I was embarrassed by the unfair trade. An ugly etching and two pieces of paper in exchange for a home! Of course it was all supposed to be about saving Cairngorm, but still, I felt as if I had set him up for a sting operation, lured him under false pretenses. Entrapment. Surely that was illegal? And yet the prospect of a home of my own was too hopelessly intoxicating. "How were your holidays?"

"That's what you wanted to ask me?" He looked at me suspiciously, as if perhaps he knew the score was about to be unsettled, irrevocably. He seemed to be enjoying it. This man had the instincts of a hunter. "Why the glum face?"

I took a deep breath, and staring at the speckled pattern of the Formica, I exhaled heavily, watched as grains of sugar trickled across the tabletop. Haltingly I described my search for the perfect home, the million and one vile dwellings I had toured before discovering the virtually ideal brownstone in the West Twenties, with its wall of brick and a fireplace in the larger of the two bedrooms, and so on, until I had sketched the entire place and I dared raise my eyes once again.

The glow steadily extinguished from Tino's face and he began to jot notes on a napkin. The waitress came and he sent her away with the flick of his wrist. He said nothing, barely looked at me, just wrote down what I said; and then, when there was nothing more to write, he drew circles on the napkin and filled them in, over and over again. My gut twisted so tight I could hardly breathe, and I wished I had never asked him for anything. "I'll call you later, little dummy,"Tino said as he jammed the napkin and the pen in the breast pocket of his waspy navy blazer.

"Wait!" I said, horrified by his swift impending escape, and checking about for sinister faces, I slowly raised the package to the table, slid it across to Tino. "I have what you asked for."

"The will! This is fabulous!" he exclaimed and snatched it up with both hands; urging the crinkled Christmas paper back just enough to peek in, he prodded beneath the wrapping with his fingers and dexterously extracted two folded pages. Forcing them open despite their creaky protests, Tino flattened them on the tabletop with the palms of his hands and quickly read the scrawled ink, flicking back and forth from one page to the other so that the paper crackled as it whipped the air.

"Does this mean we've saved Cairngorm from turning into a field of hideous council houses?" I said, elated, filled with feelings of pride and camaraderie.

"What are you talking about?"

"Because of . . . " I began unsteadily, a stab of icy fear piercing me as I locked in on Tino's mocking eyes, his stiff, hunched shoulders intimidatingly battle-ready. "The, uh, the whole reason for me getting you the will . . . " My voice shrank to a whisper as I reached the end of my sentence, unavoidably acknowledging his belittling amused gaze, the strident insistence in his eyes.

"Where do you come up with this nonsense? I have never discussed council houses in my life! I don't know the first thing about council houses, and I don't particularly want to know anything about them either!"Tino blustered. Folding the pages back into their creases and tucking them inside his jacket, he lounged back with both arms spread out along the top of the banquette like wings readying for takeoff. I wanted to say something, but the moment was so intensely claustrophobic that nothing seemed at all appropriate. I wanted to accuse him of all sorts of crimes, but it was too much of a confusion right then. In a single abrupt move Tino stood up. He kissed me on the cheek, like a slap. I watched his square shape edge through a family of five by the door, heard the bass of his voice. "Excuse me. Excuse me," he said, desperate to get away. A blast of cool air entered as the glass door closed behind him. I sat there in a daze, my heart thumping like a drum beating a macabre requiem, one hand mechanically rubbing my face where he had kissed me. The etching, half emerged from its shell of wrapping paper, lay abandoned on the table. I was impressed with this little picture and its incredible journey, and yet horrified by the veiled evil it had led me toward. I could not bring myself to touch it, and I did not take it home to Madeleine's.

Weeks tumbled into months, and I never heard from Tino. I lay on my bed at Madeleine's, smoking until my throat burned, and waited until gradually the truth registered like the aftershocks of an earthquake. It seemed impossible to me that he had decisively vanished from my life. Even more impossible was trying to calculate how far back his elaborate deceptions might have begun, and each time I attempted to do so, tears would skid across my face and I would burrow under the pillows and force sleep upon myself. No matter how many times I played the scenes over in my mind, they made no sense to me. Depression infected like a fever, burning me up, leaving me wasted and delirious, mercifully sparing me undue time with hateful, mocking reality.

Eventually I called. I tracked him down in a hotel in Venice. He sounded delighted to hear from me, full of enthusiasm, skirting neatly around the edges of the confrontation.

"Oh, Maria, don't take everything so seriously" was his idea of an explanation. "Anyway, you shouldn't listen to people when they're drunk!"

"Are you drunk or mad?" I spat, a flow of rage swarming my

consciousness, questions and alarm bells striking up symphonic chaos.

"Is that what you called to ask me?" He laughed aggressively.

"No," I said, taking in a deep draught of air, steadying myself. "I called to ask why you worked so hard to get Cairngorm for yourself. I mean, with that half of the will you're in a position to claim it. Right?"

"Better that I have it than anyone else. Especially your mother!" Tino continued, his cackling laughter mingling with the long-distance static. "Your mother's a tart!"

"Why, because she slept with everyone but you?" I snapped viciously. "Was I the next best thing, Tino? Did you do this just to avenge that cocksmith image of yourself?"

"Don't flatter yourself! You know, you royals have the worst manners!" he barked, the words hammering the inside of my ear. "Your mother got herself knocked up by Charlie Cairngorm, your father, in case you never figured it out, while she was still married to Sammy Moses! In my book that is distinctly tarty behavior! But that's none of my business, no concern of mine whatsoever! I'll tell you what is a concern, though— when your mother took Charlie off to some remote part of the world and, one way or another, managed to leave him there! I'm not the type to take a backseat when I detect foul play! So, when I met you . . . "

I could still hear Tino's jeering voice as I hung up the telephone, heard the words stamped out by a definitive clack, and I sat quite still in Madeleine's sitting room on the green-and-white sofa and vaguely heard the clock's hands muttering in their childish, lisping way.

I began to pick through the decaying memories of all the time we had spent together, and it seemed to me, as I fit the pieces in their rightful order, that it had always been an optical illusion that had seemed true by virtue of my desire that it be true. Reality is in the eye of the beholder.

• • •

"I TRIED TO WARN you!" Madeleine declared. Dragging an imitation Louis XV chair by one gray velvet arm, she sat beside my bed where I lay propped up like a dying dowager.

"Is he some sort of genius chess player thinking up moves years in advance?" I asked, dramatically waving my cigarette around. "If none of it meant anything, I'll go mad! You do realize, don't you, that I have single-handedly sabotaged an inheritance that would be wending its way to me! To me! I would have had a fucking castle, and I traded it in for the possibility of one lousy rotting floor of a brownstone! But I suppose if you come from a family that loses countries, why not a castle? Am I insane? Tino must think so, and he's probably having a good laugh about it. Do you think I should look up Prockney Hall on my next visit to England and commit myself? Do I belong in an asylum after all? What lovely irony!"

"Maria, calm down," Madeleine admonished, administering a mug of tea, her bright, soft, yellow hair fluffed around her face, like an angel's. "I warned you to keep away from Tino. You refused. I warned you not to go to France. You refused. I warned you about the apartment, but as usual you knew better."

"He offered me a home! That's like asking a beggar if he wants a hundred bucks. Of course he's going to say yes; of course he's going to be mesmerized!" I moped, sipping the tea and sucking hard on my cigarette between long, agonizingly loud snifflings, soon confusing the three moves in a comic charade. "It's so humiliating! I mean, Tino was supposed to be my ultimate weapon, my means of avenging myself against the dreadful parents, and now it's all ruined because they knew all along he was a shit! And I helped him destroy me! How will I ever face them? And don't even think about telling me to apologize!"

"How about you tell them you were trying to even the score? Now you've all been equally ghastly to each other; maybe you can sort of start again!" she said as she flicked the long skirt of her pink robe over her legs before hoisting her tiny feet to the lip of the bed. "Anyway, I've told you a million times, everyone uses everyone. You used Tino as much as he used you."

"Treachery!" I said, eyeing her meanly, stung by the possibility of more harsh truths heading my way. I slurped the last of the tea, dumped the dying cigarette in so that it fizzed to death, and handed Madeleine the mug.

"Maria, let's face it, with Tino's affections for you, real or not, you replaced the need for family and friends and employment and any kind of initiative at taking control of your life! He was the perfect panacea to growing up."

"Enough being right, it's giving me a headache!" I sulked, squirreling under the covers as much for warmth as to elude any more unsolicited wisdom. "I'm such an idiot! I could have lorded it over the dreadful parents for the rest of my life, and now I'm one of them! Now I have to admit abject failure!"

"Welcome to the human race! Maria, you know I love you dearly?" Madeleine said sternly, and somehow I felt certain I was not going to like the follow-up. "But it's time you pulled yourself together. I'm going to insist that you get yourself a decent job and a home of your own. You've got a month. And that's final."

"No!" I wailed, unable to see through a storm of tears, unable to speak from the choking sniffles. "I'm like some deranged barnacle clinging to any ship that passes by. That's all I know. The cling."

Fearing that I might work myself permanently into the upholstery with my torrential crying fits, Madeleine took it upon herself to force me out into the world. Seeing to everything from washing, painting, dressing, and hand-in-hand escorting me to waiting taxicabs that would surge off and after considerable bouncing, deposit us someplace where I would be encouraged to mingle and chat with whatever social gathering my thoughtful roommate had provided for the evening's entertainment.

At one such event I met a squat, disheveled man with a sprouting wart at the end of his nose, Tino's favorite first cousin, Angus Fortesque, alcoholic rogue par excellence. I doubt the idea would have come to me any other way, but presented as it was, I felt compelled to take advantage, and proceeded, with an ease and speed restricted to the heavily intoxicated, to seduce Angus, or rather to allow him to seduce me. I endured a fortnight of Angus Fortesque before I received the phone call I was expecting, which was merciful because Angus, wart or no wart, was an unpleasant misogynist with pompous, aggressive manners that he no doubt hoped would compensate for his meager equipment, equipment he could not seem to commandeer for any longer than a minute.

"You're a tart! You've turned out to be a tart just like your mother!" Tino's voice blasted down the telephone. His anger was the most extraordinary tonic, working immediately to relieve the pressure in my heart, like bubbles carrying oxygen to the surface. "Did you think I wouldn't find out? Did you think you could get away with this?"

"Really, now Tino!" I said, hoping I sounded measured and pleasant as I delivered lines I had waited impatiently to air. "What was it you told me? Don't take everything so seriously? Yes, that's it, don't take it all so seriously, Tino!"

"I could have done a lot for you, Maria!" He boomed so resoundingly I held the receiver a few inches away from my head, further abstracting and disembodying his anger. "I could have changed your life! But you've blown it all on a very stupid joke! You'll regret this!"

"How's that?" I said, laughter overwhelming me as his bombast sounded hollow and absurd. "I don't want your things, Tino! I don't want anything you have to give! I can get all that rubbish from my own parents. I thought you were different, I thought you were taking me away from the falseness, not right to the mother lode of it all!"

"What!" Tino said, spitting the words out as acidly as possible. "I'm not some guru, some fairy godmother! You knew what you were getting into; you're just as much of a hooker as all women! You're all the same!"

"And so speaks the great moralist!" I said, unable to quench the laughter. I felt oddly detached from the words I spoke, listening to them as if it were a voice on the radio as I twirled the shiny telephone cord in my fingers, wrapped it several times around my wrist, and watched the New York dusk close in on the windowsill, a damp ash gray cloud gripping at the windowpane, sticky light. "In case you care, I'm not the least bit angry with you, Tino. I was, but I'm not anymore. I know we both took what we had to take. I suppose you could say that everybody got fucked. Doesn't make it right, but that's the way it is. I know all this thanks to my very wise roommate. She says I wanted you to be my savior, so that I could house homeless affections intended for my mother and my father. And my petty act of vengeance with Angus was not really to hurt you; it's everything that I dare not do to my parents. This all according to Madeleine, and I happen to think she's correct. I'm sure you understand all this far better than I do, seeing as you're so much older and presumably wiser! I guess I ought to thank you!" I released my wrist from the tight plastic cord, watched it spring back into shape, and for the second and last time I hung up the telephone as Tino thundered on and on about who knows what.

EPILOGUE

New York, 1997

"HI, KID, IT'S YOUR OLD DAD CALLING."
His voice emanated from a brown answering machine parked
on the floor beside the telephone. "I'm sitting here trying to
balance my checkbook, and it looks like you haven't cashed any
of those checks I've sent you. You're screwing up my account-
ing! What's the matter, kid, don't you like money anymore?
Give me a call. Maybe we can think of a way for you to make a
living before your twenty-first birthday. That's in a month, isn't
it?" I checked my watch, Charlie's gift from all those years ago,
barely recognizable in its deteriorated state, scratched and
worn as it was; yet it was accurate enough, if you did not mind
the loss of a few minutes every now and then. According to
Charlie's watch I would be twenty-one in precisely thirty-three
days. So why do I feel like one hundred and twenty-one? This is
supposed to be the bright beginning, the great send-off, but I
feel like I should be choosing a retirement home, not a career.
Perhaps a plot, a cool solitary plot somewhere in the countryside. After all, if I have to pay rent, I might as well pay for something with a future. "Maybe Omar Lahood would like to make
a movie about our crazy family!" my father continued. "No one
would fucking believe it!"

"Maria, I know you're home. Please pick up!" Madeleine's
exasperated voice rose up from the machine, and I wondered if

231

she and my father were perhaps standing at a public phone at the corner, playing a duet of mind games. The lightbulb overhead began to flicker, disco lights against a ceiling of mirrors; a little out of date, I thought. "I'm calling to remind you about your interview at three this afternoon. I've given you an excellent reference, so please don't let me down. I exaggerated your duties for Omar Lahood just the littlest bit, so go along with it. And wear your navy skirt and the white silk blouse I gave you." The air-hostess costume, I thought, all the better to enable Madeleine to sell me into slavery.

What a foul proposition she had devised—personal assistant to Andre Drakan, excruciatingly boring financial advisor at Morgan Stanley on Wall Street. Madeleine must have lost her mind. Her sense of panache was obviously limited to clothing, floundering horribly in the world of employment. "And please call me afterward, I'm dying to hear how it went," she said, and as she hung up, I could hear her lighting a cigarette. I wanted one.

Wrapping myself in the top quilt, the one burst of color in my gloomy home, I shambled over to the narrow desk. I know exactly how the interview will go. I will go in, and I will go out, and that will be bloody well that. In an ashtray I located a butt just long enough to reignite. Returning with the glowing trophy to the futon, I collapsed into the pile of bedding. Besides, I had a job. I read, for a fee, the unsolicited manuscripts sent to the A. J. Browning Literary Company, at the corner of Fifty-fourth and Madison. Most of these atrocious assaults on literature came from bored housewives in Seattle, and I could only imagine that, due to the extravagant rains, they sat twitchy and confined and unleashed their frustrations on the typewriter. Still, it was something to do. One deep puff and I was down to the filter. I dropped it into the now-cold tea. It bobbed on the surface; brown filter, brown liquid.

I doubt my entire apartment would fill the closet in Madeleine's bright red hallway. Eyeing my dingy quarters, I tried to determine what would most efficiently enhance matters. The carpet would have to go. Any one color would be a noble improvement on the threadbare leopard. Two of the walls are painted matte black, the other two, as well as the ceiling, are covered over with mirror, smashed into a filament of cracks. I could paint the black walls a genteel cream, which would shrink the room, but no doubt lift my mood. According to a decorator friend, the dark, cavelike recesses give the illusion of depth; and illusions, as far as the world of interior design is concerned (he went on to tell me with an authoritative raise of the eyebrows), are more easily achieved than reality. Financially constrained as I am, I cannot repair the mirrors, nor can I do much about the leak. I could, I suppose, buy an electric kettle and make myself tea so that I am not obliged to dress and thunk downstairs to Kim's Korean as I do every morning.

"John Harrington here, of Harrington, Harrington and Frowsty." A deep Southern voice drawled through the machine. I trolled my fingers across the carpet, collecting bits of lint until I had a healthy handful of dust clumped together. "The Aristo Society is throwing a gala bash Saturday the twelfth, and it would be absolutely delightful if you would do us the honor of attending." I know I ought to ask him for a job; I hear the firm pays a fortune for the use of one's connections, even if they are indirectly located, via one's parents, but I loathe public relations. May as well donate your soul directly to hell. I made a fist and crushed the dust into a ball, bounced it once, twice, in my palm. Each time it landed, tiny fragments burst into the air, miniature fireworks, and returned to their home on the worn leopard-print carpet. "Naturally, you're more than welcome to bring the guest of your choice, and if it isn't too much trouble, seeing as our records seem to be deplorably out of order, we'd so appreciate it if you could provide us with a phone number for your sister." Perhaps I should sell it. What is a telephone number worth? While he spoke, a torrent poured down through a light socket. The folks upstairs were taking a shower and the water sank deeply into the carpet, completely missing the cooking pot I had placed strategically beneath it, and instead irrigating the crop of caramel-colored mushrooms pushing up through the carpet, growing like a small unstoppable forest along the wall.

Before scooping up the telephone I rubbed my palm across my stomach and watched the streaks, like tire tracks, left on my T-shirt, a sticky residue. "Mr. Harrington, if you wish to invite my sister, Miranda, I'm sorry to have to tell you that she's out of town. As a matter of fact, she doesn't even live in New York; she lives with her husband in Dallas."

"Right, of course," he said, flustered. "By the way, is your mother available?"

"I have no idea." With the tips of my toes I slid the pot over a few inches to collect the dirty water, and as it clanked, I wondered if Mr. Harrington would mistake the noise for a marble fountain in my living room. "I think she's in Europe cleaning the Danube or something. Sorry I can't help."

One thin window ushers in a beam of light, and from an angle, I can see the uppermost leafy branches of a tree that grows in the courtyard below. The tree swayed, green feathers dragged down by the rain, and I thought of a willow tree I knew a long time ago that bent over a feisty river. The single vision appeared with excess baggage, sickening me with extraneous memories. I am ill with the flu or depression or self-pity or, most likely, a combination of the three. The lightbulb right above my bed goes on and off every few minutes. Rain splatters the metal buttress of the air conditioner that juts daringly out the window, the dismal sound a suitable companion to my evil mood. How many steps away from becoming a bag lady am I? April 15 my tenure in this intolerable slum is up. Will I be gainfully employed before then? Will the money I make from selling my earrings in the Sotheby's Christmas sale tide me over the winter?

Thirty-eight Christopher Street is a shabby sliver of a building almost exactly between Greenwich and Seventh Avenues. The front is an unimpressive combination of flaking paint and narrow casements that stack up four stories high, two to a floor, all of them bending slightly to the right as if they had been blown that way by the wind. On either side are taller, newer buildings of brown brick fronted by green cloth awnings and uniformed doormen.

The first time I came to inspect, I let myself in with a set of keys kept permanently with Doris, who works the cash register at the Griddle and Spoon on the corner of Christopher and West Fourth. I agreed only after Madeleine expelled me from her own lovely home, where, to be fair, I had already eked a generous stay. "It's time to make something of your life," she recommended. "Time to pull it all together."

But why, I thought, when I have such a great propensity for pulling things apart? "More like time to head for the bridge," I replied miserably. "Time to admit failure and resign and stop wasting oxygen." Madeleine would not tolerate such gross irreverence, and I soon learned to keep these dark options to myself, poring over them in private like a dirty magazine kept under the covers.

I could not find the light switches the day I came to view my future home, and so I sat on the floor in the dark and puffed away on close to a pack of cigarettes as I contemplated what it would be like to live in a box ten feet by six, furnished only with a futon and a desk painted in orange and black stripes and a single, unsteady, canvas director's chair. I found, concealed behind a mirror-covered door, a cramped bathroom with a truncated half tub and a toilet, no sink; brush your teeth like a peasant bent over the fountain in the town square. I suppose I never expected to have to move in—I thought that it would provide peace of mind, more for Madeleine than myself, as well as put a temporary halt to the sofa hopping that has become a way of life. But indeed I did take up residence in the shabby hovel, and now I exist in subhuman splendor, wondering how I will ever get out of here, where is the life raft? If only I had never met Tino, if only I had never stolen the damn will. I dragged the covers up to my chin and closed my eyes against the offensive thoughts that picked at me like a hot poker on an open scab.

Someone pounded at my front door, the sound wrenching me from a leaden, feverish doze. The volume increased and I slid a pillow over my ears to protect my groggy head filled with marbles. More knocking. Whoever was out there took to thumping on the door, which caused the marbles to collide into one another. "All right," I whimpered as I struggled to disentangle myself from the bedding. "I'm coming, I'm coming. Stop making so much noise." Staggering around the tiny room, a balancing hand pressed against the light switches, the illumination stabbing my aching eyes, I wedged my feet into a pair of brown clogs and stumbled to the end of a short, narrow hall, where I unbolted and tugged open the door.

"Hello, darling!" My mother exclaimed cheerily, her fire-engine mouth open in a wide smile, big overpainted eyelashes fluttering excitedly. She looked huge in a blaze of dark fur and shimmering dark green eyes. The sight of her floored me. I had a strong urge to throw my arms around her, hug her until she gasped for air; equally I was tempted to slam the door in her face, thrust her out of my life permanently with the force of it. Stamping her leather-booted feet, creating a puddle, she shook the rain from the folds of her umbrella and tipped the handle, a duck's head, against the wall. "Darling, I was just thinking about you, and here you are! Isn't that amazing?"

"Not particularly. I do live here," I said uneasily. It saddened me to feel emotions overflow so immediately at the sight of her, instantly churning buried hurts, blurred, faceless feelings. I wondered if she felt them too.

"Can't I come in!" my mother said in a manner that did not require an answer. She attempted to bustle past me, so that I had no option but to back up along the tiny hallway to the one small room that is my home. She has never visited me before. But, of course, I have never invited her. Pride is an enduring commodity, and I do not like anyone to see the abysmal standard of living I have been reduced to. I wondered if the shock would propel her into a fit of maternal pity, whereupon she would insist I pack up and relocate immediately. I hoped desperately that it would, and I waited expectantly as I watched her drive a cursory eye around the diminutive chamber, my heart pumping with self-righteousness, prepared to beg for and bestow forgiveness for one iota of recognition. Blood thrummed and surged at my temples, my mouth stiff and half open as I waited for her to break, and in an instant I remembered the multitude of occasions where atrocities had been only inches from her face and she had miraculously avoided noticing them. Everything from Alison's death to Dr. Jamison to Prockney Hall to Charlie's going missing to the identity of my father to moving to America and forgetting to mention it to me and . . . well, I could go on and on. But today there was no way out. It would be utterly impossible to survey this squalor and remain unaffected, and my heart swelled with expectations, warming me from within.

"I love futons, darling," she said, looking admiringly at my heap of bedding on the floor. "They're so comfortable aren't they?"

I stared at her for a long while; all thoughts and feelings momentarily evaporated. Perhaps this flu was worse than I had imagined, and I glanced quickly about me, suddenly uncertain if my mother and I were indeed at Thirty-eight Christopher Street with the filthy leopard and the cracked mirrors and the mushrooms thrusting up through the carpet. But no, we were here; and looking back at my mother and her eerily innocent confidence, I wondered how it was possible that I could have been so menaced by someone as relentlessly ridiculous and ultimately harmless as this woman, my mother, a charming and bizarre and thoroughly ineffectual fool, and I exploded with laughter, huge, gasping laughs that gouged my stomach for lack of oxygen, so that my sides ached and I clutched at myself, stumbling back blindly into the wall of mirror, sliding down to the futon, bent double with deep sobbing laughter. And when I looked up at my mother, through a shield of tears, I saw she was laughing too, and I knew at that moment that this was our only true bond, our only common reference, to laugh. But who the hell could ever tell what Mama was laughing at?

About the Author

Christina Oxenberg was born, and briefly raised, in New York City. This was followed by prolonged stays in London, then Madrid, then back to New York before returning to London, and so on, until after fourteen schools and a multitudinous array of stepparents and their tribes of offspring, a precedent for adventure was set.

Bypassing University, Oxenberg plunged into a whirlpool of random employment, everything from researcher to party organizer to art dealer to burger flipper. Between excursions, she lives in New York City.

Taxi, published in 1986, is a collection of anecdotes about the uniquely eventful New York City cab ride.